I0544641

SYDNEY SCOTT

EVERNIGHT PUBLISHING ®

www.evernightpublishing.com

**SYDNEY SCOTT**

# DEDICATION

For every woman who has struggled through an impossible situation. I see you.

**SYDNEY SCOTT**

# ADORING THE AGENT

*Willow Creek, 2*

**Sydney Scott**

**Copyright © 2025**

**Chapter One**

*Jo*
*Two months ago*

The familiar scents of motor oil, rubber tire, and degreasing agent hit Jo's nose as she walked through the open bay door of Bob's Auto Shop. She waltzed right in just as she always had, paying no attention to the stares of the men who worked for her father. They knew who she was, and they also knew better than to reprimand her for not using the customer entrance. Jolene Farrow grew up in this shop, and even though she no longer worked there like she had in high school, she still walked around like she knew every nook and cranny of the place because, frankly, she did. She could also take apart and reassemble a carburetor faster than just about every guy on the payroll, but she wasn't going to rub that in their faces.

Jo was there for one reason and one reason only: to check up on her dad at their weekly lunch date. She never took time away from work that she didn't have to, but Jo considered these lunches with her dad as necessary preventative medicine. A grimace pulled across her face as she strode through the door that separated the garage from the main offices. Her dad might not like the type of care his daughter gave him, but he would deal with it nevertheless because he knew it would save him from having to listen to Jo go on and on about heart disease and taking care of himself like she was prone to do.

Jo pushed open the door of her father's office and stepped inside, ignoring the pang of sadness and grief that crept over her when she caught sight of the family picture on the corner of his desk. Even though it had been nearly twenty-two years since her mother had passed, Jo still missed her every day. She didn't remember much of her mama now, but she did get flashes of memory every now and then.

A glimpse of her reflection would conjure images of the woman's bright smile and loose blonde curls that looked so much like her own, as would the smell of gardenias that wafted her way as she applied the same creamy, sweetly scented lotion her mother had always worn. Jo had rediscovered the delightfully floral salve in high school and had been using it ever since. It was a small connection to her past, and even though she still had her dad and loved him dearly, it wasn't quite the same.

Jo glanced over at the man she came to see. He smiled and held up a finger as he finished the phone call he was on, the deep crinkles forming at the edge of his eyes another reminder that her dad wasn't getting any younger. At any age, Robert Farrow, or "Bob" as he preferred to be called, was the greatest. He hadn't had an easy time raising her on his own, but he did his best and that had been more than enough for Jo. To give the two of them a fresh start after her mama passed away when she was just six years old, Jo's dad moved them from Columbus to Willow Creek.

Jo hadn't minded leaving all of those sad memories behind and had looked forward to their new adventure. After buying the struggling auto shop in the heart of the town, her dad managed to turn it into a thriving business while raising Jo with lots of love and attention at the same time. They had made a pretty good life for themselves in the small city, and Jo was grateful for it.

Jo's dad placed the phone in its cradle and turned his gray eyes up to her blue ones, the color lightening a tad to a more silvery hue as he did. "Joley-bear," he exclaimed before hopping up from his chair and pulling her into an all-encompassing hug.

Bob was a burly man, and at six foot two, he towered over a lot of people, Jo included. She was only half a foot shorter than him, but even she still had to tilt her head back to peer at his face. His arms squeezed her tightly, the air rushing from her lungs speaking to his strength, but his eyes looked more tired than usual, and she hoped the dark shadows she saw were just the result of a busy work week and not a sign of something more serious.

When he pulled back from the hug, the crooked smile that greeted her eased her worries slightly. "What did you bring me today? Kale chips or boiled carrots?"

"Har-har, Pops," Jo said with a smirk, tossing the brown paper bag she arrived with onto the desk with a satisfying thud. "Lunch is served." Jo proceeded to dig into the sack and pull out the salad she purchased from

Greens on the Go, and passed it over to her dad with a smile. "I got you your favorite, Spring Harvest Salad." Jo knew very well it wasn't his favorite anything, but she wanted to keep him around as long as possible, so lettuce with fruit was the best treat she had to offer.

Pops took the container, not bothering to conceal his groan of dismay. "Just once I would love it if you would bring me a burger and fries instead of this rabbit food." Anything that wasn't dipped in batter and fried to a beautiful golden brown was "Rabbit food" to her dad, and while the unfortunate look on his face tugged at Jo's heartstrings, it wasn't enough to weaken her resolve to keep his eating on track.

Jo leveled him with a look as she pulled out her own salad. "And after I do, we can take a drive down to Willow Creek General's cardiac unit. How does that sound to you?" It sounded horrible to her, even speaking the possibility aloud enough to make her jittery.

"Not ideal," he admitted, snatching a fork from her hand and using it to spear some greens and a strawberry. After munching on the combination for a minute, he smiled sadly at her. "I'm sorry I make such a fuss of eating the salad, Joley-bear. I know you're just trying to take care of me."

"Thanks," Jo mumbled.

She bit into her lunch to avoid having to say anything further on the subject. They both knew part of the reason she got on him about his eating habits was because he was all she had left and couldn't afford to lose him too. Her dad had been in his midthirties by the time he and her mom had gotten pregnant with Jo, so he was already pushing close to sixty-five now. Between his age, his steady diet of red meat, and the stress of his job, Jo was always worried about him having a heart attack, a stroke, or something else equally as bad. Losing her mom had been sudden, and Jo didn't think she could handle going through that again.

It was a hemorrhagic stroke that had ripped Jo's mother away from her family instantaneously, and while Jo knew she couldn't have done anything to prevent that, she could do everything in her power to make sure her dad was as healthy as possible now so she wouldn't lose him too. Pops was also the reason she stayed at a job she didn't love. Being the only female sports consultant at the small marketing firm she was employed with wasn't easy, and she had to put up with a lot of sexist rhetoric, but she was good at her job and was more dedicated than half the guys there. Once she had the promotion she planned on asking for, Jo would be making more money and be able to convince her dad to retire so he could live a more relaxed life. Maybe after a few years of that she could eventually move to a firm with a less toxic working environment.

"How's work?" her dad asked, cutting into her thoughts about that very subject.

Jo never mentioned the horrible working conditions or the nicknames she had earned during her tenure to her dad, but she could always talk about some of the athletes she worked with. "Well, Greg Jennings might be moving up to the big leagues soon. At least, that's what he keeps telling us," she said with a roll of her eyes. The first baseman for the minor league baseball team in town, the Willow Creek Squirrels, thought very highly of himself, but unlike some of the other clients at Elite Sports Marketing, he actually had some talent to back up the claims. "I caught some of the game highlights on my way to work and it seems like he might just be telling the truth. He got a home run and two RBIs."

Her dad scoffed. "Call me when he ups his field

game. The last time I watched, he dropped a foul ball that even I could have caught."

The man wasn't wrong. Jo had played enough games of catch with her old man growing up to know he had the uncanny ability to snag just about every wayward ball that came his way.

Jo smiled at her dad's sass. "Next time we chat I'll let him know he needs some work," she promised. It wasn't really her place to comment on her client's performances, but she often did it anyway. For the most part, they appreciated the feedback, especially since her observations tended to be fairly accurate.

"You do that," her dad said with a wink as they resumed eating.

A silence fell over the office, but it was a comfortable one. Jo and her dad were never much for deep conversation, but they did enjoy spending time with one another. Talking about practical matters like business was one thing, but matters of the heart were a lot more complicated for the both of them. Her mom was the one with all of the emotional intelligence, and after she died, it was as if Jo and her father had just silently agreed to table those types of discussions permanently. Being in his presence was still comforting, even if she spent a good amount of the time while in it silently worrying about him.

When she had polished off her salad, Jo tossed her fork down and looked out window into the garage bay. She watched with amusement as one of her best friends, Gigi, marched straight up to her mechanic boyfriend Cooper and gave him a big kiss before pulling him out to the picnic tables for their own lunch date. Jo smiled at the happy couple, wondering if that was something she would ever have, but shrugged off the thought. Up until this year, the idea of being part of a couple wasn't something she ever would have considered, but now that surety in her perpetual singlehood wasn't as solid as it had been.

Jo's mind flashed back to the night in January where she and her friends Gigi and Millie had celebrated their birthday. All three of the woman were turning twenty-eight the next day, and they had gone out to commemorate the occasion in the same way they had been doing since they first met each other in second grade: together. It was a tradition that started with sleepovers, but had morphed into something much more fun once they all hit their twenty-one year milestone. The ability to go out to bars and clubs widened the scope of their birthday venues, and to make it fair, the girls took turns picking where they would celebrate each year.

The other two girls had veto rights because no one wanted to be uncomfortable, and while that had worked out in Jo's favor the year Millie picked a book signing, karma came around eventually and it backfired the year Jo wanted them to hit up a famous all-male revue that had been traveling through Atlanta. Jo could have gone by herself, but that would have been a lot less fun and a little more desperate, so she had chosen a baseball game instead. Her friends didn't exactly enjoy sports like she did, but as long as there were soft-baked pretzels to eat and plenty of man candy on display, they were game.

Jo didn't have much in common with her two friends when it came to hobbies or interests, but they had gotten along like peanut butter and jelly since she and her dad moved to Willow Creek in the second grade. Jo remembered marching into class, a ball cap tugged low over her eyes to shield her from judgement, displaying nothing but attitude. She had been called a tomboy at her old school, and while she didn't care about being called out for her boyish ways, it was the sneer that always came along with it that bothered her.

Deciding to own her personality, she introduced herself to the class, giving zero fucks about what anyone thought. "I'm Jo, and I like sports and cars," she had said to the other eight-year-old students. Jo had jutted her tiny chin out as if to dare anyone to challenge her, and when no one did, she took the only empty seat in the class.

It wasn't until lunch time that anyone had bothered to talk to her, and when they did, it turned out to be Gigi Davenport and Millie Legare. The girls were very nice and hadn't once commented on her plain clothes, so she figured she'd give them a shot at being her friends. Once she discovered the two shared her same birthday, she took it as a sign, a gift from her mama in heaven to help her adjust to life in a new town. The three had been inseparable ever since.

On the night of their most recent birthday celebration, they had gone down to Atlanta to see a drag show, and somewhere between ordering drinks and the performance of one Miss Heidi Haux, Gigi had decided that they were all in a rut and needed to challenge themselves both personally and professionally. Gigi wanted to put on a drag show at her tea room and date someone different than all the doctors and lawyers her parents set her up with. From the game of tonsil hockey she and Cooper were currently playing, they were way past simply dating. Millie was going to start an outreach program at the library and sign herself up for dating apps, and Jo knew for a fact Millie was living up to her challenge because she had called Jo just the other night to complain about another dating disaster.

For Jo's part, she hadn't wanted to admit that she was in a rut, but even she could see that her life was looking a lot more like "same shit different day" than she wanted, so she challenged herself to try and find an actual relationship and go for the promotion at work. So far, she had neither made progress at work nor gone on a single date like she had said she would those few months ago. Asking for a promotion would be easy enough, but the likelihood of her getting shot down due to her gender made her weary of trying. Still, it was a whole lot easier than her personal challenge.

Trying to find and go out on a date when you had been operating in hookup-only mode for the last decade was pretty daunting. When it came right down to it, Jo didn't like the idea of dating because it wasn't really something she could control. Going home with a guy and leaving while the sheets were still warm, easy to control. Finding a guy, talking to him, waiting for him to call or text, or worse, trying to initiate conversation when she was about as subtle as a sledgehammer? Hard to control and scary as hell, which was probably why she had yet to really give it a try.

A beeping sound coming from her phone pulled Jo out of her thoughts and back to the present. She checked her phone to silence the alarm that had gone off, an annoying reminder that the spark of joy from visiting her dad would once again be snuffed out and replaced by the drudgery of work. With a roll of her eyes and a groan, she stuffed her garbage into the brown bag and stood up.

"Sorry, Pops. I forgot we have some special meeting this afternoon." Jo slung her purse over her shoulder and stepped behind the desk, leaning down to kiss her dad on the cheek. "I'll talk to you later, and don't forget we have plans for this weekend."

"Breakfast at the diner?" her dad asked, a hopeful expression on his face. Breakfast at Barb's Diner was one of their traditions, but the place wasn't exactly known for its healthy food and Jo didn't want to be a bad influence.

Jo smiled sadly, hating that she would be

disappointing him but needing to keep his dedication from slipping. "Not this time, Pops. We're doing a 3K down by the river." She opened the door of his office, but stopped halfway through, peering at him over her shoulder. "I'll bring you a muffin from the store, though."

Her dad started to smile, but his expression turned suspicious. "It better not be a bran muffin," he scolded.

"No promises." Quickly sliding out the door before he could protest further, she rushed out to her 1967 Mustang convertible.

March in Willow Creek was beautiful and today was no exception. The temperature was a gorgeous sixty-eight degrees and there wasn't a cloud in sight. Jo blasted some classic rock through the radio to entertain herself as she made the commute back to work. Her office was located about thirty minutes outside of Willow Creek, but Jo didn't mind the drive most days. It gave her plenty of time to psych herself up for a long day at work as well as time to decompress afterward, which was crucial to her mental health. Of course, if she worked somewhere she actually liked, neither of those thing would be as necessary, but unless she was willing to move to a bigger city, she had to stay. Leaving her dad on his own was not an option Jo would ever entertain, and with bills and student loans to pay off, her options were pretty limited.

The drive went by quicker than Jo would have liked, but there was nothing she could do about that. Mustering up what little enthusiasm she could, she reached over, grabbed her workbag and purse, and pulled them over her shoulder as she hopped out of the car. Feet moving quickly over the asphalt as she approached the most nondescript building known to man, she glanced down at her watch and winced. There was no time to check her email before the meeting, but depending on why the bigwigs had called them to gather, maybe she could check it during when no one was paying attention. Jo had a good amount of clients, and she couldn't go too long without touching base with them before they got grumbly. The last thing she needed was one of her more high-maintenance clients demanding a special dinner or drinks because they felt unappreciated. Lunches were fine, but anything after hours was asking too much, in her opinion.

With quick steps, Jo strode through the glass doors of the office building and rushed over to the elevator, throwing her arm between the closing doors. Once they reopened and she walked through, she sighed and her shoulders sagged with relief. Reaching over to push the button for the fifth floor, she paused halfway after noticing it was already lit up.

"Are you okay? That looked kind of painful," a voice asked. It sounded smooth, like it was dripping with sticky, sweet molasses, and the southern lilt was different than her own, but just as appealing. It was the kind of voice you wanted to bathe in, letting the dulcet sounds wash your worries away.

Jo turned to the corner of the small box as the doors closed and it lifted upwards. She smiled at the handsome stranger she found there, noting the man looked well put together in his expensive suit. It wasn't the cost of the suit that impressed her, but the way the man wore it. He was clearly comfortable in his skin, and while normally the men she was attracted to skew younger, there was definitely something appealing about a man who knew who he was.

Ignoring the flicker of want that stirred low in her belly, she leaned against the back of the elevator. "It was worth it," she told him, lifting one of her feet to show off her spiked heels. "There was no way I was taking the stairs in these."

The stranger chuckled, his dark brown eyes lighting up and a smile pulling across his plump lips, showing off gleaming, straight white teeth. "I can imagine that would be challenging."

"You have no idea," Jo quipped, flashing a smirk. "I once had to run up the steps of a ballpark in a pair just like these." She chuckled at the memory of running after the manager of the baseball team to try and convince him that the player she was working with deserved more time on the field and more investment from the team's public relations team. "I had blisters for weeks."

The man's face scrunched up as if he was feeling the pain himself, but the expression did nothing to hide just how handsome he was. His square jaw was sprinkled with a dusting of stubble, a rugged look that contrasted nicely with his dark brown hair that was perfectly styled, showing off thick, luscious locks that Jo was suddenly itching to run her fingers through. Jo shook her head to try and dispel the desire that came out of nowhere. Wanting to run her fingers through a man's hair wasn't something she normally longed to do. Grab onto it as she rode him to completion? Sure, but not stroke it like he was a pet cat. Clearly, her lack of sex was messing with her brain's ability to function properly. Jo had no idea who this even was and she needed to focus on work.

"Well, I'm glad you were able to save yourself today," he remarked, his smile genuine and so warm she practically felt the heat of it against her skin.

"Thanks." The elevator dinged, breaking into the most whimsical thought she'd had in years. Whoever this stranger was, he was affecting her in ways she had neither the time nor inclination to deal with. "Have a nice day." Jo rushed out of the elevator and through the doors of her firm, not sparing a glance behind her to see the handsome man again. She had places to be and things to do.

Jo sped over to the conference room and slid into a chair next to Blake Michaels, another marketing coordinator and probably the only male around the office who wasn't a misogynistic asshole. It might have to do with the fact that he was both Black and gay, and from what he had shared with her, he knew what it was like to be marginalized. Jo, however, liked to think it was more to do with him just being an all-around decent person.

"Did I miss anything?" Jo asked out of the side of her mouth, pulling out her tablet so she could pretend to take notes while she checked her email.

Blake's smile was strained, the pain of whatever he'd already dealt with obvious. Jo admired his still trying to put on a brave face despite the circumstances, something she struggled to do with anyone but her immediate supervisor. "You haven't missed anything except The Idiot Brigade over there making derogatory remarks about their administrative assistants again," he bemoaned, scribbling a few notes on his own tablet.

The men she and Blake called "The Idiot Brigade" were the other five consultants in the office besides the two of them.

"Gross," she commented and leaned in closer to him. Sadly, the rest of their team harassing others wasn't an uncommon occurrence. The group had no qualms about spouting inappropriate comments, and as hard as she tried to just ignore it and go about her day, she never could. "Did you record it?" she asked in a whisper.

"Girl, you know I record everything," he said, sliding a small notebook out of his suit jacket and waving it to her.

Jo and Blake had started to record all of the problematic things they had witnessed or heard about at work over the last year in case they ever wanted to take their complaints beyond the seemingly toothless human resources department. Jo was certain most guys at the office had a file at least three inches thick with grievances about their behavior, but nothing ever came of it. She and Blake had talked about taking the information to a lawyer, but neither of them had other job prospects or a lot in savings to buffer them against the loss of their current jobs, so that line of thinking ended real quickly. That didn't mean they couldn't be prepared just in case though.

"Excellent," she commended, pulling up her work email and sighing at the fifty unread messages in her inbox. "Ugh. What is this meeting even about? I have a ton of work to do." No matter how early she came in or how late she stayed at the office, the work never went away. Jo was tired and needed a break, but as long as she had other people to worry about, that wasn't going to happen.

Blake leaned over to her. "Rumor has it we're getting a new consultant," he divulged, his voice low. "Twenty bucks says it's another mediocre white man."

Jo scoffed. "I'm not dumb enough to take that bet." She looked around the room at the group of them. The Idiot Brigade were misogynists, but they managed their clients well enough, so she wasn't sure why they needed more bodies around. "Why are they hiring a new person? Did we sign more clients? They better not be taking clients away from us and giving them to this new guy."

Blake looked at her wryly. "If it is a new guy, you already know that's what's going to happen, so why are you setting yourself up to get angry?" he scolded.

"I'm always angry when I'm here," Jo grumbled and slid her tablet to the side.

It was a sad but true fact that she often felt most

upset whenever she was in this building, but when dealing with sexist coworkers and bosses, it was hard not to feel that way. Jo looked around the room, noticing that no one else beyond the two of them seemed to feel that way. Then again, not everyone would lose clients when this new guy started. Jo definitely would, and Blake might too. His being male might act as shield at times, but his orientation was a rarity in the sports marketing world, so while he got treated slightly better than she did, it wasn't by much. None of the men across from them would be affected, but that seemed to be the way of the work world they currently lived in.

"Oh, we know it, Jojo Beans. Your anger is constantly written all over your face," Blake teased and winked at her. He wasn't entirely wrong though. Jo was fiercely focused at work and had little time for most of the other consultants' nonsense, which was probably why most of them called her "Ice Queen." Jo was fine with the nickname, even owning it by dressing up as a certain Disney princess for the annual Halloween party last year. None of them knew the real her, so they could call her a frigid bitch as many times as they wanted and she couldn't care less.

Jo slugged Blake in the arm for his retort just as the two founders of the firm, Charles Whitcomb and Gavin Delaney, walked into the conference room. The sight of her bosses didn't faze her, but what had her jaw threatening to drop to the floor was the sight of attractive elevator guy trailing behind them. Jo's brow furrowed in confusion, but when the stranger took a seat to the right of the two other men, things got a little bit clearer and considerably more unpleasant.

"All right, people. This will be brief, so let's get started," Whitcomb announced as everyone settled into their seats and faced forward. "You may have heard some rumors going around about a new hire." A few low mumbles went through the group, but Whitcomb held up a hand to quash them. "Well, I'm here to tell you the rumors are true. Gavin, would you like to take it from here?"

Gavin Delaney, the head of marketing and the founder she interacted with most, smiled, showing off his expensive dental veneers. Jo could only wish to have so much money that she could waste it on false teeth. "It is my pleasure to introduce you to the son of a very good friend of mine." With an open hand, he gestured toward the man from the elevator, who sat there looking slightly uncomfortable with the attention, but smiling nonetheless. "This is Archer Hayes, our newest consultant. With his education and years of experience, we're certain he'll be able to handle taking over some of our higher profile clients." Her boss turned from Archer, spearing Jo with a meaningful look.

Great, so she was losing clients. Even though she had seen the writing on the wall, it still stung. No matter how many times Jo had encountered unfair treatment, it never seemed to get better. She felt like a punching bag wearing at the seams from one too many hits. How long until she fell apart completely?

Delaney cut into her stewing in righteous indignation with a booming command. "Welcome him aboard, everyone."

Archer smiled as everyone clapped and reached out to shake his hand. It wasn't until most everyone else had cleared the room that his eyes met Jo's. Archer's smile, the one she had admired not fifteen minutes earlier, faltered as he finally realized that not everyone was happy with his presence in the office.

Gavin pointed at her with two fingers and signaled for her to come to the front of the room. Jo gave

Blake a weary look before carrying out the silent order and marching to what she already knew would be an unpleasant interaction. "Jolene, this is Archer Hayes. Archer, this is Jolene Farrow, our marketing department's top earner. She'll be showing you the ropes around here." The uncharacteristic praise from her boss was accompanied by another look that brokered no argument about the command he had just indirectly given her.

Wonderful, so now in addition to giving Archer some of her clients, she would be babysitting him as well. Her shoulders sagged with the metaphorical weight of more work, but she swallowed her anger and puffed out her chest, not willing to let them see just how much it got to her.

Jo stuck out her hand to Archer. It was time to play nice in front of the boss and while she'd never declare herself an actress, she could still put on enough of a show to keep Delaney off her back. "Nice to meet you, and please, call me Jo." She blinked over at him, her mouth twitching at the corners as she held her smile, her blood boiling with anger at the bullshit she constantly had to swallow. There was so much of it in her stomach that she was surprised she ever had room for food. If only she could cut out the malignant tumor and be free of it.

Archer grabbed onto her hand, his palm a little rougher than hers, but still fairly smooth. Jo enjoyed the warmth that wrapped around her as they held onto one another during that brief moment. Slightly taken aback, Jo shook his hand quickly and dropped it, not wanting the strange and confusing feelings to linger.

"It's nice to formally meet you as well, Jo." Archer's voice was as deep and soothing as it had been earlier, but instead of wanting to soak it up, she wanted to run as far away from it as possible.

"Fantastic," Gavin boomed. "Now, Archer. I'm

going to take you around the offices and then we'll get you settled."

The two men steered away from her and she dropped her phony smile like it was a piece of hot coal. She stared daggers at the back of the man from the elevator. The man she *had* thought of as attractive, but now only thought of as one thing: an enemy.

## Chapter Two

*Archer*
*Present Day*

The ride to work was always one of Archer's favorite parts of the day. It gave him time to gear himself up for another eight plus hours of work, and as he sang along to Bon Jovi's "Living on a Prayer" as it blasted through the stereo system of his BMW SUV, he tried to tell himself that unlike those that came before it, today would be a good day. The last couple of months at Elite Sports Marketing had been rough, to say the least. Not only were the practices of the company outdated, but the environment wasn't much better. Archer had overheard some talk and a few jokes he didn't think were particularly appropriate for the workplace, but it wasn't uncommon in the sports world for things to be a little more lax, so he tried not to put too much stock in it. He wasn't there to make waves but put his head down and work his way up the ladder.

When Archer noticed an incoming call from his father flash on the screen of his dash, he stopped his thinking and clicked the button on his car to route it to the Bluetooth speakers. "Good morning, Dad," he said happily as he drove toward his office building. "To what do I owe the pleasure?" Archer had a good relationship with his father and enjoyed hearing from him. He loved his mother just as much, but she was closer to his sister than to him and they didn't have nearly as much in common as he and his dad did.

"Just calling in to check on my boy." The reply was low and gravely, almost as if the speakers were crackling. The man hadn't picked up a cigarette since Archer's mom had gotten pregnant with him over thirty years ago, but he still sounded like he smoked two packs a day. "Things still going well at the new place? Gavin says you're a superstar."

Gavin Delaney and his father had been fraternity brothers in college, and when Archer's career had stalled out at the large firm he worked for in Montgomery, Alabama, his dad suggested he try moving to the smaller Elite Sports Management in the next state over. The decision to move hadn't been easy, but his sister had come to Georgia after college, moving to the nearby town of Willow Creek that wasn't a far commute to the new office, so Archer decided to go for it. He didn't have a wife or kids tying him to Montgomery, so he left his parents and started a new journey. He wasn't sure how much of a superstar he actually was at work, but he did have some bigger clients than he'd had in Alabama, so there was that.

"Things are going well I think." His voice wavered slightly as he responded to his father's inquiry, and as soon as he heard a small huff on the other end of the line, Archer knew he'd been caught out.

"You think, or you know?" The man was the head of a media company in his home state, and he hadn't gotten to where he was by mincing words, a tactic he also used on his own children, much to their dismay. It was hard to keep sneaking out of the house as a teenager a secret when your own dad could pull the truth from you in under thirty seconds.

Archer sighed. "I know it's going well, Dad. It's just that the firm seems a little…" He paused, not wanting to say too much lest it get back to his boss. The men still talked on the phone occasionally, more so now that Archer worked for Delaney, and he wasn't positive his dad wouldn't give him up. "Old school," were the words he settled on. He could have said "antiquated" and possibly even "sexist" and still be underselling things. As far as Archer could tell, Jo was the only woman not in an administrative role and had been since the company started, and that was just the most glaringly obvious lack of progress in the workplace.

"Old school how?" his dad prompted.

Archer's dad might have grown up as part of the old boys' network, but he was far more progressive than that. He had a fairly diverse company and had always told Archer that you either change with the times or they pass you by. It was something Archer kept in mind for when he would possibly start his own sports marketing firm, something he had been thinking about more and more lately. After getting nowhere at his last place of business and his current one seeming behind the times, Archer wondered if he shouldn't bump up his timeline.

"It's probably nothing," he hedged, not wanting to get to into it too much before work. No need to start the day in a poor mood if he didn't have to.

"All right. Well, just remember every company does things differently and don't try to change anything until you get the lay of the land." His dad coughed and cleared his throat. "I have a meeting to get to, but your mother wanted me to tell you she misses you and to make sure you're eating enough."

Archer chuckled, smiling that his mother still worried about her thirty-two-year-old son getting the right amount of food in single a day. "Tell her I miss her too, and I definitely am eating enough." The take-out boxes in his fridge were proof enough of that, though he would never think of telling his mom he ate out all the time.

"Okay. Keep up the good work, son. Bye now."

Archer said his goodbyes and clicked off the call, continuing on his way to work with a smile on his face and a lightness in his chest he hoped to carry over throughout the day.

It was nice to have people who loved and supported you even from a whole state away. He sometimes wondered if he should have stayed closer to his aging parents, but Archer wanted to get his career settled so he could think about starting a family of his own soon. Of course, in order to do that he would have to date, but he had always been so focused on work that he hadn't had so much as a hookup in almost four years. The word *hookup* immediately brought the image of a certain blonde-haired coworker into his mind, but he shook it away furiously as he pulled into the lot at work. There was no way that was ever going to happen. Work colleagues were a no go, and for reasons she had never made clear, Jo hated him anyway.

Archer glanced at the clock on his dash as he parked his car. It was just about 8:30 and he was glad that traffic had been with him. Most of his colleagues showed up around nine, but as the new guy, Archer wanted to make an extra effort to show he was dedicated to the job. He entered the building and stepped into the elevator, smiling as he watched the doors close because it reminded him of his first day, when a beautiful woman had thrown herself between the doors to catch a ride. Archer sighed tiredly. He couldn't help but think of Jo every time he rode the elevator. It was a shame that the smiling, funny, charismatic woman he had chatted with for those brief moments as they rose to the fifth level had disappeared into thin air the moment he had stepped into the conference room two months ago.

Archer would never forget his first day on the job. He had been introduced as the new guy by the partners,

Whitcomb and Delaney, and was greeted with applause and handshakes from just about everyone in attendance. Then his eyes met the bright, blue orbs of Jolene Farrow, and even though her eyes were ablaze with fury, the temperature of the room felt like it dropped twenty degrees from the iciness of her expression. He wasn't sure what he had done to earn her ire that day or every day since, but he must have done something.

The last two months of Archer's work life have consisted of meeting with current clients, talking to potential clients, and dealing with a woman who seemed determined to hate him, no matter how friendly he acted toward her. He had asked a few of the other consultants about it, and they had simply replied that she had a reputation for being difficult. They called her "Ice Queen," a name Archer thought was apt. After a while he stopped trying to be friendly to Jo and just went along with his day. He spent a couple of weeks trying to ignore the glares and grumbles from her, but it was difficult. His inability to ignore her irritation toward him forced a change in tactics. If she was going to hate him, she should at least have a good reason, so he gave her one. Archer now went out of his way to annoy her whenever possible. It was probably childish, but it was also the one thing that kept him sane at work.

Archer had planned his attacks wisely, watching her closely to learn her habits and schedule. Jo was at work before him and stayed late most days, so she drank a good amount of coffee. He discovered that she always went into the break room for a refresh around 10:00 in the morning, so he would make sure he went in for one five minutes before that, emptying the carafe and not making a new pot for her. Seeing her disgruntled look when she had to make a fresh pot every time she went for a refill had become one of the highlights of his day. Jo was actually pretty cute when she was annoyed, her nose twitching like a bunny's and her cheeks flushing red.

Currently, Archer had started to imagine what other situations he could see her blushing in, wondering if the freckles he spied on her skin would disappear under the pink hue or stand out more because of it. Jo would be a spitfire in the sack, of that he had no doubt, and as much as he loathed the animosity she sent his way, he couldn't help but think of how wonderful a hate fuck between them could be. Archer got so lost in those lustful thoughts that he hadn't realized the elevator had been sitting at the fifth floor until the doors started to close again. Shaking off the amorous fog his mind had wandered into, he shot out of the elevator and strode through the glass doors that separated his firm from the other businesses in the building.

The lights were all on, the smell of coffee and paper filled the air, and the sounds of Jo arguing with someone or something drifted to his ears. Archer breathed it all in and smiled at the start of another glorious day where he could annoy his favorite coworker. He marched past the mostly empty cube farm designated for interns and administrators before turning the corner that would lead to the marketing consultants' offices, stopping dead in his tracks as he beheld the marvelous sight in front of him.

Jo was on all fours in front of the copy machine, cursing a blue streak and trying to pry something from its depths. She was wearing a skirt, a rarity as she favored pantsuits most days, and it was currently riding up just enough to give Archer a good look at her toned thighs. Images of his hand running along the inside jumped to the forefront of his mind, and when Jo reached her arm into the machine and her skirt hitched, a flash of lace at the top of her pantyhose made an appearance.

His teeth clicked together instinctually, the need to drag them down her legs with nothing but his mouth increasing by the second and causing him to thicken in his pants. Sporting wood in her presence was practically a regular occurrence at this point, not even her perpetually sour mood enough to overcome his physical attraction. He shifted on his feet and started to recite baseball stats in his head to quell his desire. It had been too long since he'd gotten some release if he was lusting after the one woman who would never look at him with anything other than disdain.

Needing to do something with the pent-up energy, Archer shuffled closer, being sure to make as little noise as possible. Jo was so preoccupied with the copier that she hadn't noticed him even as he was a few inches away, providing him with another perfect opportunity to rile her up. He leaned down closer to her, catching a hint of the floral scent that seemed to follow along wherever she went. Not that he noticed that kind of thing or had stopped by the perfume counter at the local drugstore to try and match it, a completely normal thing for him to do.

When she still didn't notice him, a smirk pulled across his face as he got closer to her ear. He ignored the impulse to nip at the lobe, keeping his focus where it belonged. "Need some help?" Archer's smirk widened into a full-out grin when Jo nearly jumped out of her skin and bumped her head against the copier.

"Jesus Christ," she exclaimed. She flopped onto her backside and leaned against the copier, one hand clutching her chest and the other rubbing her head.

Archer smiled wryly. "No, just me I'm afraid, though I have been told I have the looks and presence of a god, so you're not too far off." He'd had his fair share of lovers and never once been compared to a deity, but a little false confidence never hurt anyone.

Jo's eyes rolled so far back in her head Archer was afraid she might lose them entirely, and he absolutely loved it. Teasing her was easily the most fun he'd had since moving here and maybe even a little before that. He would thank her for making his days go by quicker if she weren't also the reason they dragged along sometimes.

"Well, compliments from your mama don't count," she grumbled with a sigh. She peered up at him with a scowl, the small vee that formed between her brows not marring her face in the slightest. As he continued to stare silently, Jo started making a shooing motion with her hand. "If you aren't going to help with the paper jam, you can go along your merry way."

Archer leaned down to look inside the machine—the paper was wedged in there good and tight. His eyes flicked over to her face, and when he saw she was staring at him, her eyes filled with a curious interest, his became transfixed. Jo's face was beautiful, there was no question about that. Her oval face made up of porcelain skin, sky blue eyes, rosy cheeks, and full, pouty lips was enough to drive any man wild, but it was the smattering of freckles across her nose and cheeks that held his attention. They looked like stars sprinkled across a blank canvas of sky, and he found himself wondering why he was waxing poetic about a woman who hated his guts.

Archer's eyes found hers once again, but her scowl was firmly back in place, as if she too had remembered that they didn't like one another. For a moment, Archer was tempted to reach over and smooth out the small wrinkle between her eyes just to piss her off, but he was still thrown by the conflicting emotions that were running through his body, so he backed off. He was irritated that she hated him without cause, but he was also incredibly attracted to her, which messed with him more than he'd like to admit. He needed to get out of there and focus on his job, not continue to let the two halves of him wage an internal war neither would win.

Archer straightened up, reaching down to pat her head like she was a small child, the patronizing gesture a parting gift to himself before he went back to work. "I think you can handle this one, Champ," he taunted her before striding over to his office and shutting the door.

Archer plopped into his brown leather chair and sighed, scrubbing a hand down his face. He opened up his laptop and checked out his emails, trying to make a to-do list for the day, but his mind kept drifting back to Jo. How was he going to handle that type of situation should it happen again? There had been that moment when she looked at him without animosity, and it gave him hope that there could be something between them other than pettiness and barbed words. Archer thought about it for the first hour of his day, and at the end of that time, he was still no closer to figuring out what he would do should there be a repeat of what could have been a wonderful moment. What he had discovered, however, was that he was desperately hoping it would happen again, and soon.

## Chapter Three

*Jo*

*Stupid Archer and his stupid handsome face.* It was the chorus of the song Jo sang in her head just about every day of the week, the "I absolutely, one hundred percent hate this man and am not attracted to him in the slightest" song. Of course, that last part was categorically untrue, but people told themselves lies all the time, so why should she be any different? Archer Hayes and his dark brown eyes that reminded her of her favorite brand of chocolate, his fantastic head of hair that she was just dying to get her hands on, and his gorgeous smile that she wanted to wipe off his face with a fierce kiss. *Stupid, stupid, stupid,* she reminded herself as she worked on the paper jam that had quickly become her all-time nemesis. Jo had already torn one nail trying to get the damned thing out, and she was pretty sure it would happen to the other nine if someone didn't help her with this.

"Why do we still need paper anyway?" Jo grumbled to herself as she continued to work on the copier. "We live in the digital age," she declared as she gripped onto the last shreds of paper and pulled them free. "Woo-hoo."

The exclamation rang out around the mostly empty office, but having no one witness her victory didn't dampen it in the slightest. Some of the accountants and tech people had trickled in as she worked on the paper jam, and of course no one had offered to help her. It wasn't Jo's fault everyone thought she was a salty bitch. Well, the perma-scowl she wore probably didn't help, but she saved her smiles and politeness for people who actually deserved it, and with a few exceptions in the form of her friend Blake and some of the administrative assistants, none of those people existed in her office.

Jo sighed heavily as she crumpled up the destroyed paper and tossed it into the bin next to her. She hadn't always been so jaded. When she first started at Elite Sports, she had been bright-eyed and eager to please, so focused on putting her head down and getting the job done that she hadn't noticed some of the more toxic traits of her work culture right away. After a while though, those traits became more and more apparent. Except for Jo, the consultants were all men, and they all liked to comment on her demeanor, telling her to smile more or try to get her to fetch coffee for them, sexist things like that. They also constantly hit on their administrative assistants, a fact that explained why there was such high turnover amongst the group and why it was now comprised almost exclusively of men. No woman in her right mind wanted to work there and Jo couldn't blame them.

There seemed to be no consequences for any concern great or small. Jo knew people went to human resources to complain, even having done so herself on a few occasions, but when absolutely nothing changed, she learned try to stop caring and just do the work. Jo had hated that there was basically no recourse for her when it came to the work culture, but because of that fact, she simply hardened herself up even more than she already had been, saying only what needed to be said and shutting down any inappropriate behavior with a glare or curt comment. It didn't stop it from happening in other parts of the company, but it mostly stopped it from happening around her. It was only a small consolation, but it was something.

Jo finished putting the copier back together before

dusting off her hands and pulling herself up to standing. She looked down at her knees and swore under her breath. They were red and dimpled from the Berber carpet, and she hoped that it would go away before anyone could see and make a snide comment about spending time on her knees or something equally inappropriate. That would be pretty on-brand for some of the guys in the office, but luckily she scared most of them, so maybe they would leave it alone.

Jo opened the repaired machine and was able to successfully copy the endorsement contract for one of her clients, taking the warm papers back to her office and relaxing into her swivel chair, or trying to, anyway. The chair was ancient, the flaking leather a constant source of irritation against her skin, and it would invariably tilt at one odd angle or another. Whenever she had put in a request for a new one, she was told "it wasn't in the budget." Of course, the male consultants had better furniture and offices that actually locked to give them privacy, but whatever. Jo would just add it to the long list of reasons this place sucked, move along with her day, and ignore the crick that was forming in the small of her back as she tried to hold herself upright.

The next few minutes flew by in a flurry of emails and promises to grab lunch with some of her clients over the next couple of weeks. Client lunches were probably the best part of the job because she got to eat out on the company's dime. Jo smiled as she made a note to look at some of the ritzier places for her next few lunches, but the smile fell off her face when a meeting reminder sounded on her laptop. Ugh, another useless strategy meeting. These meetings happened at least once a month and consisted of the founding partners wanting to strategize about how to get more clients and ended with them sticking to the same tired approach that kept the company at the level they were currently at. She leaned back in her chair to pop her back and grabbed her tablet and notepad before heading out to the conference room.

Jo walked in and was greeted with a curious glance at her knees from Lowell North, one of the slimier consultants on the payroll. He smirked, raised one black brow, and opened his mouth to say something, but Jo stopped him with narrowed eyes and pursed lips. He immediately raised his hands up in surrender. "Sorry, Ice Queen. I didn't mean for you to get all frosty on us already," he jeered.

Trent Chadwick, another consultant, chuckled and playfully wrapped his arms around his chest, mock shivering as if they were in the arctic tundra. "Did anyone else notice the temperature drop? I think my balls just froze off."

"As if you had any to begin with," Lowell shot back at his friend, and when Trent replied with a middle finger, the two laughed and a few of the other consultants joined in. The Idiot Brigade was in rare form today.

"Just because we work with athletes doesn't mean we have to act like we work in a locker room, gentlemen," Gavin Delaney remarked as he strode to the front of the room.

That was all the reprimand that the consultants would get, and while it was a nice reminder for them to behave, it wasn't nearly enough. Jo was pretty sure it was just something their boss said to make himself seem like a leader, like he was above it all, even though she had heard whispers about Delaney that she hoped were just rumor, but knew were probably more than that. If shit rolled downhill, then Delaney must be King of Turd Mountain with how bad things were with his underlings.

After taking her seat, Jo watched as the last few consultants, including Blake and Archer, trickled in and took seats around the conference table. Blake sat next to her and elbowed her side, a bright smile on his face. "Congratulate me. I just signed my first LGBT client," he raved in a hushed voice.

"That's amazing," she mouthed back and scribbled a note on a scrap of paper before sliding it to him. *Tell me more over our coffee break?*

Blake read the note and nodded, but Gavin clearing his throat had them turning back to the front. What little fun she'd had was already over, but at least there was the promise of more time with her friend later on.

"If we're done passing notes, children," he scolded. "I'll begin." Jo ignored the smirks and stifled chuckles from the jerk consultants and tried to concentrate as Gavin droned on and on about "mixing it up out there" and "really going for it" as well as other motivational catchphrases that really meant nothing when there was no actual plan behind them. When he finally ended his diatribe about "getting their heads in the game," he asked for ideas and Jo shot her hand up in the air just as she did at every meeting. She tried to get her ideas across all the time to no avail, but she would try again anyway. Giving up on changing the culture was necessary to keep her sanity, but performing her job to the best of her ability was something she could never stop doing.

Gavin looked around the room and when it became obvious no one else had anything to say, he finally called on Jo. "Go head Jolene." He'd nodded his assent, but his voice was already primed to dismiss whatever idea she had.

Undeterred by her boss' lack of interest, Jo straightened in her chair and put on her most persuasive voice. "I really think we should reach out to more female athletes, female-led teams, and female athletic directors." A few groans erupted around the room, but she ignored them and barreled ahead. "Blake and I are the only two consultants who have female clients, and even then I only have two and he has one. We are ignoring a key demographic, and if we represented more women, we could get them the exposure and endorsements they need to create more interest in their respective sports. We have a huge opportunity to change the culture of athletics and we aren't taking it."

"I'm all for exposing more females," Lowell said with a snicker. Jo gave him a look that could wither a rose and he coughed before continuing. "I just don't think that's the direction this company should go in. We need to hit the major leagues a little harder, get more of the big names in men's basketball and football."

"I think Jo's idea has merit," Archer chimed in. Jo whipped her head in his direction, surprised to see someone other than Blake agreeing with her. To see Archer putting himself out there on her behalf put her off balance. Jo shook her head, there must be some other angle for Archer to speak up like this. "Female sports are getting more and more popular, and we don't want to be left behind."

"That's a good point, Archer." Gavin stroked his chin thoughtfully as he actually took time to consider the idea, *her* idea. "Maybe look into some numbers and report back to me with more on what you're thinking."

Jo had to rest her head on her chin to keep her jaw from dropping. While she liked that Gavin was finally seeing value in what she had to contribute, she hated that he was giving the credit and the assignment to Archer. No matter how many times she got passed over, she couldn't seem to make peace with it. Jo liked to tell herself that she was over it, but every time it happened, she felt her blood pressure skyrocket and her fists clench. It would take a year of kickboxing classes to exercise away all of her pent-up anger.

"Shouldn't…" Archer started, looking over at Jo with confusion, but Gavin interrupted him before he could finish.

"Ultimately though, I agree with Lowell," Gavin replied, surprising no one. "Let's stick with the direction we have for now. Everyone put your ears to the ground and let me know if you hear of any big names looking for new marketing representation." With that, he strode from the room, officially ending the meeting.

Jo shook her head and frowned, her teeth gnashing together like a cement mixer. A warm hand pat her shoulder and she looked over to see Blake smiling sadly at her with sympathy in his eyes. "Sorry, Jojo Beans. You'll get 'em next time," he assured her before standing and leaving the room. Jo had heard enough empty platitudes when her mom had passed and every time she mentioned it after to last a lifetime, but even though she and Blake both knew his promise was an empty one, it was nice to hear him to say it.

Jo glanced out of the clear walls of the conference room over to Gavin's office. He might not listen to her about female athletes, but he would listen to her when it came to her getting a promotion, and she was fired up enough at the moment to finally go demand it. She turned back to the table, gathering her tablet and notepad before standing up and making her way out of the room. A hand on her elbow stopped her, and she swung around with every intention of giving whoever was touching her what for, but she stopped when she saw it was Archer. She flicked her eyes down at his strong-looking hand before looking back up at him with a raised brow.

Archer dropped his hold on her elbow and took a cautious

step back, smiling sheepishly at her as he did. "No harm meant." His voice held a slight tremor, and Jo wondered if maybe her resting *don't fuck with me* face needed to soften a little bit. She didn't want anyone messing with her, but the idea that Archer found her to be that terrifying didn't sit right for some reason. The man had been nothing but a nuisance since he'd show up, but at least he wasn't as outright horrible as most everyone else. He shuffled his feet along the floor, cheeks turning a shade pinker as he continued to stare at her. "I was wondering, since it was your idea and all, if maybe you have time to help me run those numbers Gavin requested about the female athlete demographic."

The scowl Jo always wore at work deepened. Of course he was asking her to do his homework for him. Typical of this office, and here she had tried to give him the benefit of the doubt and actually listen to what he had to say. She'd shown him the ropes weeks ago, but it seemed like she still wasn't done babysitting. "So, you want me to do all the work for you so you can take all of the credit?"

Archer reared back, the accusation she'd thrown hitting him harder than she expected it to. "Whoa. Th-that's not..." he sputtered, looking flustered, but Jo held up a hand to stop him.

"Save it," she ground out between her clenched teeth. "You already have all my big clients, so why not have all my ideas too, right?" She flicked her finger across her tablet to access her email. "Would you like me to attach the spreadsheets with projected revenue growth tied to an increase in female representation, or would you prefer I simply hand over all of the scouting reports and interviews I did with potential clients? Just how much of my hard work would you like to pass off as your own?" It wasn't his fault that their boss constantly overlooked her, but he still seemed to be trying to take credit for her work and that pissed her off.

Archer's scowl nearly matched her own and he raised his hands in surrender. "You know what? Forget it." He walked out of the room, taking all of her righteous indignation with him.

Jo slumped against the wall and sighed. Between the meeting and another short spat with her rival, she was exhausted and it wasn't even lunchtime. At least the glass she was leaning against helped to cool her overheated skin. As she felt her blood pressure return to normal, she replayed the interaction over in her mind and realized two things: she may have overreacted to Archer's request for help, and she probably owed him an apology. Jo wasn't going to acknowledge either of those things at the moment though because she had a promotion to demand.

With a curt nod of her head, she brushed aside the talk with Archer and marched over to Delaney's office. Charles Whitcomb was a partner, but he oversaw the financial reporting and the schmoozing of investors, so it was Gavin who would ultimately approve her moving up to senior consultant. Jo stopped at the desk of his administrative assistant, Janine. The woman was in her late forties and was always kind to everyone, so her working at that office made little sense to Jo, but she wasn't going to drive away a friendly face by asking too many questions of the woman.

Pasting a polite smile on her face, Jo tapped the edge of the desk. "Hey, Janine. Does Gavin have a minute?"

The woman peered over her purple-framed glasses to look at a day planner and returned Jo's smile, though hers looked far more genuine. "If you hurry, you can catch him before his next meeting." The woman tipped her head toward the double doors that lead to

Delaney's office.

Jo stepped over and knocked on the frame of one of the open doors. "Gavin? Can I have a second?"

Gavin looked up from his computer and smiled at Jo. It looked more perfunctory than friendly, but she was used to that from her boss. Was anyone here actually happy to see anyone else? Jo seriously doubted it. "Certainly," he said. "Come on in." He gestured to one of the plush seats in front of his large, wooden desk and Jo held back a groan as she slid into the comfortable chair. Why couldn't she have one of these in her office?

"Thanks." Suddenly nervous, Jo felt her mouth go desert dry as she tried to think of the best way to get what she wanted.

Gavin looked at her expectantly and she clasped her hands in her lap to stop them from shaking. As much as she tried to always act like a badass, she still got anxious when it came to certain things, like asking for something when the outcome was less than sure. She hated it when she wasn't in control, and this was one such occasion. Gathering her courage, Jo took a deep breath and decided to just go for it.

"Gavin, I think it is long past time that I was promoted to senior consultant. I've been with the company for over five years now, and I have done excellent work. I bring a lot to the agency and will continue to do so with the new title and more responsibility." She exhaled, happy to have said her peace.

Gavin leaned back in his chair and stroked his dimpled chin with a finger. Jo had seen his thinking face enough times to know that he was at least considering her idea, but she had no read on what his reaction might be, and that bothered her. "You have been with us a while, and I know you do good work, Jolene."

Jo's shoulders stiffened and she tried not to visibly cringe at the use of her full name. Her mother had named her after the Dolly Parton song, and while Jo enjoyed the tune, she didn't really love the moniker. It was far too old fashioned for her, but it clearly resonated with her boss.

"I'm not sure it's been enough, though." The small sliver of hope she had been holding onto that he would actually approve her moving up slipped through her fingers. She should be used to disappointment at work by now, but not being recognized for all her hard work hurt.

Jo peered around the room as she gathered her thoughts, seeing walls covered in all of the man's accolades, but noted that none of them were dated from the last decade. Getting the approval from a man who was stuck in the past ultimately didn't matter, but getting the raise so her dad could retire sooner did. She looked back to Gavin and asked the question she already knew the answer to. "What more can I do to prove myself?" Jo was already doing everything she could think of and really had no idea what else could be done beyond signing the hottest player in the NFL or NBA as one of their clients, and the odds of that happening were slimmer than Blake's fashionable ties.

"Well, that's the question now, isn't it?" he said vaguely, smiling at her in what she assumed was supposed to be a friendly gesture, but it looked completely out of place on his weathered face. He stood up and she followed as he walked her to the door in a clear dismissal of both her and the promotion. "I think that if you keep at it and land us a few big clients, we can revisit this conversation again in the future." Jo nodded and turned to leave, but Gavin called back to her. "And Jolene?"

"Yes?" she asked hesitantly, afraid of what else he might say. If he told her that she needed to take her clients out to dinner more often, she might lose it.

"It wouldn't kill you to smile a little more often, sweetheart," Gavin winked before shutting the door to his office.

Jo rolled her eyes as she sighed wearily and passed Janine, giving the woman a small wave before slipping back over to her office and shutting the door. She leaned a hand on the corner of her desk and held back tears. They were tears of anger, frustration, and most of all, exhaustion. She was just so tired, so worn out to the core of her being from working herself to the bone and getting nothing in return. Where was she supposed to find some big client all while doing what she had been all along? She already came in before anyone else and left long after they were all gone. What more could she do?

Jo blinked away the moisture in her eyes, pulled her phone out of her pocket, and swiped over to the folder that held all of her hookup apps, whining in frustration when she remembered that the folder was now empty and she no longer had her favorite means of working off all of this frustration. Her friends wouldn't know if she cheated and went back on her promise of no hookups, but she would. Somehow, knowing that she failed at a challenge she made for herself was worse than her current predicament. Jo felt like she needed to prove something to herself, so she swiped away from the empty folder and over to her texts, opening the group chat she shared with Gigi and Millie.

Jo: **Is it Friday yet? I need pizza and wine pronto.**

Gigi's reply came almost immediately. Either the tea shop was slow today or she too was eager for an escape. For her friend's sake, Jo hoped it was the former.

Gigi: **Two more days and then its pizza, wine, and eye**

candy from *Top Gun: Maverick.*

Her chest, which had felt in danger of caving in, lightened considerably, and Jo chuckled at her friend's reply and let her thumbs fly across the screen.

Jo: **Are we sure Millie can handle the shirtless beach scene? I hope you have a fainting couch at the ready.**

Millie: **Ha ha. I can handle it. I've seen all three Magic Mike movies after all.**

Gigi: **You saw the last one without me?** ☹

Millie: **It was on one of my dates. I think I accidentally matched up with a gay guy because he seemed way more interested in Channing Tatum than me. We're taking a cooking class together next week though, so there's that.**

Jo sighed at Millie having another unsuccessful date and watched as Gigi's reply came in.

Gigi: **No dating gay men, Mills. You're supposed to be falling in love with someone, not finding a new best friend.**

Jo: **Yeah, you don't need more friends. You have us.**

Millie: **We can talk more about it on Friday.**

Jo chuckled and turned off her phone. She was excited to see her best friends this week, and not just because she needed the stress relief. Maybe they could help her come up with a few ideas for how to find a big client, because she was tapped out both creatively and physically. If she didn't come up with something soon, she would have to make peace with the fact that her career was going nowhere fast. As horrible as being stuck at the worst job ever was, Jo would never leave her dad. Pops was the only family she had left, and while she might not need much in her life, she did need that.

## Chapter Four

*Archer*

Fridays always seemed to go on in a never-ending loop of phone calls and emails from clients, managers, and talent scouts. Archer groaned and rubbed his dry eyes that felt like sandpaper against his eyelids. It seemed as though he had been staring at the computer screen in front of him for hours, and when his eyes flicked over to the tiny clock in the bottom right corner, he saw that he actually had been. The one bright spot was that it was just after 4:00, and he would be leaving soon, but not nearly soon enough for how weary his body felt. Archer always took off slightly early on Friday so that he could have dinner with his sister and her family, and he was really looking forward to it after the long week he'd just had. His sister, Caroline, had moved to Willow Creek after she finished her finance degree in Alabama so that she and her then boyfriend, Todd, could be closer to his family. They got married one summer later and they have lived in the suburbs of the small city with their two boys ever since.

Archer had loved living in Alabama, and it was still taking some time for him to adjust to his new reality. His former firm was much larger, so Archer was used to having a lot more resources at his fingertips, like his own administrative assistant rather than the one he shared with three other consultants. He ended up doing his own admin work most days just to save time. No use sending an email that would take half a day to get a response to when he could just file something himself. It didn't help that some of the other consultants spent half their time flirting with the female admins instead of working, keeping them distracted most of the day as well.

The culture at work bothered him, but as the new guy, he wasn't sure what he could really do about it. It didn't help that he had basically been given the job because of his dad's relationship with the boss. Gavin Delaney had gone to college with his dad, and Archer hadn't minded using the connection to get himself a job. He had actually been pleasantly surprised with how welcoming the two founders of the firm had been when he arrived. Archer had figured he would need to start from the ground up as far as finding clients was concerned, but the partners explained that due to his education and experience, they were transferring some of their bigger clients that the other consultants were having trouble handling over to him. Archer felt like he would be spitting in Delaney's face, and his father's too, if he made complaints to human resources, so he kept his head down.

Everything seemed to be working out in his favor, but it still felt like something in his life was missing. If he asked his sister about it, she would tell him he needed a woman, and while that would be nice, he wasn't sure that would fill the void. Maybe he just needed to get out of the office more. Archer hadn't really bothered to explore his new city much yet, sticking mostly to the area surrounding his house and the closest grocery store. He should call his sister or brother-in-law and go grab a beer some night away from the kids. A night out with adults he didn't work with might be just what the doctor ordered.

Archer looked at the clock once more, lamenting the fact that only five minutes had passed since the last time he checked. He navigated to his email and was typing up a maintenance request for his squeaky office chair when something hit him square in the chest. Startled, he looked down into his lap to see the tiny rubber snake he had placed on Jo's office chair earlier. Archer smiled at it and swallowed a laugh before schooling his features and tilting his head back up to meet the gaze of the woman herself.

Her arms were crossed, pushing her modest chest up and creating a line of cleavage that peeked out just above her silk tank, and a look of exasperation was painted on her face. "I grew up rolling around in the dirt and catching toads near the creek," she said matter-of-factly. She reached up and swept a stray curl behind her ear, looking utterly bored with both him and his pranks. "You'll have to do better than a rubber snake if you really want to rile me up."

Archer smirked and placed the snake in his laptop bag so he could be sure to return it to his nephew. She may not have been impressed, but it did it managed to get her in his office, so as far as he was concerned it was *mission accomplished.* "Is that a challenge?" He didn't mind admitting that he was behind the pranks. It was fun, having to think of new and interesting ways of getting under her skin. Messing with her coffee was by far the easiest, but he also discovered that he could annoy her by adding googly eyes to just about anything in her office and taping a twenty pack of pine-scented car air fresheners underneath her desk. Watching her hunt around for the source of the smell for half the morning had brought a smile to his face and still did anytime he thought about it.

Jo sighed, tilting her head to look at him sardonically. "You could take it as a challenge, or you could leave me alone to do my work instead of having to come over to your office twice a day to complain about your childish behavior," she sassed.

Oh, how he would love to kiss the sass right out of her, but as that wasn't an option, he had to settle for schoolyard pranks.

Archer rested his hands behind his head and leaned back in his chair. "You could always just stop complaining," he suggested. In reality, he would be devastated if she actually took him up on the offer and stopped coming around to scold him.

Despite her chilly demeanor and the chewing out she gave him in the conference room the other day, Archer found himself consistently drawn to the woman. It was frustrating beyond reason, and he was certain a psychologist would tell him he had unresolved issues or something he needed to work out, but neither of those things mattered whenever she popped her pretty face and smart mouth into his office. It was like all of the horrible interactions they had since that first day couldn't erase his initial impression from his mind. She was smart, funny, and sexy as hell. It really was a shame that she hated him so much. Archer had the feeling they could be something really great together if she could knock that chip off her shoulder.

"If I couldn't complain about work, I would have nothing to talk about," she quipped.

He sincerely doubted that was true. Jo seemed like the type of woman who probably had an opinion on everything, and a very strong opinion at that. Archer wondered how he could find out what those opinions were, but his musings were interrupted by his phone alarm chiming. Shrugging off his musings on Jo, he shut it off and started to pack up his things for the day.

Jo huffed from the doorway. "Leaving so soon? Must be nice."

"I'm having dinner with my sister and nephews," he explained.

Even though he didn't owe her an explanation, Archer didn't like the idea of Jo thinking of him as a slacker, not wanting to add to the large pile of reasons she'd conjured to dislike him. It shouldn't matter, but her opinion of him was really important for some reason. Maybe it was because so few people held her good opinion, but he couldn't help wanting to be one of them. Though it could just have easily been that he'd spent too much time at work. No matter. A home cooked meal and some good company was going to be a great way to kick off the weekend and set himself to rights.

"Seeing as how you have the maturity level of a five-year-old, maybe while you're with the kids you can ask them to teach you some manners so you can learn how to play nice with the other boys and girls in the office," she clucked with a smile, her eyes lighting up with mirth.

Jo really was a beautiful woman when she let go of all the frustration she seemed to carry around everywhere. He liked to see it and hoped to keep the fun going. "Great idea," he shot back, powering down his laptop. "I'll ask them for some tips for you as well. Maybe they have some thoughts on how the Ice Queen can thaw out a little bit."

When the small smile she had been wearing slipped off her face and her shoulders slumped slightly, he immediately regretted his choice of words. Where there was once a playful smirk now sat pressed lips and an expression on her face he couldn't quite decipher. If he didn't know any better, he would have called it hurt, but Jo was the toughest person in the office. Even she would regularly made jokes about freezing her colleague's hearts if they had them, so he wasn't sure why his using the same nickname would matter.

"Have a good weekend," she said flatly, before

marching out the door.

"Jo..." he started, shoving his laptop in his briefcase and gathering the rest of his things to go after her, but as he stepped out of his office and looked down the hall, Jo was nowhere to be found. He shook his head at himself and locked his office. "Way to go, Hayes. That was some real Busch League behavior," he grumbled into his chest.

Playing goofy pranks was one thing, but calling her names, particularly one given as a means to isolate her from the rest of the consultants was another. Whatever positive ground he had made with Jo over the last few minutes just slipped out from underneath him. Hopefully his sister had some beer at her house because suddenly Archer found that he needed a drink, hoping it would help him forget the hurt look on Jo's face, and the fact that he'd been the one to put it there.

****

"Caro, I'm here," Archer called out as he opened the door to his sister's home. She always left it unlocked when she knew he was coming over, the small gesture making him feel even more welcome than he already had in her home. He slipped off his oxford shoes and kicked them over near a bench in the entryway were they joined an army of sneakers.

Archer ambled down the hallway in just his socks, loving the feel of the soft carpet underneath as he rolled the sleeves of his button-down shirt up to the elbow. It was nice to finally be away from work and relax a little. As he entered the kitchen, his oldest nephew, Timothy, was sitting at the table playing a handheld video game. The kid was mesmerized, not stirring at the sound of his voice or his coming further into the kitchen, so Archer just patted his head as he walked by before going over to his sister and leaning over to give her a hug.

"What's up, sis?" He glanced around the room and noticed his brother-in-law and other nephew were missing. "Where are Todd and Trevor?"

Caro smirked as she plated up some family style pasta. "Trevor had a birthday party for someone in his kindergarten class, and Todd was excited to take him, so it's just the three of us tonight."

Archer raised a brow at his sister. There was no way his brother-in-law willingly signed up to attend a kid's birthday party. He was a great guy and was good with kids, something he had to be as a high school science teacher, but there was a reason he taught teenagers and not elementary school children.

Caro shrugged a shoulder. "Fine. He lost rock, paper, scissors and had to go. Besides, you were coming over and we all know you would rather hang out with me anyway," she proclaimed with a smile.

"Do we all know that, or do you just think that?" he asked, getting a cooked noodle whipped at him as a reply. He peeled it off his face and ate it.

"You're such a child," his sister commented, and he was instantly reminded of the similar comment he had received from Jo just half an hour before. Would he ever be able to go more than five minutes without thinking about her? He hoped so, or he was in for one miserable existence.

"That's what they tell me," Archer replied. Eager for a distraction from his earlier interaction with Jo, he pushed off the kitchen island and helped his sister carry the food over to the small dining table in the corner.

Caro's kitchen was a rosy pink color with a white wooden dining table. It reminded Archer of an old-timey ice cream parlor, and he idly hoped Caro had some mint chocolate chip in her freezer for dessert. He didn't have much of a sweet tooth, but he needed something to obliterate the mess of feelings in his brain.

"Hey, screens away, please," Caro said to her son.

With a disgruntled groan, his nephew reluctantly ended his game and joined the rest of them in reality. After that, the three of them sat down and chatted while they enjoyed their meal of spaghetti Bolognese, garlic bread, and a garden salad. His sister didn't have beer, but she had red wine, so Archer made do. It hadn't erased the earlier interaction with his female colleague from his mind, but it took the edge off his discomfort.

After his nephew had gobbled down his food like a starving man and disappeared upstairs to organize his Pokémon cards, Archer and his sister enjoyed the rest of the meal in relative quiet, talking about her kids and their family plans for summer. During a break in conversation, he polished off his glass of wine, and looked across the small dining table to see his sister giving him a thorough once over.

"What?" he asked, suddenly feeling very self-conscious. Archer and Caro were close enough that she could easily get a read on him, a fact he lamented as she continued to study him.

Eventually, Caro clucked her tongue and nodded to the now-empty glass. "Tough week?"

Archer sighed, not bothering to hide just how much work was affecting him. "It wasn't tough, per se. Just long and monotonous." He picked at the crust of bread that remained on his plate before pushing it away. "The firm I'm at now is just a little behind the times and it's an adjustment."

Caro frowned, two little lines forming between her eyes. "Behind the times how?" she asked, swirling her wine glass before taking a sip while she waited for his reply.

Archer turned his thoughts over in his head for a

minute while he thought of the best way to put his observations into words. "In some ways that don't really matter and others that do." He blew a harsh breath out through his lips and continued. "Like, the offices could use a face lift and there are some computer programs that would make things easier that just aren't being employed. While all this is going on, we're expected to woo big clients away from larger firms when we're kind of a dog and pony show."

Caro chuckled at his characterization of his workplace. "Well, have you suggested those changes?" she asked, looking at him intently.

Archer scoffed. "I'm the new kid, remember? I think I need to be there at least a full year before I start trying to change everything." He'd briefly entertained the idea a dozen times already and already dismissed it, and this time was no different. "No, I'm just going to keep my head down and focus on work."

His sister frowned and Archer could see the worry tinged with disappointment shining out from her eyes the same hue as his own. "You should be focusing on something more fun. Like dating." She reached a hand over and touched the sleeve of his button-down, her face growing more concerned the longer she looked at him. "I want a sister-in-law and my kids need cousins, but I haven't heard you once talk about a date or sound even remotely interested in a woman in a really long time," she complained.

When he heard the words "date" and "woman," he immediately thought of Jo again, and while he was attracted to her physically and loved to tease her, there was no way they would ever make a good couple. She clearly despised him and was not afraid to show it. He was also fairly certain he had never heard her talk about her personal life, so he wasn't even sure if she was currently dating. Hell, she could be in a relationship or even be married for all he knew. Suddenly his mouth tasted sour and his stomach felt heavy, the thought of Jo being taken not sitting well. Either that or he had too much pasta. He was going to attribute it to the latter, despite knowing full well he could digest carbs easily.

"No, I'm going to focus on work. Maybe after I'm fully settled I can think about dating, but not before that," he vowed.

Caro sighed and stood up, gathering the empty dishes and walking them to the sink. "That all sounds well and good, Arch, but I think getting out onto the dating scene would help you feel settled, and if things work out, maybe you could be happy too."

Archer hummed noncommittally and walked over to help her with the dishes.

Later that night as he was sitting on the couch in his apartment, Archer considered downloading some dating apps and looking at what was out there for him, but somehow, the idea still held little appeal. It didn't take him thinking about it for long for him to come to the reason why. Jo's bright blue eyes flashed through his mind and he smiled sadly. The one woman he couldn't stop thinking about was one woman who wouldn't date him, not in a million years.

Determined to put her out of his mind, Archer got off the couch and locked his door. When he got into his bedroom, he walked over to the window to close the curtains, pausing for a moment to look up at the night sky. As he did, he could help but notice a few scattered stars already shining brightly. *Just like Jo's freckles,* he thought as he drew the curtains together, the realization that he was already in deep coming a little too late. Resigned to his fate, all Archer could do was keep going and hope he didn't drown.

## Chapter Five

*Jo*

Jo's living space was never the ideal place to hold girl's night, but it was her turn to play hostess, so she and her two friends did their best to squeeze in to the small studio apartment that she rented. The complex itself was pretty small, but it was one of the most secure in the area. Pops had insisted that if Jo wasn't going to live at home after graduating from college, something that was unthinkable to her given her penchant for hooking up, she needed to be somewhere he would know she was safe. It was a touching thought, and she loved her dad for thinking of her, she just wished that the space itself was a little bigger.

On the plus side, Jo's apartment was nicely decorated with cream walls, a chandelier over the small living area, and some strategically placed windows helping to create a bright, welcoming atmosphere. A sliding, dark wood barn door separating the bathroom and walk-in closet from the rest of the apartment and a stained glass window above the sink of her small kitchenette were lovely touches that made the place feel just the slightest bit luxurious. Still not luxurious enough for her and her friends to really spread out, though.

"Sorry, Jojo," Millie said, apologizing for the second time in as many minutes when she accidentally elbowed Jo in the side. It hadn't hurt in the slightest, but it was damned inconvenient.

The three friends were currently on her small sofa, drinking wine and snacking on cheese, crackers, and chocolate. Enough chocolate that it was practically another guest at their little party. After the week she'd had, Jo was ready to consume at least a few pounds of the sweet stuff until she felt better.

"Stop apologizing, Mills," Jo said to her friend with a smile. It was the first genuine one she'd worn all day, and she hoped that a little more time with her friends would bring out more of them. "It's not your fault I live in a sardine can." A beautiful, but incredibly tiny sardine can.

"A very cute sardine can." Gigi echoed Jo's own thoughts as she grabbed a dark chocolate truffle from the platter on the coffee table. She took a bite and chewed it with more force than one would think necessary for a smooth, creamy chocolate treat. Gigi was normally a dainty eater, but right now she looked like she wanted to destroy the bittersweet confection.

"You okay, Gi?" Jo asked. Millie was the calmest of the three of them and Jo was definitely the most volatile as far as harsher emotions went with Gigi landing somewhere in the middle. To see such an outward display of frustration from her was slightly concerning. "You're biting into that truffle like it has personally offended you or something."

Gigi seesawed her head and sipped her wine. Once she had finished the glass, she rested it against her chest, seemingly needing it as a comfort object. "I think something's wrong with Cooper," she sniffed, holding onto the glass tighter. "He's been acting weird ever since we had dinner with my parents."

Jo snorted. "Anyone would be weird after spending time with Clifford and Theodora. The fact that he met them and hasn't run in the opposite direction practically makes him a superhero. Marry the man," she told Gigi, looking down at her own empty glass. How many had she already drunk? If she was talking about marriage, probably a few too many. She wasn't opposed to the institution, but she'd never seen herself participating in it either. Jo put her glass on the table and pushed it away.

Gigi smiled wistfully. "I'd like to, actually," she admitted, a blush forming in her cheeks.

"Really?" Millie asked, already bouncing in the seat next to her. Anything romance related energized their librarian friend, and this time was no different. "That's so amazing. I'm sure the weirdness is probably nothing, but you could always talk to him about it."

Gigi nodded, biting her lip. "Maybe after my drag brunch next week." Her friend turned to look at the two of them, eyes hopeful. "You guys are still coming, right?"

Jo lightly punched Gigi's shoulder at her thinking she even had to ask. "Of course we are, silly." Jo leaned over to grab a truffle, and stuffed the entire thing into her mouth. "We already have tickets," she mumbled, her mouth full of deliciously rich chocolate.

"Good." Gigi sighed wearily but her eyes danced with amusement. "I'm a little nervous, but I'm super excited too." Gigi was putting on her first-ever drag queen brunch at her tea room, The Happy Kettle. The Kettle was a gorgeous tea room that was a beloved fixture of the community. Normally Gigi only served high tea at her shop, but next week she would be serving up hot drag queen performances as the culmination of her birthday challenge to bring something a little different to their small town.

"It's going to be amazing," Millie gushed, giving their friend a hug, or rather, as much of a hug as was possible given the close quarters of the small sofa. It looked more like two T-rexes trying to wrestle, the sight bringing another much needed smile to Jo's face.

"Thanks." Gigi seemed more relaxed, which was

always a good thing. Girls' night wasn't much fun when they were all anxious or upset about something. Gigi looked over to Millie. "Want to tell us about your latest date?"

Millie blew out a slow breath, and Jo had a feeling that her latest date had probably gone about as well as her others, which was to say not well at all. "Can I not? It was kind of a disaster and I don't really want to relive it right now," she pleaded.

Jo leaned her head on Millie's shoulder, offering her what little comfort she could. She felt awful that her friend, the sweetest, most loving person she had ever met in her entire life was having a horrible time trying to find her person. Who wouldn't want a smart, gorgeous woman who was also probably the best cook and baker in the county? Though, it certainly didn't help that Millie was still hopelessly hung up on Gigi's brother, Ford. At least she was branching out and trying to date other people, since the likelihood of her and Ford getting together was almost zero. He was too under his overbearing parent's thumbs, much like Gigi had been before dating Cooper.

Jo reached over and patted Millie's leg, wishing there was more that she could do. "It'll happen for you, Mills. I just know it."

Millie smiled sadly. "It would be nice if it would happen soon, but I guess I can wait," she conceded, clasping Jo's hand to give it a little squeeze before letting it go and sipping her wine. Millie had only had about a quarter of a glass, as per usual, and Jo idly wondered what it would be like if Millie ever drank a little too much. In all their years of friendship, she had never seen it and wondered what kind of drunk Millie would be. Probably one who still made sure everyone else was taken care of before passing out comfortably in her own bed. "So, Jo, how are you doing without, you know...?"

Millie trailed off before making a lewd gesture with her hands.

Jo snorted. "You can say sex, Mills," she teased, smiling when Millie blushed, her cheeks turning a deep red.

"I know that," she whispered before leveling Jo with a shrewd look. "You didn't answer my question though."

Jo exhaled slowly through her pursed lips. How did she put into words just how hard it was to not been getting some much needed release in the form of no-strings attached sex? "Honestly? It sucks, big time. I can't remember being this worked up, and no matter how much I exercise or how many sex toys I go through, it doesn't take the edge off." She rubbed a hand over her face and rolled her shoulder, wishing the act did more than just loosen her muscles slightly. "It doesn't help that I have to deal with the new guy constantly annoying the ever-loving crap out of me," she admitted. Archer did annoy her. Stupid, handsome, irritating, gorgeous man.

"Uh-huh," Gigi said with a smirk, her eyes flicking over to Millie, and the two of them shared a knowing look.

"What?" Jo asked her friend, narrowing her eyes to try and decipher the expression on her face.

Gigi shrugged a shoulder. "Nothing. It's just, you seem to talk about this new guy an awful lot. It just makes me wonder if maybe there isn't something there. He does seem to be the only guy to ever really keep you on your toes," she sang, reaching out for another truffle.

Jo huffed. "I'm on my toes all the time because he's always pranking me. I have to stay vigilant, or he wins." Archer was a prankster, and while part of her secretly liked the attention, the part of her that liked winning did not. Jo had always been competitive, and while she might not be succeeding at work in the traditional sense, she could at least be the victor in whatever battles occurred between them.

"Wins what?" Millie asked sarcastically. "This little imaginary war you're fighting in your head."

Jo took Millie's wine glass away from her and put it on the table. Her normally sweet friend was getting a little too sassy for her liking. Or maybe it was more about Jo not liking being called out so accurately, but she wasn't going to think on that for too long and instead set the facts straight. "It is not imaginary," Jo insisted, tossing up her hands. "He stole my clients and is getting credit for my ideas. How is that not a real war?" Jo had worked so hard for so long and it all got swept away and given to someone else. It was maddening.

Gigi scratched the underside of her ponytail. "Yeah, but wasn't that your jerk boss's doing? Not exactly new guy's fault if you ask me."

Jo sighed. Gigi wasn't wrong, but it was more complicated than that. *Wasn't it?* "I mean, yes, it was Gavin's idea. I know it's not really Archer's fault that he's benefitting from Delaney's stupid, sexist ways, but I can still be mad at him for pranking me." She crossed her arms over her chest, as if she could hide the fact that she secretly enjoyed it. As she did, Jo remembered what had bothered her the most of all of Archer's transgressions. "And he called me the Ice Queen earlier today," she spat out petulantly.

Millie rubbed her hand up and down Jo's arm slowly. It was warm and soft, much like the woman herself. Jo may not have a mom anymore, but she did have the next best thing in her friends. "That doesn't sound very nice, but I thought you didn't care when people called you that," she reminded her.

"I don't," Jo insisted, and she didn't, for the most

part. There was something different about when Archer said it though. He was different. The other consultants were always rude and had been since she started, but pranks aside, Archer had actually been pretty decent, so it hurt when he used the same moniker the other guys did. She didn't really want to examine why, but by the look she saw on Gigi's face, they weren't going to let her get away with not going there.

"It seems like it hurt your feelings when he did it, though. Was that the case?" Gigi asked. Already getting to the heart of things.

"Yes," she admitted, quietly. Jo liked everyone to think she was tough, and she was most of the time, but every now and then something or someone would sneak its way in and bruise her heart a little bit. It turned out Archer was that kind of someone. She wasn't sure how he had gotten past the walls she'd so purposefully constructed around the more sensitive parts of herself, but he had, and she hated how vulnerable it made her feel.

"Do you think that maybe there's a reason that it hurt when he said it, but no one else?" Millie asked, prompting her to think about her feelings. It was a bit sad that her two friends had to hold her hands and lead her to her feelings all the time, but Jo didn't do emotions well. Emotions were messy and unmanageable, and she didn't do things she couldn't control.

Jo hadn't needed to think too hard about the reason why her feelings had been hurt. She had known from the moment they met in the elevator that there was something different about Archer, but she really, really didn't want to think about what that might be or how that made her feel. It was so much easier to hate him, or at least pretend like she hated him. He truly was annoying sometimes, like an overly energetic puppy, but it was in a sort of loveable way. The word "loveable" caused her chest to tighten, and she didn't enjoy the feeling, so she busted out her favorite coping mechanism: deflection.

"I'm sure there's a reason, but like you not wanting to relive your nightmare date, I'm not ready to dive down that particular rabbit hole just yet." Jo hopped up off her couch and grabbed her laptop, which had been resting on top of her unmade bed. Jo never made her bed. What was the point of making up a bed she was just going to sleep in later that day anyway? She was hardly ever home enough to enjoy her tiny apartment, and that included the sight of a made bed. Jo sat back down on the sofa and pulled up a dating match website that had a satisfaction guarantee. "Now, how about instead of me thinking about my feelings, you two help me make a dating profile? You can help me weed through the fuckboys and choose a suitable match."

Gigi and Millie looked at one another, silently communicating again. Jo knew what they were thinking, of course—the three of them had been friends for too long for her not to. They were thinking that she was just avoiding the inevitable and burying her feelings instead of having to deal with them. They were right, but that wasn't going to stop her from doing it anyway. An hour later when she had her profile set up and already had some messages, her friends helped her go through them, not another mention of Archer from either one. Too bad he was still the only guy she was thinking about the whole time she scrolled through profiles, and for a long time after her friends had left for the night.

****

Sunday was probably Jo's favorite day of the week. She had breakfast with her dad, usually stopping by her old house to make him an egg white omelet, oatmeal soufflé, or something equally nutritious and that he would actually eat, grumbling about it needing salt and bacon the whole time. This week, Pops had managed to convince her to meet him at Barb's Diner down near the garage. Since Jo needed to work on her car anyway and wasn't allowed to at her apartment complex, she figured that she could cave on his request just this once.

Jo swallowed her comments about sticking to his diet as she watched her dad mop up the pool of syrup on his plate with a giant piece of pancake. She didn't want to be the person who was constantly nagging him about food and exercise, but she was worried about him. At his last check-up, his doctor had put him on blood pressure medication, and while he was taking it religiously as far as she knew, Jo still wanted to make sure she could do everything within her power to make sure her dad stuck around for a very long time. Jo missed her mom, and the pain of it was something she still carried with her, but she had always been a bit of a daddy's girl, even more so after her mom passed. Her dad was basically her whole world, so losing him as well just wasn't an option. What was all of her hard work at a place she didn't like even for if not to keep him around for as long as she could?

"Stop watching me eat, Joley-bear," her dad muttered as he gnawed on a slice of undercooked bacon. "I'm doing just fine, so you can tuck your worries away."

Jo smiled apologetically. "Sorry, Pops," she muttered. Forking off a piece of her pancakes with strawberries, she tried to enjoy the sweet, sugary flavor, but it tasted a bit like cardboard in her mouth. It was hard to enjoy what you ate when your stomach was knotted with worry, and right now hers felt like it was tangled up like a pretzel. "How's the garage doing?" she asked, hoping to get her mind off her thoughts about losing her dad. Maybe hearing him talk about how great things were at the shop would help alleviate some of her fears about him working himself into an early grave.

Her dad smiled, put down his fork, and took a sip of his pitch-black coffee. "It's good." He took another slow sip of the warm, caffeinated beverage before continuing. He'd always been one to savor the little things while Jo ate like the food would disappear at any moment. She tried to be more like him, but she just didn't have the time. She worked so he wouldn't have to much longer, and she was okay with that. "We've got a lot of business coming though since summer is just around the corner. The books look good, and all the guys seem happy, especially Cooper. I haven't seen that boy stop smiling since he started seeing our Miss Gigi."

Jo smiled, the pressure in her chest feeling lighter after hearing how good things were at his shop. "Yeah, they seem pretty happy." She drank from her own coffee cup, the warm liquid helping to wash down the sticky sweetness from her breakfast.

Pops inspected her from across the table, his cloud-gray eyes narrowing as he did. "You could be happy too." He looked at her imploringly before attacking his pancakes once more with gusto.

"I am," she replied automatically. She was happy, wasn't she? Jo didn't really love the job she spent most of her time at, and she was always worried about her dad, and despite the time she spent with Pops and her friends, she was actually pretty lonely and had been for a while. Hooking up served a purpose, but she had never used it to make a connection with another person outside of a physical one. Maybe one of the guys she was messaging through the dating site would work out to be someone she could connect with, if she ever found the time to actually meet up with one, that is.

Pops looked at her skeptically. "Are you really, Joley-bear?" His expression was full of doubt as he gazed at her. "It seems like you're either working on your clients, working on your car, or working on my health. I don't see a smile on your face nearly often enough," he lamented as he pointed at her with his fork. "I want to see you *actually* happy."

Jo turned her head to look out the window. It was less about the view of the street and passing cars and more about making sure her dad didn't see the tears that had started to pool in her eyes. She spent all her time worrying about her dad, and here he was worrying about her. How had they gotten here? As nice as it was that he cared about her, Jo couldn't let him worry. Pops needed to focus on taking care of himself. Jo took a deep breath and steeled herself. She was an adult and could handle things, so she blinked away the moisture in her eyes and cleared the emotion from her throat before turning back to face him. "I'm good, Pops. I promise."

Jo could see the lingering doubt in her dad's eyes and she didn't blame him. Her life wasn't exactly where she wanted it to be, but there was nothing she could really do about that at the moment besides try to distract herself with other things. A picture of Archer flashed into her mind, but she dismissed it as quickly as she could. Not him. It was too complicated and messy. They worked together, and he annoyed her anyway, so why was she still even thinking about him? Frankly, it was ridiculous.

Refocusing on the man in front of her, Jo tried to put on her happiest smile for her dad "Can I work at the garage today?" she asked, changing the subject. "I promise I'll set the shop back in working order for tomorrow."

"Sure thing," her dad said, smiling back at her. His worries seemed to be gone, at least for the moment, and that was all she needed to keep her going.

Jo enjoyed the rest of the morning with her dad as they talked sports and made plans to go see a minor league game before the weather got too hot to make it enjoyable. Later when she arrived at the auto shop and drove her car into the bay, she felt a little better about everything. She just hoped the feeling would last. After all, for her, it didn't come around all that often.

## Chapter Six

*Archer*

Sundays were the greatest as far as Archer was concerned. No work, no real responsibilities other than making sure he had enough food in the apartment for the week ahead, and nothing but time to do whatever he wanted. After sleeping in until 8:00, a rarity nowadays, he spent about two hours watching sports on the plush leather sofa in his family room. As nice as the morning was going, it would have been even nicer to not be alone. If he had a girlfriend, he wouldn't be spending so much time on the couch, or at least, the time he did spend there would be a lot more enjoyable.

Archer thought of having Jo in his apartment with him and groaned as the idea tried to take root in his mind. Ugh, he could not stop thinking about this woman and it was going to drive him insane. Frustrated beyond measure, he leaned over to snag his phone from the coffee table, and texted his sister to see if she was up for a hike. Some fresh air and exercise might do him some good. At the very least, it would distract him from his thoughts of Jo.

Archer: **Hey, Caro. You up for a visitor?**

The reply came almost immediately.

Caro: **Not at the moment. Trevor and Timothy are at a sleepover, so Todd and I are having couple time.**

Archer knew what that meant and shuddered. Despite him have similar thoughts about Jo, he didn't care to hear that from his sister.

Archer: **TMI.**

Tossing his phone to the side and with no other

69

plans on the horizon, Archer finally dragged himself back to his room to get dressed and head out for the day. Maybe he would enjoy a hike on his own or go try a new brunch spot. He brushed his teeth and threw on whatever clothes were clean and mostly unwrinkled, giving himself the sniff test before grabbing his phone and a water bottle from his fridge. After hopping in his car, he pulled out of the parking space and pointed it toward the river. Hiking or running along the water and breathing in the fresh, summer air might be the ticket to clearing a certain blonde-haired, blue-eyed lady from his mind.

The drive was a short one, but about a mile out from the trailhead, the engine of his car started making a weird pinging noise. Archer glanced out the window and spotted a sign for an auto shop, so he quickly changed lanes and pulled into the parking lot. The place looked like it was closed, which would make sense for a Sunday, but one of the bay doors was open and a vehicle was lifted up slightly. Maybe someone was there who could help him out, or at the very least, point him in the direction of another shop that could service his car. With a thirty minute commute, the last thing he needed was for his only mode of transportation to be out of commission.

Archer hopped out of his vehicle, enjoying the warm air hitting his skin as he did. As he walked closer to the shop, he was able to get a better look at the car in the bay. It looked just like one he had admired a few times on his walk through the lot at work. Archer knew next to nothing about cars, but it was obvious that whoever owned the beautiful, vintage automobile took great care of it. He had always figured it belonged to someone who worked in one of the other businesses that occupied the building, but now he wasn't so sure it wasn't someone he already knew. The chances of two people owning an aqua Mustang convertible in the same area were pretty slim.

Archer stood right outside the bay doors. He didn't want to be a bother to the person working on the vehicle, but it really was a spectacular looking car and his curiosity at who owned it was getting the better of him. As he moved inside, his eyes widened, but not at the sight of the car in front of him. The antique ride was definitely worth admiring, but it was the taut torso encased in a clingy white tank top as well as the long, lean pair of legs sticking out from beneath the car that had all of Archer's attention.

Lengthy stretches of smooth, porcelain skin were visible all the way from the bottom of the woman's tiny, cut-off jean shorts to the converse sneakers on her feet, sneakers that were currently bopping along to the classic rock pouring out of a radio on one of the workbenches. Archer was definitely a leg man, and this pair had him thickening in his shorts and picturing them poking out from under his bedsheets instead of the car. The legs started to look familiar to him, and after another minute of staring, it finally dawned on him who the car's owner was. Archer had stared at Jo often enough to know her legs anywhere.

A wide smile spread across his face and he approached the side of the car with soft feet. He crouched down right next to where Jo was lying on a roller bench, completely unaware of him being there. Archer raised a fist and knocked loudly on the side of her car. "Hey there," he boomed, his voice echoing in the cavernous garage.

"Jesus Christ," Jo shrieked before rapidly rolling out from under the car and bolting upright. When her face appeared, her eyes were wide with shock and she was breathing hard, a wrench wrapped so tightly in her fist that her knuckles were white. Jo's beautiful blue eyes blinked rapidly as she looked at him with confusion.

71

"What the hell are you doing here?"

Archer rolled his eyes and stood. "Nice seeing you too, Jo," he said, offering her a hand to help her up. She batted his gesture away with a wave of her grease covered hand and stood up on her own, dropping her wrench in a toolbox before grabbing a clean rag and wiping her hands off on the terrycloth fabric.

Archer took a minute to appreciate the woman who stood in front of him as she cleaned up. Jo always looked beautiful, but it was in an untouchable kind of way. Her shields seemed to be up permanently, and she wore her professional clothes like a suit of armor, protecting herself from whatever it was a woman like her might actually be afraid of. Right now though, in just her tank and shorts, her mass of blonde curls pulled up into a ponytail and a grease smudge across her cheek, she was accessible, approachable. To put it simply, she was stunning.

"What are you doing here, Hayes? The shop is closed on Sundays," she said flatly as she tossed the now greasy rag over on the workbench.

Archer hated that she only ever used his last name. It wasn't uncommon among sports consultants and he did it with everyone too with one notable exception, but he really, really wanted her to call him "Archer" if only to hear the way it would sound in her smoky voice. "My engine is making a funny sound and I was hoping someone would be around to help me out with it," he explained, gesturing around the shop they were both standing in.

"We're closed," she repeated, her brow furrowed into a scowl. At least this one wasn't as deep as the one she usually wore in his presence, the vee between her eyes more gulch than canyon. Maybe he had caught her on a good day.

Jo's words finally registered. "We?" he asked, suddenly needing clarification on that part of her statement. Did a boyfriend own the shop? A husband? The thought of Jo with another man made his stomach turn. Probably a symptom of a much larger problem headed his way, but he would deal with that later.

"My dad owns the shop. I worked here in high school and a little in college, so I still always think of it as being a 'we' thing." She sighed, leaning against the side of her car.

Archer took a long look at her and frowned slightly. Jo was tired, the purple shadows under her eyes and slump to her shoulders proof enough of that. He wasn't exactly sure why he was acting like that was news to him when he'd witnessed firsthand just how hard she worked all the time. The woman was a machine, clocking longer hours than anyone in the firm, and on her day off, here she was working on her car. Did she ever make time to just relax? Probably not, so he really shouldn't be bothering her anymore.

"Well, I'll try and find a place that's open. See you at work." He was more than a little bummed at not being able to spend more time with her but also didn't want to cause her any more trouble than he already had.

"Wait." Archer turned at the sound of her voice, finding Jo eyeing him suspiciously for a moment before shoving off the side of her car. "I can take a look at it for you."

"Really?" Archer asked, his voice filled with hope. It would be great to get his car looked at, but he was more excited at the prospect of being around her for even a few minutes more. Work Jo was a tough nut to crack, but maybe weekend Jo was a little easier to get to know. Archer hoped so because he needed to know more about the woman he couldn't seem to keep his mind off of.

"Sure. Why not?" she replied with a shrug. "It's not often I get a chance to peek under the hood of a BMW."

Jo smiled and it made his heart kick against his ribs. It was one of her special smiles again, the kind he had been craving since the only other time he had seen it. It was the same smile from that first day in the elevator. After that, he still got the occasional smile from Jo, but they were her sassy ones, smirks, and the kind of smile that was really telling you to *fuck off,* but this smile was different. The happy expression currently lighting up her whole face was something he wanted to see all the time: her authentic smile. It had her rosy lips pulling all the way back, giving him just a hint at how she looked when she was truly happy, and he made a silent vow to get her to make it again as often as he could.

"Glad I could provide you with the opportunity," he told her, walking next to Jo as they approached his car. Archer messed with his key fob for a moment and popped the hood. "I just hope it's an easy fix."

"It should be. More often than not, the sounds you're hearing are something minor, but you never know," she intimated, her smile pulling even wider. "Maybe you'll need a whole new engine." Her eyes were filled with glee and he couldn't help but return the smile she'd bestowed upon him.

"The fact that you are so excited at the prospect of me having to spend that kind of money is a little scary," he admitted with a chuckle. Truthfully, Archer would gladly part with half his bank account if meant he got more pleasant interactions with Jo, and more of her genuine smiles. Both had pushed away the loneliness he'd been feeling better than any hike along the river could.

Jo simply shrugged her shoulder. "Just giving you a hard time." She smirked at him before ducking under the hood of his car.

Archer tried not to think about the phrase "hard time" as she was bending over his vehicle, her firm ass on display for him. He swallowed thickly and shifted on his feet, trying to hide the evidence of his arousal. It seemed to be a permanent problem whenever she was around, though he would happily deal with it. Jo started poking around the engine, and Archer figured he would watch what she was doing. Maybe he would learn something. It was unlikely, but it would definitely keep him from fantasizing about her if he was focusing on the parts of the car and not the parts of her body.

"What kind of gas do you put in your tank?" she asked, peeking over at him with a furrowed brow.

Archer shrugged a shoulder. "Unleaded." He had no idea what the type of gas had to do with his engine noises, but that was why she was the mechanic, not him.

Jo smiled sadly at him. "Well, there's your problem. This kind of engine needs a higher octane, so you're going to want to put premium gas in your tank. Unless you actually want to totally screw up your car," she explained, leaning back to close the hood and wipe her hands on another clean rag she'd pulled from her pocket.

"That's it? Just a different gas?" Jo mentioned solutions being simple most of the time, but he hadn't been so sure. Clearly, the woman knew what she was talking about, something he should have known based on her stellar performance at work.

"That's it. Fill her up with premium and the knocking should go away as the new gas cycles through," she explained.

Archer stared at her in awe. The woman had

shown she was more than capable at work, basically running circles around the other consultants, and here she was on weekends tuning up her own car and fixing his as well. "Wow. Thanks," he told her, genuine gratitude lacing his tone. "I feel like I should pay you for helping me or something." Maybe she would let him take her out to lunch, but he was a little afraid to hear her say no to that, so he stowed the idea.

Jo snorted. "We can call this a freebie. Besides, even you couldn't afford the kind of service I can provide," she teased before winking at him, and with that one small gesture, Archer could tell that he was done for. Jo could tease him or continue to treat him like a pariah, and he would still follow her around like a lost puppy. He was so weak where she was concerned. He was also currently thinking of the different kinds of ways she could service him and not his car. Archer knew very well she hadn't meant it as a euphemism, but his brain and his body were certainly taking it as one. Jo seemed to catch on to what she had said and her cheeks pinked slightly. "Ugh, that's not what I meant," she whispered, shaking her head.

Jo's eyes flicked to his lips and his moved to look at her rosy mouth. At that moment, he would do just about anything to get a taste of it. "Whatever you need to tell yourself, Freckles," he quipped, flashing her a cocky grin. Archer couldn't help calling attention to the little flecks that graced the skin along the bridge of her nose. He was obsessed with them, and the endearment for her felt natural and very fitting. At the very least, he was sure it would annoy Jo, and she always looked so damn cute when she was irritated with him.

Right on cue, her nose scrunched as she mulled over her new nickname. Jo still wouldn't look at him, but he could swear he saw the corners of her mouth twitch as if she had wanted to smile. Her phone rang and she slipped it out of her pocket, breaking the spell he'd seemingly cast on her. "I need to get this."

"I guess that's my signal to go." Archer smiled, backing toward his driver side door. Better to leave while they were on good terms before one or both of them brought them back to square one. "Thanks for the tune up."

"No problem," Jo said with a smile of her own before answering her phone. "Hey Pops..." Her conversation trailed off, and Archer watched as she walked back over to the garage and leaned against the wall. When his eyes met hers, her smile turned a little shy before she ducked away from him, so he hopped in his car to make his way over to the gas station to follow her advice.

Later that evening when he was lounging at home, Archer would find himself revisiting his time with Jo, and his mouth would pull up into a big, dopey grin every time he did. She had been right about the fuel being the problem, and since he'd followed her instructions, his car was running even better than normal. Her intelligence and capability fascinated him beyond measure, but her beauty, her humor, and the way she teased him were completely wonderful as well. He was utterly transfixed by her and didn't see that changing anytime soon. It wasn't until he was staring up at the ceiling of his bedroom that he realized most of the day had disappeared in thinking about Jo, and he spent the rest of that night wondering how on Earth he could ever convince her to date him.

# Chapter Seven

*Jo*

Two weeks had passed since Jo had seen Archer at the garage, and ever since then, his pranks on her at work had gotten fewer and farther between. What used to be daily occurrences were now sporadic at best. He hadn't messed with her coffee once in the last week, and while she should have been happy that Archer had stopped annoying her so much, she kind of missed it, if she was being honest with herself. The cling wrap blocking her door and the whoopee cushion on her chair had been a little irritating, but they broke up the monotony of her day. Jo also noticed she had been smiling more with each small prank, even sighing wistfully when she spied the deflated whoopee cushion lying in her desk drawer yesterday.

Which was why after nursing Gigi back from her almost break-up with Cooper yesterday, Jo went to one of the antique store downtown and purchased a little surprise for her favorite coworker. Or was he a friend now? Their time at the garage had been brief, but relatively friendly. Jo was so out of practice when it came to real interactions with men, however, that she wasn't sure what they were now. All she knew was that every time she thought of the two of them being friends, she found she liked the idea. They were probably more like frenemies at best at the moment, but maybe that would change.

Jo stood patiently at the community printer out near the copy machine, pretending to be waiting for an important document when in reality she was waiting for

Archer to arrive at the office. She could have just stayed at her desk, but she wanted to greet him and get a better view of his reaction as he discovered the present she'd left for him on his office chair. When the elevator dinged, Jo's lips pulled into a grin and she felt a sense of giddy anticipation in her chest. If this was what Archer felt every time he pranked her, it was no wonder he had been doing it so often. She felt almost like she had before her mom passed, not a care or worry in the world beyond feeling excitement for what came next. This feeling could easily become addictive. Planning this friendly little prank had been really fun, and it had been far too long since Jo felt this kind of liveliness.

Jo peeked over her shoulder and watched Archer stride out of the elevator. He was impeccably dressed as usual, his dark navy suit looking like it had been tailor-made for him, and judging from the BMW she had looked at a couple weeks back, it probably had been. She knew he came from money, but other than his fancy clothes and luxury car, he didn't flaunt it or act like he was better than anyone because of it. It was nice and reminded her of Gigi. Just because you were born well-off didn't mean you were better than anyone else, and she appreciated that he seemed to believe that as well.

Archer walked passed her, a friendly smile on his handsome face. He turned, glancing over his shoulder briefly, and when his cocoa-brown eyes met hers, she sighed internally. *Reel it in, girl,* she said to herself. Jo was trying to work her way up to having a friend, nothing more than that yet. He could probably smell the desperation on her, but all she could smell was his bergamot cologne, and she was suddenly tempted to push him into his office and stick her face into his neck to get a deeper inhale.

"Morning, Jo," Archer said, his tone open and

friendly as he walked over to his office door and took out his keys.

Jo hummed happily in reply, still too dazed from his appearance to articulate anything more than that. She creeped closer, watching him enter his office and flip the lights on. He dropped his messenger back on top of his desk and removed his suit jacket, the light blue button-down beneath it pulling across his chest and biceps. *Damn, he looks good.* Jo tried to remind herself that developing a crush on a coworker was a bad idea, but when he peeked his eyes up and over to her once more, a grin on his face, all those reminders disappeared. Then he winked at her, causing Jo to squeeze her legs together to ease the building pressure from imagining his strong arms holding her up against a wall as he pounded into her.

"Shit," she whispered to herself. It was a good thing Jo had a date tonight, because she was in serious danger of jumping her colleague's bones if her dry spell lasted any longer. Tempting as it might be, work was already enough of a mess without adding that kind of complication on top of it.

Archer's high-pitched squeal pulled her out of her thoughts and brought another smile to her face. "What the absolute fuck?" he barked as he stumbled backwards out of his office. When he turned to Jo and saw her hand covering her mouth to stifle her laugh, his eyes narrowed. He took three big steps and was directly in front of her, his chest brushing up against hers and pushing her back, the printer hitting her behind as she leaned away from him. "Something funny, Freckles?"

Jo practically melted against the table when he called her that again in his smooth, low voice, but she mustered her resolve and stood her ground. She could turn into a pile of horny goo later. "I'm just out here waiting for a contract. Nothing funny about that," she lied and straightened up to face him.

Archer leaned in closely enough so that she could smell the coffee and mint on his breath, a combination she had never thought about before but was suddenly curious to taste. Of course, only if she could taste it on him. She licked her lips instinctually and tried not to whimper when he tracked the movement with his eyes, the brown going a shade darker as he did.

Archer shook his head lightly, his eyes meeting hers again. "You mean to tell me that you had nothing to do with the completely vile item that is currently on my office chair?" he questioned, his tone dubious.

Jo shrugged a shoulder innocently just before he circled his hand around her wrist. The movement caused goosebumps to erupt all over her skin, every inch of her being becoming acutely aware of how good his fingers felt on her body. Jo found herself wanting to lean into him, but before she could, Archer dragged her into his office. He kicked his chair, spinning it to face the two of them, before backing away from it slowly. "So this wasn't put here by you. This, this absolute soul-sucking nightmare?"

Jo stifled her laugh at his over-the-top reaction and kept her cool despite the man next to her causing her whole body to heat up. She clucked her tongue at him, and walked over to pick up the doll she had purchased yesterday. It was an ancient, Victorian porcelain doll with a cracked face, black eyes, and a faded, yellowing gown covering its little body. There had been the possibility that Archer wouldn't find it as creepy as Jo thought he would, but she bought it anyway and was pleasantly surprised to see him freaking out so much more than she could have hoped.

Jo held the doll up to her cheek and turned to him with a pout. "I think you hurt her feelings."

Archer's face paled and he took another step back. "F-feelings? That thing looks like it wants to push me down a flight of stairs. The only feeling it has is murderous rage." He made the sign of the cross, or attempted to. Jo wasn't religious, but she was pretty certain it didn't involve tapping your nose and belt buckle. "Do you not watch movies? Dolls are always evil."

Jo tutted softly at his dramatics. "Aww, come on now. I think that's a bit of an exaggeration." She held the doll out toward his chest, wiggling it back and forth. "I think you two should kiss and make up."

Archer back hit the doorframe as he tried to escape. This prank had worked out better than Jo thought it would. Not only was she getting the reaction she hoped for, but the way he was currently leaning against the door had him looking all kinds of delicious. His hips were pressed forward, one of his hands gripping the doorjamb, and she could almost picture herself kneeling in front of him as she gave him more pleasure than he could handle. Jo might not be able to date him, but he did provide all kinds of wondrous material for her spank bank.

"Her face is cracked, Jo." Archer's voice was higher like he was legitimately afraid of the doll, and the sound cut into her lust-filled brain and brought her back to reality. "I'm pretty sure I would cut my lip if I even attempted to kiss that wicked thing," he said, attempted to climb the wall as she walked toward him just to create some space. "Keep it away from me."

"Relax." Trading places with him, Jo tried not to laugh when he walked back over to his chair and brushed it off with his hand, ridding it of antique doll cooties. "I won't let little Anastasia hurt you."

Archer sat down, his expression haunted. "You named it?"

Jo scoffed. "Of course not, silly. She told me her name," she explained before holding the doll's face up to her ear. "What was that, little Annie? You want me to do what?" she asked, glancing down at the doll before looking over to Archer with a grave expression. The amount of joy she was deriving from this little interaction was obscene, but she wasn't going to stop now. "I don't think she likes you very much."

Archer pointed a finger at her. "You're evil," he insisted. The tone of his voice was dead serious, but Jo caught the corners of his mouth twitching. He wanted to laugh but wouldn't give her the satisfaction. Fine, he could keep his dignity. For now.

"I think that's a bit harsh," she countered, strolling over to the wastebasket just inside his office and tossing the doll inside.

Archer balked. "You can't just throw that away in here. You have to burn it and bury the ashes." He powered up his computer and looked back up at her, his gaze curious. "How did you get in here anyway? I always lock my door."

Jo snorted. He was so cute when he was naive. "Please, Hayes. I can take apart and reassemble an entire car. You really think I can't pick a lock, especially one as ancient as this?" She flicked the doorknob that was straight out of the 1950s. "At least you have a lock that works on your office."

Archer's brow furrowed, a frown pulling his mouth down. "I thought you just always left it unlocked."

"Nope," she said, popping the *p*. Jo leaned down and grabbed the doll from the wastebasket. She'd had her fun, so there was no need to torture him with its continued presence. The odds that it would spook him had been high, but she had no idea it would wig him out as much as it had. *Two dollars well spent*, she thought to herself as she straightened up, shooting a smile over to Archer as he sat at his desk. "It looks like our work here is done," she announced, waving the little doll's arm at him in farewell before leaving his office.

"Remember to burn that thing or I won't sleep for a month," Archer called after her.

Jo chuckled in reply, enjoying that things seemed to be getting back to normal between the two of them. Well, their version of normal anyway, and as the day went on, Jo found herself liking their version of normal a whole hell of a lot.

****

The sound of Jo's feet pounding against the belt of the treadmill and her breath coming in quick bursts were the only noises filling the silence of the gym in the basement of her office building. Normally when she was alone in the gym, she would blast some AC/DC or Metallica to keep her motivation up, but today, Jo had all the motivation she needed. The date she had gone on the night before went horribly awry, and now there was so much unreleased tension that had built up in her body over the course of the evening that she needed to work off the frustration in the only way she had available to her at the moment. It was no wonder Millie was having such a hard time finding a match for herself out there. If last night was any indication of the state of modern dating, things were bleak, and Jo wasn't exactly hopeful that they would get better anytime soon.

Maybe Jo's expectations had been too high going into the date in the first place. After talking to Guy (and yes, that had been his actual name) for a couple of weeks, she had thought they would have had a great time. Their banter while messaging had come easily enough, and they had a decent amount in common. They both liked sports, both were into cars, and they both had jobs that were very demanding. Guy mentioned that he was a doctor, so he would understand that work came first sometimes and wouldn't feel bad if Jo had to cancel plans to work late, and she would be just as understanding if he had to do the same. All in all, it should have been a great time. When Jo showed up at the restaurant and saw another woman at the table, however, she knew things were off to a bad start.

The situation would have been much easier to take if the appearance of two women was because he had double booked the date. If that had been the case, Jo could have just gone home and ordered a pizza. No big deal. People dated more than one person at a time and the mix-up would have been totally understandable, not desirable, but understandable nonetheless. A double booked date, however, was not the situation Jo found herself in. Instead, her date had been with Guy and his *mother*. Why he thought that bringing his mom along on a first date was a good idea was beyond her, but he had, and Jo dined with the two of them for almost two hours because she didn't want to hurt the older woman's feelings by turning tail and leaving abruptly.

Guy's mom, Deidre, had seemed like a lovely woman, but Jo hadn't expected a meet a parent on the first date, so she felt thrown off her game from the get-go. She also hadn't expected to spend most of the night listening to her date's mom brag about his accomplishments as a Doctor of Puppetry, an area of study Jo hadn't known existed until last night. When Guy bragged about being a doctor and how much he prided himself on the number of lives he had saved, Jo just assumed he was a medical doctor, not a doctor of puppetry, the art of making and using puppets for entertainment. When Guy said he saved lives, she thought he meant literally keeping people from dying, not making them laugh or keeping them entertained with his felt-covered friends, as she had later discovered.

It wasn't his profession that bothered Jo, though when she admitted to never really being much for puppet theater, she could see that it bothered him, but it was that deception about the whole thing that really got to her. Guy must have known how it came across when he talked about the demands of being a doctor. Before they met up for their date, he had messaged at length about the long hours and the immense responsibility he felt at having the fate and happiness of others in his hands.

There was also the matter of having brought his mom along without asking her about it first, so at the end of their evening when Guy smiled and talked about how he would message her later, Jo just kept quiet and nodded, hoping that she could think of a nice way to break things off without hurting his feelings, or his mom's. Deirdre had been a pretty sweet lady, but Jo wasn't getting involved in that whole mess.

Jo shook off the weirdness from the night before and punched the buttons on the treadmill to lower the speed, slowing the pace of her run to more of a brisk walk. Her eyes wandered over to the weight bench as she stomped her irritation, and she decided that some strength training was just the ticket to burn off tension from the night before. Between her run, the weights, and a nice, warm shower afterwards, she should be feeling a lot better when she got back to work.

Jo slammed the stop button and hopped off the machine, turning and running straight into a wall of hard muscle when she did. "Fucking hell," she spouted, leaning back to look up at Archer. He was wearing a smirk and the tightest exercise shirt she had ever seen. It hugged every bulge and dip in his athletic body. All the tension she had worked out over the course of her run returned momentarily, but the stiffness she felt was of a different kind now. As she let her eyes wander over his taut torso, she had to work extra hard to resist the urge to reach her hand out and run it along the hard planes of muscle she was currently staring at.

"Good to see you too, Freckles," Archer said, stepping to the side to let her pass.

It was good seeing him, and not just because he was bending down to stretch his legs and his basketball shorts clung to his tight ass in the most delicious way. Lately, being around Archer also had the strange effect of lightening her mood, and as someone who spent her time more often grumpy than not, it was a good feeling. Archer bent down further, popping his booty out a little bit more. Jo wondered if he was doing it on purpose, but if he was she didn't mind. He had a phenomenal rear, and at that moment, Jo wanted to bend down and take a bite out of it. Instead, she mumbled incoherently and hustled over to the bench press, racking and securing her weights.

Jo didn't lift a lot, just enough to keep her strength up, so when Archer walked over and took the spotting position, she placed her hands on her hips and glared at him. "I can bench fifty pounds without a spot, thank you very much."

She took her position on the bench and grabbed the bar, but before she could lift it up, Archer's hands fell on top of hers and stilled them. Jo looked up at him and saw a playful smile on his face. Before it would have irritated her, but now she felt herself eagerly awaiting whatever it was he would say next.

"I know you can. I've seen you do it many times," he admitted, the tips of his ears turning pink. Was he embarrassed that he had watched her? Or that he had admitted it? Either way, the shy smile was endearing, and Jo found herself liking him even more than she already did. "But we're the only two in here right now and I would feel responsible if you were to get crushed under here, so indulge me."

Jo smirked up at him. "So this is really more about assuaging your possible guilt than it is about preventing any harm to myself?" He nodded with a grin and she chuckled. "Have it your way, Hayes," she replied, lifting and bringing the bar down to her chest before pressing it up again.

"I usually do," he said softly, winking at her as he held his hands just below the bar. Her grip wobbled slightly when he winked at her, his smirk widening after it happened. Ugh, he knew what he was doing to her. Jo probably would have cared more if the she didn't enjoy the feelings he was causing so much. Now that she had stowed her ire toward him, she could see that he was actually pretty great, definitely handsome, and just the right amount of flirty to keep her interested.

After a finishing her set, Jo stood up and stretched her arms over her head. She saw him checking her out in the reflection on the mirrored walls and smiled before peering at him over her shoulder. "You want a go?"

Archer's eyes flicked up from where they had been, which was staring at her ass in her tight running shorts, and into her eyes. "W-what's that?" he stammered out.

Jo walked back to him and pushed at his chest lightly with her pointer finger. "I asked if you wanted a go. You know, with the bench press?" She nodded at the machine next to them.

Archer exhaled slowly and moved his body, plopping it down on the bench. "Um, sure," he mumbled before scooting back and lying down under the bar.

Jo took up position just above him, but instead of spotting the bar, she gripped it and ducked underneath, moving her head so that her mouth was near his ear. "Did you want me to make it harder for you?" she whispered breathlessly in his ear, watching his Adam's apple bob along the sculpted column of his neck as he swallowed.

"W-what?" Archer breathed, his voice low and strained. Archer wasn't the only one who knew what they were doing when it came to flirting. Jo knew exactly how to get a man worked up, and even though it had been a few months since she'd had occasion to do it, it was just like riding a bicycle, and boy did she want to take this man out for a spin.

"Did you want me to make it harder for you?" Jo repeated huskily, making sure he breath fanned against his skin. Dammit. She was turning herself on a little in the process of teasing him. This was a bad idea, but she couldn't seem to bring herself to stop. Talking and teasing with him had eased more tension from her body than her entire workout had before. "You know, add some plates so you can bench more weight?"

"Oh." The single word was choked out before he scooted to the end of the bench, bolting upright. "You know what," he squeaked, grabbing his towel and water before backing toward the men's locker room. "I, uh … I just remembered I have a call at one o'clock that I can't miss."

Jo glanced at her watch. "It's only just after twelve," she informed him, a smirk forming on her face. When it came to working men up, apparently she still had it.

"Yeah, but uh, I have some prep to do and I need a shower after all that working out." His words came out in a flurry as he moved to cover his groin with the towel. Apparently she'd worked him up quite a bit more than she'd intended. "Later." After that curt goodbye, he practically ran from the room.

Jo chuckled to herself and grabbed her own things before heading into the women's locker room. She had been looking forward to a nice warm shower, but after her interaction with Archer, she knew it was going to need to be an ice-cold one to cool her down. If this was how she felt after five minutes of light flirting, how would she feel if they did more than that? Jo tried not to think too much about it as she cleaned up and got ready to head back to work, but she found that no amount of cold water could keep her from feeling the way she did.

The sexual feelings were very familiar to her, but it was the other emotions that were mixed in there as well that felt new. It was like her body was stirring after a very long nap, with old feelings returning the more she awakened. The light fluttery sensation that was in her chest was one she hadn't felt for a long time, probably since high school, and she liked having it back. Now all she had to figure out was what she planned to do about it.

## Chapter Eight

*Archer*

The cool air of the apartment felt nice against Archer's damp skin as he strolled in from his early morning run. He wasn't normally a morning exercise person, preferring to squeeze in a workout during his lunch hour, but he had too much pent-up energy and he needed an outlet for it. It had been a couple of weeks since he had seen Jo at the auto shop and they'd had their first hospitable interaction, and Archer couldn't stop thinking and fantasizing about the woman, especially after yesterday's little run-in at the gym. He knew she had been teasing him, getting him back for his pranks like she had with that creepy ass doll on Monday, but his heart and his body hadn't really cared what her motivation was.

When Jo leaned over him on the bench press, looking like an avenging angel fresh from the battlefield, her shiny, golden curls clinging to the side of her damp face and her eyes bright, her flowery scent washed over him and he nearly lost it. Archer had not only gotten uncomfortably aroused at the sight of all her exposed skin and the sound of her breathy whispers, but his heart had beat rapidly and his mind raced with thoughts of cuddling on his big couch, holding hands as they walked along the river, and going to ball games together. The images and arousal had caused him to panic and flee from the gym like his feet were on fire. Even after taking the coldest shower of his life, he still felt aroused, so he avoided Jo the rest of the day just to be safe.

Archer walked back into his bathroom and turned

the water to cold. He didn't even bother with hot showers nowadays. It was icy cold showers all the time and he was getting sick of it, but it was no use. He could go and look for someone else to date or even just hookup with to take the edge off, but he didn't want someone else, he wanted Jo. Archer stepped into the icy spray and nearly shrieked as the water hit his skin. The temptation to take himself in hand to thoughts of Jo was ever present, but instead he quickly washed his hair and body so that he didn't have to spend any more time in the water than necessary. When he was done and toweled off, he dressed in his typical uniform of a dark suit and white button-down, and grabbed a protein shake from his fridge before heading out for the day.

Half an hour later, he was walking into the office. Sadly, the two founders of the firm had called yet another meeting and Archer had to head straight into the conference room to take part in that. He hated not having time to check his messages and emails at the start of his day. It made him feel rushed, and he hated feeling rushed. That could explain why he was taking his sweet time with Jo, but he knew it was more than that. Archer was worried about getting rejected and then having to work with her after the fact. That would be beyond awkward and he couldn't stand the thought of losing the fun little back-and-forth he and Jo had at the moment.

Archer walked into the conference room to see almost everyone at the table. He took an open seat next to Blake Michaels and smiled in greeting. "Good morning," he said to the man. He hadn't interacted with many of the other consultants much, but Blake seemed like a nice guy and he worked hard, so the two of them at least had that in common.

"Morning." Blake flashed a toothy grin filled with genuine interest. "How are you settling in?"

"Good, good," Archer replied automatically. It had been good for the most part. He still felt that the firm could update some of their practices and the offices themselves, but overall it had been okay. "I think I finally have the lay of the land, but if you have any tips, I'm all ears."

Blake nodded in thought before dipping his head toward Archer's. "I'm not sure what tips I have other than keep your head down and focus on the work." Blake's eyes flicked across the room to some of the other consultants, who were joking around and laughing. "And be careful who you associate with."

"Because..." Archer led, trying to understand exactly what Blake was saying. He didn't really associate with anyone outside of maybe Jo, but even that thread was tenuous at best. Archer was curious what the other man was getting at. He'd noticed inappropriate behavior from some of the other consultants, but it would be nice to know whether or not he was reading into things.

Blake sighed, the spark in his eyes dimming considerably. "All I'm saying is that some consultants have complaints against them, and you might not want to be lumped in with those kinds of people," the man warned, confirming Archer's suspicions.

Archer hummed in reply. He hadn't noticed any behavior worth complaining to the higher-ups about, but like Blake had recommended, he had been focusing on the work, not the environment. Maybe he needed to pop his head out of the sand every now and then. "Thanks. I'll definitely keep that in mind."

Blake smiled, turning back to his notepad, and Archer took a sip from his travel mug to get a hit of caffeine.

Lowell North coughed loudly to draw everyone's attention. "Bust out your parkas, boys—the Ice Queen cometh," he said with a smirk.

Archer hadn't needed to turn his head toward the windows of the room to know who Lowell was referring to, but he did it anyway, knowing full well it was to have an excuse to look at the object of his infatuation. Jo strode over to the conference room, shoulders back and a fiercely determined look on her face. Her blonde curls were down and bounced as she walked, a jolly contrast to her serious expression. She looked every bit the queen of some arctic tundra as she marched toward the room in her white pantsuit with matching white camisole. There was a strip of lace across the top of her tank, just below her cleavage, and Archer found himself wanting to trace along it with his finger, or better yet, his tongue. He cleared his throat and took another sip of his coffee, catching Blake smirking at him from his seat.

"Good morning, your majesty," Lowell called to Jo as she entered the room.

She smiled coolly in reply and took the only open seat available.

As Jo sat down next to Jerry Finch, the man grabbed at his arms and shivered. "Brrr. There must be a cold front coming in because I'm freezing," he jabbed before laughing at his own bad joke.

Jo raised her middle finger to him, not sparing him so much as a glance as she opened up her tablet and started taking notes.

"Aw, don't be like that, Jolene," he pleaded with a mock pout. "Give us smile."

Archer could see Jo gearing up to say something in reply, but she shouldn't have to defend herself against those idiots, so he spoke up instead. "So, Finch. I hear that Sal Verona might be seeking other help with his brand marketing. Is that true or just a nasty rumor?" Sal Verona was a boxer and probably Finch's biggest client, and while Archer hadn't heard any such rumor, he figured that he could mess with him the way he had messed with Jo.

Jerry turned to him, looking furious. "That's bullshit. Where did you hear that?"

Archer shrugged a shoulder and clucked his tongue. "I've just been keeping my ear to the ground like we were told. You might want to give your guy a call," he warned ominously.

Jerry pulled out his phone and tapped at it furiously, but he was forced to pocket it when Whitcomb and Delaney walked in.

"Good morning, all," Charles Whitcomb said, running a hand over his graying brown hair. It was slicked back in a look straight from the '80s, just another reminder that Archer was stuck in some sort of time warp. "Let's get started."

Archer's phone buzzed in his pocket and he slid it out to surreptitiously check his messages. It was a text from Jo, and when he raised his eyes to hers, she wasn't even looking in his direction, her focus completely on the meeting.

Jo: **I could have handled that.**

Archer should have known that she would be upset at him for butting in, but he had hoped that she would see it as the friendly gesture it was. He started to type out a reply as another text came in.

Jo: **But thank you for doing it. The look on Finch's face alone was worth it.**

Archer looked up again to see Jo still focusing on the bosses, but her mouth ticked up in the corner with a smile. He shot over a simple reply.

Archer: **Anytime.**

He meant it, too. Anytime he could be there to help her out, even in a small way like putting one of the idiots they worked with in their place, he would. Archer pocketed his phone and tried to focus back in on the meeting when really all he wanted to do was stare at the person across from him.

"So we're going to set up a little competition between the eight of you, or rather, four teams of two," Whitcomb said.

Archer's brow furrowed in confusion. He really should have been paying closer attention to the meeting.

"We'll select the teams, and we have everything set up for Saturday morning, so be sure to cancel any weekend plans you have," Gavin Delaney added.

Archer huffed, displeased with the last-minute change to his schedule. He was used to pulling extra hours when needed, but he had wanted to hang out with his nephews this weekend. It looked as though that wasn't going to happen, though there was one big upside to that and it was glancing in his direction. Spending time with Jo was no small consolation prize, and Archer found himself suddenly looking forward to the overtime.

"Now, let's draw the teams," Whitcomb announced, sounding oddly gleeful. Since he spent most of his time dealing with finances and never really leaving his office, Archer half wondered if this might just be the highlight of his day. "First we have Lowell and Trent." The two men high-fived like they had just won the lottery and Archer tried not to roll his eyes. Jo didn't bother to hide her eye roll and his mouth twitched when he clocked it. Next to him he heard Blake whispering something that sounded like "*please not Jerry*" just as Whitcomb announced the next team. "All right, next we have Blake and Jerry."

Blake groaned and lifted his head to look at Jo. She made a frowny face at her friend just as Whitcomb announced that she would be partnered with Archer. Her eyes flashed to his and he thought he read a mixture of excitement and relief. He supposed he was the better option than the three consultants who were left, but he would take it nonetheless.

"That leaves Bill and Tom," Whitcomb finished, and everyone looked around at their partner.

Most people seemed happy with their pairing, but they weren't given much time to digest it as Delaney started talking again as soon as his partner had finished. "Now that you're all paired up," their boss said as he passed out paper with a map and directions on them, "make sure you're on time for the laser tag tournament. The winning team gets a very special assignment."

Everyone smiled as the two partners left the room before dropping the pretense and breaking out into their own conversations.

"Laser tag? What are we, twelve?" Blake asked as he gathered up his things.

Jo snorted and closed her tablet. "I'm stuck on the prize for the winner being more work." She sighed, her head shaking in dismay—understandable, since as far as Archer could tell she was the hardest working woman in the office, maybe on the planet. "Not the biggest incentive for us to try our hardest."

"You two are just bitching because you know you're going to lose," Trent remarked before he bumped Lowell's fist. "You're looking at the winning team, everyone, so you might as well not bother even showing up."

"Care to make a side bet?" Bill asked him, and the two talked dollar amounts as everyone else packed up their stuff.

Jo rolled her eyes again and stood up to leave as Delaney's assistant, Janine, entered the room. "Jo, you have a delivery." She held out a small vase that was filled with an arrangement of berries on sticks. Jo looked at it skeptically before taking it. "Someone must really like you," Janine told her before leaving the room.

"Ice Queen has a man? Was it love at frost sight?" Trent joked and Archer couldn't stop from groaning at the lame pun.

"None of your business," Jo shot back before leaving the room and going back to her office.

Even though he had just heard her tell someone else to butt out, Archer couldn't help himself or keep his curiosity at bay, so he gathered up his things quickly and followed her out of the room. He walked up to her office just as she was peeling off the jacket of her pantsuit. The camisole left a lot of skin exposed and Archer had to shake himself a bit to stay focused on the task at hand and not on counting the freckles that were sprinkled across the tops of her shoulders. He wanted, no, needed to know whether or not she was with someone, and getting that answer had just become his top priority. Archer raised his fist and knocked on the frame of her door, his breath catching as her bright blue eyes shot up to his.

"Oh, it's just you," she said as she sat down in her office chair and put her head in her hands.

"Just you" wasn't really the best way to be described by someone you were interested in romantically, but it was better than an icy glare or a direct command to leave her the hell alone. "Mind if I come in?"

Jo raised her head but kept it propped on one fist. "Sure." When he grabbed a seat across from her, she slid the vase over to him. "Strawberry?" she asked with a sad smile.

Archer reached over and plucked a berry from one of the sticks. Before he raised it to his mouth, he looked at her one last time. "Are you sure? I'm pretty sure these weren't meant for me."

Jo nodded and he popped the berry in his mouth. She watched as he licked his lips clean of the sticky, sweet juice before sliding the card that came with the arrangement over to him. "They may have been meant for me, but I don't feel right about eating them," she groused.

The small white note sat between his fingers for a moment before he read it aloud. "We had a berry good time with you the other night. Hope you change your mind, Deirdre." Archer looked up at Jo with a furrowed brow. "Who's Deirdre?"

Jo leaned back in her chair and chuckled lightly. "Deirdre is the mother of the man I had a date with the other night." She twisted her chair back and forth slightly, looking somewhat defeated. Archer hated seeing it. "She came along to chaperone us."

Archer sat back in his chair and barked a laugh. "You're joking." He wasn't really happy that she had been out on a date with another man, but clearly if he brought along his mother and Jo didn't love it, he couldn't really be considered competition. It looked like his prospects weren't totally bleak where she was concerned after all, thank God.

"I wish I was," Jo replied with a sad smile. "I messaged him yesterday to say I didn't think we made a good match and he seemed okay with it." She flicked her finger at the little note in his hand. "I guess his mom wants a second chance."

Archer chuckled and handed the note back to her. "What are you going to do?"

Jo moaned and leaned her head back to look at the ceiling. "Ugh, I don't want to do anything, but she was a nice lady, so I'm going to have to message her son again."

"For another date?" Panic arose in his chest at the thought that might be the case. Archer may not be ready to ask her out himself, but the idea of her out on a date with another man made the sweet taste in his mouth turn bitter.

Jo looked at him wide-eyed. "God, no. To tell him to keep his mom in check." She twisted the vase on her desk, admiring her gift. "This was really sweet though."

Archer snagged another strawberry and popped it in his mouth. "Is it better than getting a bouquet of flowers? I mean, at least you can eat these." He was genuinely curious what would impress a woman like the one across from him. Jo always seemed so tough and determined that he wondered if she ever even felt like she needed anything from another person.

Jo grabbed a stick with a berry on top and spun it slowly in her fingers. "I wouldn't know." She looked at him with a resigned expression. "No one's ever given me flowers before."

Archer narrowed his gaze at her. "No way is that true," he insisted. She had to have gotten flowers at least once in her life. Jo was amazing. A woman liked her deserved flowers whenever she wanted them.

"It is," she breathed out before standing up and grabbing the vase. "Want another one before I take these to the break room?"

Archer just shook his head and watched her walk out of the office. He stood up and finally went to his own desk to try and get some work done, but he had a hard time concentrating on the matters at hand. His thoughts kept drifting to the woman down the hall, the one who had never been given flowers, perhaps never been given much of anything else by a man. The thought that maybe because she acted like she didn't need anything or anyone she was never given anything really bothered him. Archer spent most of the day wondering what else she might actually want or need that got overlooked, and whether or not he could be the one to give that to her.

## Chapter Nine

*Jo*

The building that would house the competition between the teams of consultants looked like it was being held together with spit, glue, and a prayer that the whole thing wouldn't collapse. It was in an old strip mall off the highway about ten minutes south of their office building, and while Jo hadn't minded the longer drive this morning, she did mind that her bosses dragged her out here on a Saturday to possibly be buried alive under the rubble of a collapsed Xtreme Laser Tag and Fun Center. Jo snorted as she hopped out of her car, wondering exactly what constituted the "fun" part of what she would be doing today.

"As if laser tag wasn't enough, we have a whole fun center at our disposal," Archer chimed in next to her as if he had been reading her mind. He looked especially good in his black t-shirt and basketball shorts. His hair was a little messier than usual, and Jo liked the more casual look on him. She idly wondered what he would look like first thing in the morning, but his speaking again stopped that train of thought quickly. "You ready for some laser tag?" he asked as they strode into the facility.

"Only if it's the extreme kind," she quipped and walked up to the counter to check them in. As they waited for the rest of their colleagues, she turned to him with a curious gaze. "What's the difference between regular and extreme laser tag, do you think?"

Archer smiled wryly at her. "Jo, please. It's obviously the advanced equipment we've been entrusted with that designates that what we are about to take part in is totally extreme," he said, holding up the vest and laser gun that looked like they had been around since the early '90s. He gestured for her to spin around with his finger. "Turn around and I'll help you with your vest."

Jo did as he asked and he helped clip her into the vest that smelled vaguely of teenage male—a frightening combination of sweat and Axe deodorant spray. She was wearing black yoga pants and a tank top, so when Archer's fingers lightly brushed the exposed skin on her shoulders, she shivered in response. His fingers closed over her shoulder and he spun her back around, his dark brown eyes reflecting concern. "Are you cold? I have a hoodie in my car."

Jo smiled weakly. No one had offered her their coat before, and even though it was just a hoodie, she found herself feeling warm in the center of her chest at his thoughtfulness. She shook her head, her curls bobbing in their ponytail. "I'm okay. Thanks."

He nodded and spun around so she could clip him in. As she did, the rest of their group arrived and registered before making their way back to where Jo and Archer stood.

She leaned up next to his ear and made her voice low. "Ten bucks says one of them makes a 'is that a gun in your pocket' joke."

Archer turned to her, a knowing smirk on his face. "I'm still a little new, but even I know enough not to take that bet," he replied, holstering his gun.

"Party pooper," Jo griped before walking over to Blake and giving him a hug. "Sorry you're stuck with Finch."

Blake shrugged a muscled shoulder. Even on a day off he was a snappy dresser, trading his colorful suit combinations for a bright pink tank and stripped biker shorts. "It's the pits for sure, but I already have a plan in place to make the day worthwhile." He grinned, his expression becoming increasingly mischievous.

"Oh? Do tell." Jo smiled wickedly, leaning in to hear whatever diabolical plan her friend had come up with.

"I don't want any extra homework from teacher, so I'm going to spend the whole time shooting my teammate in the back. Guaranteed loss." Blake raised his hand for a high five and she slapped it. Blake really was one of the best parts of the office. Jo hoped he never left.

"Loving it," she told him, already anticipating the little tantrum Blake's partner would throw when they lost. Finch deserved a little payback for all the crap he'd thrown her way over the years.

"What about you?" Blake asked, his eyes lighting up with mirth. "What little scheme do you have going on today?"

Jo smiled genuinely. "No scheme," she admitted, pulling on the black beanie she had walked in with. Blake barked a laugh as she tucked her curls under the hat. "I don't want the extra work, but I'm still competitive as hell." She gave a finger wave to Blake before walking back to Archer.

"Get it, girl," she heard Blake call over to her and she chuckled at her friend, though she was pretty sure he wasn't just talking about scoring the win during laser tag.

Archer scrunched his nose up at the sight of her hat. "What's with the cat burglar get up?" he asked, his mouth twitching.

Jo patted the top of her beanie. "I don't care about the prize, but I do care about the win, and dark clothes are better for hiding in black light," she stated as she poked a finger into his hard chest. *So muscly*, she thought before mentally slapping herself. "Don't mess this up for me,

Hayes."

Archer held up his hands in surrender and she gave him a curt nod, turning to the front of the room where her bosses were now standing.

She peeked over at him quickly and held out her phone and keys. "Do you mind holding these? My pants don't have any pockets." She wiggled a little to show off the clingy material, and when she looked back up to Archer, his eyes were still on her ass. Jo hadn't meant to give him a show, but now that she had, she was happy to see that she had flustered him a little bit. She flashed him a smile and when he finally looked back up at her, his cheeks had turned pink.

"Yeah, I-I can do that."

Jo handed him her things and he shoved them in his shorts pocket, clearing his throat afterward.

"Thank you," she sang to him before their attention was called back to the front.

Gavin and Charles were both at the front, dressed in what could only be called country-club attire. Both men wore brown slacks and collared shirts with little polo players on the front. This was probably their first stop before a round of golf and martinis at the clubhouse. Too bad they didn't invest more of their money into their own business—then maybe she would have a chair that didn't squeak and tilt and weird angles.

Gavin coughed into his fist before speaking. "Good morning to you." When there was no reply, he gave them all a stern look and waited for a chorus of "good morning" to come back to him before continuing. "As you know, this is a little competition, and the winning team gets a promising assignment, so give it your all and you just might be making big steps in your career as a result."

Gavin elbowed Charles in the side and the older

man looked up from his phone. "Good luck to all," he muttered before his thumbs were back on the screen.

All of the consultants lined up to enter the arena. Archer walked next to her, and when his arm brushed hers, her body erupted into a full-out shiver. *Who knew something so simple could light her up like that?* He leaned down to her, his warm breath fanning across her neck and his voice just above a whisper. "Wouldn't it make more sense for a juicy assignment to be handed out based on how good we are at our jobs?"

Jo ignored the ache building in her core, smiled, and patted his cheek gently. "It's cute that you think this place operates on a meritocracy," she said as they stepped up to the doors of the arena. "We don't use logic at Elite Sports, Hayes."

Archer smiled at her, bemused, and she turned away from him before he could catch her blushing. Jo wasn't used to feeling so weirdly shy around a man, but the new sensations it provided were incredible. Going from zero to fucking had been effective for her in the past, but after getting away from that and spending time with Archer, she found herself craving the slow burn instead of the fire that ended too quickly.

A kid who couldn't be older than seventeen stepped to the front, pulling Jo from her thoughts as she listened to him explain the rules of the game. They would play three rounds lasting ten minutes each, and the team with the most hits at the end would be declared winner. Jo looked around at the other pairings and they all seemed as singularly focused on winning as she was. Well, everyone except for Blake, who already had his gun aimed at his partner's back. She stifled a giggle and tried to regain focus. The teen let them know they would have two minutes to find a spot in the arena, and when the flashing lights went off, they would start the game.

The area doors opened and they rushed inside before scattering around like cockroaches when the lights came on, which was interesting considering it was pitch black with the exception of a few black lights that lit up people's light colored clothes and the spots of random graffiti on the walls.

She turned to Archer with a raised brow, hoping he could see it in the darkness. "Divide and conquer, or stick together?"

Archer pressed his lips together in thought before leaning down to her ear. "Let's stick together and see how it goes for the first round," he suggested, and she nodded before ascending a staircase to her right.

Archer followed her up, his hand on her lower back light but warm enough that she felt it through her clothes. If that was his way of branding her, Jo didn't really mind. She nearly stumbled at the thought, but Archer was right there to keep her steady. Nodding her thanks, she refocused and they scouted around for a bit before hitting the jackpot. In one corner of the second floor was a crow's nest of sorts, the perfect spot for picking off the competition.

"Score!" Jo shouted with a smile and rushed over to the small nook, Archer squeezing in next to her. There wasn't a ton of room, but if their bodies had to press together every now and then to make it work, she certainly wasn't going to complain. He was all hard muscle covered by soft skin, and she felt herself wanting to rub up against him more than she should. They stood next to each other in silence for a moment before his breath brushed against her skin.

"You always smell like some kind of flower," Archer confessed softly. "I like it."

Jo tilted her head up slightly to look at him, seeing that his eyes were already on her. "You do?" she asked, even though he had just admitted as much.

Archer nodded in the dark and brushed a lock of hair that had escaped her beanie back behind her ear. Jo's eyes flicked to his plump lips and she licked hers involuntarily in response to the sight of them. He leaned closer to her, and just when she thought he might kiss her, lights flashed to signal the start of the game.

The next half hour went by quickly, and from what Jo could tell, she and Archer did pretty well. They were able to maintain their spot in the crow's nest for the first two rounds, but after getting hit right at the beginning of the third, they had to abandon their small nook and split up to cover more ground. Once the game was over, she and everyone else were making their way out of the arena and back to the registration area, looking far more sweaty and bedraggled than she thought they would have given the short amount of play time.

Jo peeled the beanie off her head and ran her fingers over the damp strands of her hair. She pulled the locks up into a sloppy bun to cool the back of her neck and looked over to see Archer staring at her again. She shrugged a shoulder. "I know. I look a mess," she said, wiping her brow.

His head shook. "I never said that," Archer told her, smiling to himself before looking to the point board.

"But you thought it," Jo remarked with a small chuckle, but Archer just kept shaking his head.

"Actually, I was thinking…" he started, but he was interrupted by Gavin clapping his hands to announce the winner.

Argh, Jo could kick her boss in the shins right now. What was Archer going to say? It's not like she could ask him now without looking thirsty as hell, but she really, really wanted to know what he was thinking. That probably wasn't a good sign, but she was choosing to ignore the little red flag that was waving around in her mind that read "work and romance don't mix," at least for right now.

"All right folks," Gavin started, his eyes filled with amusement. Jo wasn't surprised the man got a giddy thrill out of making his employees run around like rats in a maze on his day off, but he didn't have to revel in it. "After calculating the scores, it seems that Mr. Hayes and Ms. Farrow are our winners, and by quite a margin as well." He started to clap, and once again, the others begrudgingly joined in. Blake looked genuinely happy for her, but his wide grin could also be because he had been able to hit his own partner about two hundred times. "Archer, Jo. Come see me. The rest of you, have a great weekend and we'll see you Monday."

Jo and Archer got a few displeased looks from their colleagues as they passed by, but she ignored them and walked over to the boss.

"So what's this big assignment?" Archer asked Gavin as they approached.

She glanced around for Charles, but he clearly had better things to do than stick around for this thing.

Gavin smiled at the two of them. "I'm assuming you're both familiar with Georgia's Liberty University." Jo and Archer looked at each other, wide-eyed. Anyone who lived in the state had heard of Liberty. It was the most prestigious private college in Georgia and they were renowned as much for their sports program as they were their excellent academics. Gavin laughed at their reaction and smiled. "I'll take that as a yes."

"It's the best sports college in Georgia," Archer said, stating the obvious. Jo was impressed that he had already brushed up on the local colleges when he'd only lived in the state for a few months.

"That it is," Gavin proceeded. "And they're

looking for a new firm to be in charge of their sports marketing."

"That's a big get," Jo breathed out. It was big enough for a raise and possible promotion too, she thought. "What happened with their old firm?"

"That's not important." Gavin waved away her question with his hand. She ignored the fact that he basically brushed off her inquiry in favor of listening to what else he had to say. If it meant her getting a promotion, she supposed she could put up with a little more of his nonsense. "What is important is that the athletic director called me himself and said he was interested in coming to us. I told him I'd get my top two people on it, and that's the both of you. I had confidence in all of my consultants, but I needed a team who could work together well to take out the competition, and you illustrated that beautifully today."

Jo glanced at Archer to see the same skepticism from earlier on his face, so she bumped his elbow with hers to get him more on board. "Congratulations, partner," she exclaimed, smiling at him and pleading with her eyes for him to be good with this. Jo needed the raise to take some of the edge off the worry she had for her dad. If she made more money, she could help him retire sooner and maybe move to another firm after another year or so.

Archer smiled back before turning to Gavin. "Will we be making a pitch the director only or a whole team?" If they managed to land Liberty U as a client, it could be a boon for their small agency and their careers.

Gavin smiled. "There will be a formal pitch in a few weeks in front of the director as well as a few very important people at the university."

"Okay, so we go in with everything we've got." He looked over at Jo. "Go big or go home, right?"

Jo wasn't sure if it was a phrase Archer normally used or if he busted it out for their boss's benefit. The man did love his little catchphrases.

Gavin clasped Archer on the shoulder. "That's the spirit," he gushed, his smile displaying his shiny fake teeth. "You'll have to be pretty impressive. Back in my heyday we didn't have fancy computer presentations and the like. We just met over drinks and talked things out until we made the deal."

Jo frowned, glad that she wasn't back in Gavin's heyday. Hashing things out over drinks wasn't how she liked to do business, and it sounded sketchy as hell anyway. "When exactly is the pitch?"

"No specifics yet, but I want this to be your top priority." Gavin nodded and clapped his hands together loudly, as if they were dogs who needed to be called to attention. "Get it done," he commanded before leaving the facility.

Archer turned to her with a grimace. "What are we supposed to do about our other clients while we make this our top priority?" he asked as they walked out to the parking lot.

"Try to squeeze it all in, I guess." It wasn't like she wasn't already burning the candle at both ends, so what was one more item on the list? "Maybe I can buy a cot and start sleeping in my office."

Archer chuckled. "Hard pass. I am willing to do a lot of things for my career, but giving up my pillow top mattress is not one of them," he insisted.

Jo tried not to think about how good he would look on that pillow top mattress, every inch of him on display and all spread out for her to feast on, but it was difficult. Instead, she reverted back to teasing him. "You are so spoiled." She rolled her eyes good-naturedly just as her phone pinged. It was still in Archer's pocket, so he reached in and held it out to her along with her keys. "Thanks." She grabbed the phone and saw a notification from her dad on the screen. It looked like the garage was slammed and he was cancelling their plans for lunch.

The disappointment must have been showing on her face because Archer reached out and touched her forearm. "Everything okay?"

Jo's arm tingled where he had touched it, and she smiled at another unfamiliar feeling that she was slowing getting addicted to. It had been a very long time, maybe forever, since anyone had given her that warm, sparkly feeling, and she really liked it. "Everything is good," she assured him, waving her phone at him. "My dad just cancelled our lunch date. No biggie."

Archer nodded and shuffled his feet on the pavement of the parking lot. "Well, I guess I'll be heading off."

Jo nodded, jingling her keys nervously. She didn't want to say goodbye, but wasn't sure what else to do. If this were a bar and she wanted to take Archer back to her place for a romp in the sheets, she would have no problem sealing the deal, but simply interacting beyond hookup territory was so foreign to her. "Okay," she finally replied with a shrug of her shoulder.

Archer kept nodding and backed away slowly. He started to turn around, but Jo stepped forward, trying to gather up some courage.

"Hayes," she called out to him, and he faced her once more, his expression filled with curiosity.

"Did you need something else?" Archer's voice sounded hopeful and it gave her the little push she needed to ask for something she had actually been wanting to do for a while but hadn't known how to bring it up.

"Um," Jo replied nervously. "If you don't have any plans, I was going to see if you wanted to grab lunch.

I mean, we'll be working together on this project and all, so it would probably be good for us to try and make it through an entire meal without squabbling with one another."

Archer's eyes widened and she panicked, wanting to pull the words back into her mouth immediately. She knew how to flirt and how to get a guy to take her back to his place, but she had no idea how to ask a guy out on a date. Not that this was a date. It was just her doing what was best for her career, and landing a big client wouldn't happen if they were still in a weird space.

"If you're busy—" she started, but Archer cut her off.

"I'd love to," he said emphatically before wincing slightly. "I mean, that sounds like a good idea." He chuckled awkwardly and she smiled. It was endearing, a word she'd probably never used to describe a man in her life, but it was the only one that fit. Archer had definitely endeared himself to her, and while she wasn't sure what to do about it, Jo was certainly starting to enjoy it. He nodded at his SUV. "Want to follow me home and you can drive us from there?"

Jo's eyes narrowed in suspicion. "Angling for a ride in my cool as hell car, huh?" Most people saw her car and wanted a ride, something Jo was used to and didn't bother her in the least. In fact, the image of Archer in her car was kind of nice, fitting.

Archer shrugged his shoulders. "I'm not even going to pretend it's anything else," he confessed with a smile.

Jo returned the smile and stepped back from him, turning and walking to her car. She peeked over her shoulder at him a few times before she slipped inside and caught him doing the same to her. With a smile and wave, Jo followed him out of the parking lot. Another unfamiliar feeling started up in her belly, and Jo smiled at the return of something else she hadn't felt since she was a teenager with a crush: butterflies. She had thought the winged creatures had gone extinct for her, but it seemed she was wrong and spent the rest of the drive enjoying the fluttery feeling, hoping that it wouldn't go away anytime soon.

## Chapter Ten

*Archer*

June was sweltering in Willow Creek, but the breeze blowing through Archer's hair as Jo drove the two of them around town in her convertible helped cool him off considerably. It wasn't just the temperature that had Archer feeling hot under the collar—it was the woman next to him, too. He slid his eyes to the driver's seat and checked her out as discretely as possible. She looked relaxed, her left arm resting on the door of the car as she leaned back and steered with one hand. Stray curls that had fallen from her messy bun danced around her beautiful face as the air rushed past them. He let his eyes wander south and run over her body, enjoying the slight curves that were on display in her tight tank top and yoga pants.

When Jo had handed over her keys earlier and wiggled her ass for him, Archer practically melted into a puddle. It was a good thing he had been was wearing loose basketball shorts or she would have seen him staring to pitch a tent. The last thing he needed was to give her more fuel for her teasing, though in truth, he actually liked it. It was nice to see her let loose and enjoy herself fully. Jo was always trying to take control of whatever situation she was in, but it was fun to be able to flip the script on her every now and then. So many ideas came to mind at that thought, and Archer had to pinch his arm to stop from imagining them in the bedroom, him in complete control and her at his mercy.

"You okay over there, Hayes?" Jo asked as she turned her head to look at him for a moment before casting her gaze back to the road. "You've been pretty quiet since we dropped off your car."

Archer had been quiet, but not because anything was wrong. He had been so intent on studying every facet of the woman next to him that he forgot about things like making conversation or acting like a normal human being and not someone who was infatuated with their coworker. "I'm good," he replied, shaking his head and flashing her his trademark, charming smile. "I think the laser tag took more out of me that I thought."

Jo snorted. "Should I steer us toward the senior living community? If we hurry we can get you the early bird special before you have to tuck yourself in for the night," she taunted.

Archer rolled his eyes, not that she would see it behind his sunglasses. "Funny," he said, his voice flat. "I'll have you know that I'm only thirty-two."

"Could have fooled me." Jo smirked as she pulled the car into a parking lot for a place called Barb's Diner. Archer had seen and driven past the restaurant many times but never gone in—the place looking too much like a greasy spoon for his liking.

Jo slipped her car into park and turned to look at him, her right arm resting over the top of her chair. If he moved a little closer, her fingers would be brushing his shoulder. Archer was tempted to do it, but scolded himself for acting like a lovesick teenager. Jo slipped her sunglasses into her hair, pushing the loose curls away from her face as she narrowed her gaze at him.

"What?" Suddenly feeling self-conscious, he ran his fingers through his tangled hair. Her bright blue eyes continued boring into him and he squirmed in his seat under her intense scrutiny.

Jo nodded her head to the diner. "I know it doesn't look like much from the outside, but they have the best food in town." She pulled her keys out and opened her car door, shooting a sardonic look at him from over her shoulder. "I promise to take you somewhere else if your delicate sensibilities are offended."

Archer scowled and exited the car, rounding the hood to meet her at the front of the diner. "Who says my sensibilities would be offended?" He crossed his arms over his chest in challenge.

Jo stepped closer to him and crossed her own arms, which pushed her small breasts up to say hello. The effect was not lost on him and Archer wanted to greet them both personally, preferably with his tongue. Once again, he was glad he still had his sunglasses on so she didn't catch him noticing just how hot she was.

"You drive a BMW, your suits look tailor-made," she remarked before flicking at his wrist. "And I'm pretty sure the watch you're wearing would cost me half a month's salary."

Archer looked down at his Ferragamo watch and frowned. It had been a gift from his dad, but she wasn't wrong about the cost of it, or his car, or his suits for that matter. He hoped he didn't come across as a snob, but clearly if she was worried about what he thought of the diner, he had. Hell, Archer had even been thinking about where else they could possibly eat from the moment they arrived. It was disconcerting to have someone read you so easily, but her ability to do so was probably what made her such a good marketing consultant.

"Fair enough." Placing his hand on the small of her back, he led her to the diner entrance. "How about I set my opinions to the side until I've had some food?"

Jo nodded curtly and went to open the door, but he beat her to the handle and opened it for her. She looked annoyed, but not mad, so he guessed that was a win. Archer slipped off his shades and blocked her from entering with his other arm.

Her blue eyes met his. "I thought we were reserving judgement," she challenged.

"We are." He smiled before leaning in closer to her, stopping just short of their noses touching. "But that means that you have to not judge me based on all those things you just listed." Her brow furrowed in confusion. "I may come from money, but I work just as hard as everyone else, so no preconceived notions about me either please."

Jo nodded slowly, a smile pulling at the corners of her mouth. "I won't judge you for that. I'll just judge you for letting a game of laser tag tire you out, old man," she jibbed gleefully before ducking under his arm and heading into the restaurant.

Archer chuckled and followed her inside. He would take pot shots about his age all day if it kept that bright smile on her face. He walked up next to her as she stood at the hostess stand. "Still only thirty-two," he reminded as he gently nudged her arm with his. "That's only a few years older than you, Freckles, so take heed of this little glimpse into the future because back pain, creaky knees, and heartburn are all coming for you too."

Jo laughed and smiled brightly at him. "We'll see," she said as the hostess finally approached.

"Hey there, Jo," the older woman greeted like they were old friends. "Are you meeting your daddy today?" The hostess looked over at him and grinned widely, her brows arching. "Oh, I see you're with another kind of daddy."

Archer barked a laugh and stuck out his hand to the woman as Jo stood next to him, mouth agape and cheeks pink. "I'm Archer, ma'am. We're coworkers."

"I'm Annabeth, and it's really none of my never

mind, anyway," the woman said as she smiled and shook his hand. "Though it is nice to see Miss Jo out with a man who she isn't related to." She grabbed two menus from behind the small hostess stand and walked toward the row of booths. Annabeth leaned over to Jo as they walked. "Good job, honey."

Jo groaned as she plopped into the red vinyl seat of their booth with Archer sliding into the seat across from her, smiling at her discomfort. Jo looked up at Annabeth with pleading eyes. "We are really just coworkers, Annabeth. Please don't tell Pops the next time he sneaks in here for a burger." She pointed at the older woman with a mock glare. "Don't think I don't know about his little weekly burger runs. You're all enablers, I hope you know."

Annabeth held her hands up in surrender. "Sorry sweetheart, but you know how much we love seeing your daddy. I promise to slip a few carrot sticks onto his plate next time he's here." Jo nodded in thanks as their hostess turned waitress whipped out a small notebook and grabbed a pen from somewhere in the mop of pink hair that was piled on top of her head. "Now, what can I get ya'll?"

"Um," he started, opening his menu to get a look at it. Archer had no idea what to order from this place, and as much as he liked to think he wasn't a snob, he did have pretty exacting tastes when it came to meals.

Jo snapped the menu out of his hands and handed it back to Annabeth. "We'll both have a double cheeseburger and fries. One chocolate shake and…" she trailed off, glancing across the table and giving him a once over. "One strawberry milkshake."

Annabeth smiled at Jo and tucked the menus under her arm. "I'll get that put in for you," she said, chuckling as she walked away from their table.

Archer looked over at Jo, his brows near his hairline. "How do you know that's what I wanted? I could be a vegetarian or vegan for all you know." He wasn't, but once again she was totally taking over. Archer didn't mind it so much because he had been floundering with his order, but he was curious to know why she always felt the need to control everything.

Jo lifted a shoulder nonchalantly. "I know you aren't a vegetarian or vegan because I've seen you with your little packed lunches of chicken skewers at the office, and everyone likes a burger and fries. The strawberry milkshake was a guess."

Archer furrowed his brow. "Lucky guess," he grumbled. He did prefer strawberry milkshakes, always had. They were refreshing and reminded him of summer, his favorite time of year. "I'll let you get away with it this time because I've never been here and you know what's good, but don't start thinking that because I'm letting it slide that you can just walk all over me all the time."

"Oh, I don't think it," Jo remarked, leaning across the table with narrowed gaze. "I know it." She smirked and leaned back into her seat, unfolding a napkin and placing it on her lap.

Archer hummed silently. "We'll see about that."

Jo smiled and looked out the window, and as he admired her beauty, he was once again bombarded with images of the two of them in a very different environment. He wanted her to give up control to him, but not because he wanted her submission. Archer wanted to see her free from all the worries and obligations that seemed to be tying her down, and he desperately wanted to be the one to help her get there, the one to give her that release along with a great deal of pleasure. He shifted in the booth and grabbed a glass, filled it with water from a pitcher on the table, and took a long drink. He really needed to get his thoughts under control around her or he would give himself away. Dating a coworker was not a complication he needed in his life right now, but it was all he could think about.

A change of subject was in order, and Archer grasped onto the first on he could think of. "So you come here with your dad?" Talking about family was a sure fire way to kill his libido.

Jo turned back to him, a small smile on her face. "Not all the time, but every now and then we meet here for breakfast on Sundays." She shook her head, but her smile was pleasant. "My dad and I are close, and Sunday mornings became our thing a while back. Most of the time I make him breakfast at home, but everyone deserves a treat every now and then."

"A treat?" His eyes pinged around the older diner. The inside looked more updated than the exterior had, but Archer couldn't imagine that this was the place most people came to treat themselves.

"Yeah," Jo smiled wistfully. "Growing up, my mom would make pancakes on Sunday mornings, and after she passed, making pancakes in the kitchen just wasn't really the same, so we stopped doing it." She shrugged a shoulder, though her eyes held a bit of the pain she must feel at having lost a tradition along with her mom. Archer's heart kicked painfully in his chest at the thought of Jo having gone through that. "I know it's silly, but I guess we come here for pancakes every now and then as a small way to stay connected to her."

Archer bowed his head slightly, trying to express his sympathy for her. "I'm sorry to hear about your mom." He wanted nothing more than to reach across the table and grab her hand, but didn't do it in case it would scare her into retreating back into herself. This was one of the few times he'd caught a glimpse of the vulnerable

Jo, and he wanted more of the real her. The fact that she trusted him enough to show her soft underbelly to him made him feel more accomplished than he had even after being at the top of his class in graduate school, and he didn't want to screw that up. "I don't think it's silly to want to keep that connection."

"Thanks," Jo said quietly, running her finger through the condensation that had formed on her water glass. "How about you? Are you close with family?"

Archer's head tilted in thought. "I suppose I am." He shifted in his chair to get more comfortable, settling in for a long conversation he was actually looking forward to. "I moved back here partly to be closer to my sister and nephews. My parents are still back in Montgomery, but they're pretty busy with work and their social calendar. I was working all the time there and I wanted a slower pace."

Jo nodded and smirked. "Well, you don't get much slower paced than at Elite Sports," she said before taking a sip of her water. "I've been there for almost six years and I'm still a junior consultant."

"Really?" That surprised him. Archer knew she was a junior consultant, but he hadn't known she had been there for that long. Between that and the fact that she was always the first one in and almost always the last one to leave, she should basically be running the place by now.

Jo bobbed her head slowly. "Yes, really. It seems like everyone else has moved up except for me. Though I guess I shouldn't be surprised with how sexist Delaney is."

Archer's brown furrowed. "Sexist?" He had noticed a few things that he wasn't entirely comfortable with, but he wasn't sure he could go as far as to label their boss that. "I haven't noticed anything that bad."

Jo sighed, spearing him with a look. "You're a white male in the prime of his life. You don't have to notice these things because they don't really affect you." Her face was resigned, like this was just a fact of life that she had slowly accepted.

Archer leaned back, affronted. "I don't know how true that is," he protested, but when he saw the impassive expression on Jo's face, he wondered if he was wrong. He had witnessed firsthand how she was taunted by their coworkers, and her ideas were often overlooked or credited to someone else in their meetings. The culture wasn't great, and that came from the top down. "So why do you stay? If it's so bad."

Jo rubbed a hand down her face before leaning a cheek against her fist. "There aren't a lot of options for sports marketing near town, and I can't leave my dad." Her eyes looked sad and her mouth lifted in the corner. "He's all I have left, and it's worth putting up with a lot of crap if I can live closer and spend time with him, help him take care of himself."

Archer nodded slowly, finally putting some of the puzzle pieces together. Jo tried to control everything so she wouldn't end up alone. The thought of her feeling afraid and lonely made his heart ache again, and while he longed to comfort her, he wasn't sure how to do that with their relationship being what it was.

A plate piled high with a burger and fries slid in front of him, disrupting his thoughts. "Here you guys are. Holler if you need anything else," Annabeth said after dropping off their food and milkshakes.

"Thanks, Annabeth." Jo picked up a fry, dipped it in her chocolate milkshake, and popped it into her mouth, groaning in pleasure. Normally that kind of sound coming from her would have Archer feeling all hot and bothered again, but right now he was just bothered. He was upset that such a smart, funny, beautiful woman was working herself to the bone for a company that didn't appreciate her so that she could take care of her dad. Who took care of her? "What? Don't tell me you don't dip your fries in your milkshakes. It's completely normal," Jo insisted, popping another fry covered in ice cream into her mouth. "Salty and sweet is the best combination."

"Whatever you say, Freckles." Archer followed her lead, dipping his own fry into his shake and enjoying the mix of salted strawberry flavor as it hit his tongue. When he finished chewing he smiled at her. "Okay, you win. You get to order all my food from now on."

Jo smiled and nodded at his plate. "Just wait until you taste the burger. It's the greatest thing in the world," she said before lifting her own and taking a large bite.

Archer smiled and did the same. And while the burger had been one of the better ones he'd ever had, he didn't think it was the greatest thing in the world. That title belonged to the woman sitting across from him. Jo was the best thing to walk into his life in a long time, and Archer planned to do everything he could to ensure she never walked out of it.

## Chapter Eleven

*Jo*

The racks at the boutique Gigi had dragged her and Millie to contained very little clothing in a style that Jo felt comfortable in. Dresses were draped as far as the eye could see, and while Jo wasn't against dresses per se, she never really chose to wear one unless she had no other option. Maybe it was the tomboy in her, but she would rather be in pants just about any day of the week. On the occasions Jo wore one of the few skirts she owned, she was always tempted to slip a pair of biker shorts underneath just to add that extra layer of comfort.

She picked at the flowy fabric of a light pink dress in front of her. "Remind me why we're here again." Jo looked to her two friends, who were currently browsing through the rack next to her.

"Well we certainly aren't here to complain about shopping," Gigi said to her, giving her an exasperated look before turning to their friend. "I'm so excited for your date, Mills. You said he's an author. That's incredible since you love books so much."

Millie lifted a shoulder in a light shrug. "I guess." She lifted a blue dress up to show Gigi, looking not at all enthusiastic about her choice. "What about this one?"

Gigi scrunched up her nose and shook her head. "No, you need something that shows a little more skin, not something that looks like my mom would wear it to the country club. This guy sounds like he has real potential, so you need to really put yourself out there."

Millie blew out an exaggerated breath. "Can I just cancel? He wants to meet at some fancy French restaurant. I never feel comfortable in those places."

Jo frowned at her friend. Millie grew up in a trailer park with parents who could barely hold down jobs, so she had always been nervous when it came to money, but Jo had thought she was past all that. Apparently her financial insecurity was still alive and well. Jo walked up to Millie and squeezed her shoulders in a side hug. "You deserve a nice night out just like everyone else. Besides, when was the last time you treated yourself to a new dress and a fantastic dinner?"

Millie twisted her lips up in thought. "I don't know. Does the artisan pizza dough I made the other night count?"

Jo chuckled because she would think that fancy pizza dough was a treat too. That happens when you live off take out and frozen dinners like she did.

Gigi smiled endearingly at their friend. "I don't know if it counts if you had to make it yourself."

"Hmmm. Then I guess it has been a while." Millie picked up another dress, eyed it for a moment, then shook her head at it. "Most of my other dates so far have been pretty run of the mill and we never went anywhere that was more than fifteen dollars a plate."

"Well, then now is your chance to really make a night of it," Gigi enthused before pulling an ice-blue halter neck cocktail dress from the rack and presenting it to Millie. "And you should totally wear this."

Millie looked at it skeptically. "That looks like Jo's ice princess costume."

Jo snorted because it totally did, but she tried to cover it with a cough when she caught Gigi's glare in her direction. Jo straightened her back and turned to Millie. "First of all, I'm an ice queen, not a princess. Secondly, this will look amazing on you." It would, too. Jo might be taller than both her best friends, but she had always been a little jealous of their curves since her body skewed more toward athletic and slender. Jo was more watchband than hourglass compared to her friends.

"I don't know." Millie grimaced as she looked over the dress, a weary look on her face.

"Just try it on, please," Gigi pleaded with a wounded puppy expression that usually got her just about everything she wanted, a look Jo couldn't pull off in a million years.

"Okay," Millie sighed before grabbing the dress and heading into a changing room.

As soon as she was gone, Gigi swung around and pointed at Jo. "You're next." With a smile, she grabbed Jo's hand and steered her over to the professional clothes.

"Whoa, whoa, whoa," Jo protested, trying to dig her sneakers into the floor to stop her friend, but the woman was surprisingly strong for such a short thing. "I don't have a date lined up and I already have plenty of work clothes."

Gigi stopped in front of a clothing rack and looked at her with a wicked grin. "I know, but I'm guessing nothing in your closet was chosen to help entice your new project buddy into a little something-something."

Jo fought a smile as she crossed her arms over her chest. "I don't want a little something-something with him." It was only a small lie, so she felt no guilt over it. After their lunch the day before, Jo found herself thinking about Archer more and more. Most of those thoughts ranged from simply favorable to overtly sexual in nature, but they still worked together and it was a bad idea. "I don't date colleagues."

Gigi shot her a wry look. "You didn't date colleagues because you didn't have one that you liked before. Now you do and you need to get it, girl," she insisted.

"I need to get something, all right, but it isn't a date with Hayes," Jo grumbled at her friend. "What I need is to focus on my career and forget about men altogether." It was easier said than done, especially when you were sexually frustrated and your coworker seemed to be designed just for you. Archer Hayes wasn't the type of guy she could see herself just hooking up with. She could see a future with a guy like him, and for someone who had never thought past a romp in the sheets with anyone, that was a very scary thing.

Gigi's hazel eyes shone with concern when they met Jo's. "I worry about you, Jojo." She stepped closer to her and rubbed her arm gently. "You're one of the toughest people I know, but you're working so hard at a place you hate all to take care of your dad. Let other people help you every now and then."

Jo smiled sadly. "And how would a date with a coworker help my situation?" It was nice that her friend cared about her so much, but Gigi had lived a fairly charmed life and didn't really understand how hard it was to be the only one your parent relied on.

Gigi shrugged. "At the very least, it would get your mind off things for a while." She sifted through the rack in front of her, and brought out a black pencil dress. The V-neck was deep and the hem shorter than she would normally wear, but it was still professional-looking while being sexy at the same time.

"I don't have the boobs for that dress," she stated matter-of-factly. Her breasts weren't nonexistent, but she wasn't nearly as endowed as either of her two friends. She blamed her extra height and genetics.

"Come on," Gigi pleaded. "You helped give me a push when I needed it, and now I'm doing the same for you. You like this guy, so show him what he has to look forward to when he makes a move." She dangled the dress in front of her with a smirk

Jo took the dress and looked at her friend. "What you're really saying is that you're all gaga for your boyfriend and you want Millie and me to get coupled up so you can feel better about ditching us in the future," she retorted.

With a grin and a nod, Gigi pushed her toward the fitting rooms. "Exactly," she replied cheerfully and the two chuckled as they walked through the store.

They got to the fitting rooms just as Millie was stepping out in her dress. She looked gorgeous, but completely self-conscious as she showed off the flowy dress to her friends. "On a scale of one to ten, how silly do I look?"

"Zero," Gigi replied immediately before giving their friend a hug to bolster her confidence. "You look amazing, as you always do."

"Thanks," Millie said shyly, pushing the bridge of her nose where her dark-rimmed glasses usually sit. She blinked rapidly. "Ugh, I'm still not used to contacts. Do I really look okay?" She looked over to Jo, knowing that she would give her honest opinion.

Jo chuckled and nudged her friend's arm. "You're stunning, Mills. You're going to knock this guy right off his feet." How a woman as pretty, smart, and good in the kitchen as Millie wasn't already married with four kids was a mystery to Jo, but life was weird. Just look at her, actually thinking about a future that included a husband and maybe even a kid or two for herself.

Millie smiled and went back into the fitting room to change. "What about you, Jojo?" Gigi asked her with a smile, nodding to the dress in her hands. "You going to knock your guy off his feet."

Jo just smiled and opened the door to another

changing room. "Yup, and just think of all the fun things we can do once he's down on the floor," she said, closing the door to the sound of her friend's giggles. Jo always knew how to get a laugh out of her friends, but as she tried on the dress and twisted this way and that to look at herself in the mirror, she realized she hadn't been joking.

****

The sun shone brightly, and even behind her sunglasses, Jo winced as the light pierced her eyes. It was Monday, the start of another week, and while everything in the parking lot and the front of the office building where she worked looked the same as it always had, something felt different about today. Jo didn't bother trying to tell herself it was because it was she was wearing the sleek, black dress that she had bought yesterday because she knew the real cause. She felt different because she had acknowledged the fact that she had started to develop feelings for a certain coworker, and while she still wasn't going to go for it in the traditional sense, she wasn't going to fight her attraction to him any longer either. If things naturally progressed between the two of them and they ended up on a date, or in bed, or whatever, so be it.

The elevator ride to the fifth floor was a quick one, and after striding through the doors, Jo found she wasn't the first one in the office. The smell of roasted coffee permeated the air, and when she walked around the corner, she nearly smacked into Archer.

"Whoa," he said, moving his coffee mug just in time to avoid a spill on his light blue button-down. When he looked up at her, he smiled happily. "Good morning, Freckles. Looks like I finally beat you into the office."

Jo scoffed. "First and last time, probably," she replied with a smirk. It was difficult for her to not immediately go into ball-busting territory with him. It was who she was at her core, but she also wanted to be more than that where he was concerned. "But congratulations on your accomplishment." Needing something to do with her hands that wasn't reaching out and pulling him into a kiss, Jo snagged his coffee mug from him and took a sip. She flinched at the overly sweet liquid and shot him a look. "How much sugar do you take in this?"

Archer grabbed his mug from her with a roll of his eyes. "It's one teaspoon at most. Sorry not all of us like our coffee to taste like bitter sludge," he snarked before taking a drink from his mug, his lips touching the same spot hers had. Millie must be rubbing off on her because the idea of them sharing a drink seemed romantic instead of germ infested like it normally would have.

"Black coffee keeps me on my A game," Jo informed him, retreating away from her fanciful thoughts about shared drinks and lips touching to slip into the break room and grab her own mug from the cabinet. "Speaking of A game." Jo poured herself a bracing cup of liquid caffeine. "What brings you in so early?"

"I'm so glad you asked." Archer's smile caused those new butterflies to take flight once again. The man had an amazing smile and should wear it all the time. "Follow me." He spun on his shiny black shoes and headed back toward his office.

Jo hiked her bag higher on her shoulder and followed him. Archer strode toward his office with purpose, but that wasn't where Jo's focus was. She was currently ogling his backside, which was magnificently displayed in his tight trousers. Whoever his tailor was deserved a big fat tip because the man did good work— the high, tight ass bouncing in front of her was highlighted so beautifully it deserved to have poetry written about it.

Archer fell into his office chair, cutting off her fantastic view, and spun his laptop to face her. "I've been putting together a dossier on Liberty U. I spent a good amount of time yesterday doing a deep dive into their previous sports marketing campaigns and I think I have an idea."

Jo looked over the information he had displayed for her and nodded. She took a seat across from him, having some difficulty crossing her legs in the dress she bought. It looked great on her, but it wasn't the most practical as far as daily activities were concerned. When she caught Archer looking at her legs though, she decided the little bit of discomfort was worth it. This time. There was no way she was letting Gigi take over her wardrobe for more than one day. Jo took a sip of her coffee and bounced her leg on her knee, watching with amusement as Archer followed the movement, his deep, brown eyes sparking to life.

"You have an idea?" she prompted.

"Hmm?" Archer asked before shaking his head, and as he cleared his throat, she smiled at her ability to discombobulate the man. "Yeah. I mean, yes I do." He clicked over to another document and showed her what looked like the beginnings of an outline. "Liberty's previous marketing was pretty outdated. Lots of references to power, strength, that sort of thing. There was also a lot of focus on the male athletes."

"If they want more of the same, they had the right idea contacting Gavin," Jo remarked. Her boss's idea of innovation didn't extend past the credit-card-accepting vending machine he had installed in the break room four years ago, so it made sense that Liberty would extend an invite to his firm for a pitch.

"Exactly, but I don't want to go that route, and I don't think you do either," Archer said firmly.

Jo nodded. "You are absolutely right about that. Centering a campaign on hotshot athletes is definitely not my style." That had been done ad nauseam and Jo wanted to really do something noteworthy. She put her mug down on his desk and leaned forward. "What's your idea?"

Archer smirked and tapped at the top of the outline that was displayed on his screen. "I think we should focus on a more diverse group of athletes, the women, minority, and LGBT athletes who deserve a chance in the spotlight and can show that Liberty isn't just a college full of white guys playing football."

Jo chuckled at his spot-on assessment. That was what Liberty was known for, but times were changing and the university and their marketing needed to change with them. "This looks really good, Hayes." Jo looked over the information on his computer once more, impressed once again with his knowledge and hard work. She glanced up at him and smiled. "I like it."

Archer's shoulders relaxed and he sighed, seemingly in relief. "Good," he breathed out. "I was afraid you would come in here and tell me it was crap."

Jo stood up and tutted at him. "I'm really not that scary." She was totally that scary, purposefully so, but she was trying to be different with him. She shook her head solemnly in mock disappointment. "And here I thought you knew me."

"I'm trying to," Archer said with a wide smile. "As long as you'll let me, anyway."

Jo's cheeks warmed with a blush and a smile tugged at her lips. She wasn't sure how to reply to his remark without giving herself away, so she simply raised her mug to him in cheers and fled from the room like the totally mature and put-together woman she was.

As soon as she was back at her desk, she took a

deep breath and fanned herself to cool off from the flood of emotions that were bubbling up. She really, really liked this guy, and it was throwing her completely off-kilter. Needing a bit of normalcy, she booted up her laptop and shuffled around in her planner to see what her day looked like. After a few minutes of checking her planner and emails, a calendar invite popped up on her screen. It was from Archer with the title "working dinner," scheduled for that evening. Jo smiled and immediately hit ACCEPT. It wasn't a date, she told herself as she navigated to her email. It was a working dinner, nothing more, but the smile that stayed on her face for the next hour told a much different story.

# Chapter Twelve

*Archer*

The plan for the start of the week had been for Archer to put his nose to the grindstone, focus on the new assignment while still giving his other clients all the attention they deserved, and to interact with Jo as little as possible to avoid his feelings deepening and possibly causing awkwardness between them. That plan went right out the window as soon as Jo walked in this morning looking like sex on a stick. Archer thought Jo looked amazing in her pantsuits, and even the yoga pants and tank combo she had been sporting on Saturday had gotten his engines revving, but there was something about seeing her in a dress that made it impossible for him to focus on work.

The moment Archer laid eyes on Jo wearing the little black number that showed off just a hint of cleavage and hugged her body like cling wrap, he knew his plans for the day were shot. He had needed to focus all his attention on not drooling on himself when she grabbed his coffee mug and drank from it. With rapt attention, he had watched as her rosy lips rested against the edge of the mug, and when her pink tongue darted out to lick away the coffee remnants, he had rushed them back to his office so that he could hide the proof of just how much she got to him behind his desk.

After their brief meeting to go over the dossier he had put together, Archer thought about just trying to communicate with her via email, but it was no use. He couldn't go more than ten seconds without picturing her back in his office, her long, smooth legs on display and her buttery-blonde curls brushing against her shoulders. Other imaginings flashed through his mind as well. The most prominent was a show of him locking up his office and sweeping everything off his desk before laying her out over the top of it, ripping the clothes from her body, and exploring every inch of her delicate skin with his hands and mouth.

It had only taken about five minutes for Archer to cave and send out a working dinner invite. Jo was on his mind all the time, even more so since their lunch on Saturday, and he was done fighting the urge to get to know her better, to explore these feelings that he hadn't had for a woman in what seemed like forever. Jo was everything he could ever want in a woman and then some, and now that she was finally softening and allowing him to actually get to know the real her, the Jo behind all the armor, he was helpless to resist.

Archer glanced at the clock. Time had seemed to drag all day, but it was finally nearing 6:00 and his palms sweat with nerves. It wasn't like this was a date, just a couple of colleagues working on a project while eating some food to keep their energy up and brains firing on all cylinders. His mind knew that, but his heart wasn't getting the message and was currently trying to beat its way out of his chest, the emotions too strong for one organ to contain. Archer took deep breaths to try and calm himself, but it didn't do much to squash the nerves or anticipation.

A message from the internal communication system popped up on his screen and he smiled when he saw who it was from.

Farrow, J: **So what's for dinner, Hayes? I'm thinking take-out from the Thai place across the street. Do you like Thai food, or are you someone who I will no longer be associating with?**

Archer shook his head at her sass but smiled at her message. Jo definitely had strong opinions, but he liked that. When someone as unyielding as Jo let you past some of her barriers, it meant something, and it made him feel special that she was letting him in more.

Hayes, A: **I happen to love Thai food, so you can still associate with me. You may change your mind after you hear my opinions on pizza toppings though.**

Archer didn't bother turning away from the message bubbles to try and get back to work. He knew anytime he was engaged with this woman, she would always have his full attention.

Farrow, J: **I'm almost afraid to ask, but go ahead and hit me with it. I'd rather know now than have you surprising me with sardine and onion pizza next time we have dinner.**

Archer couldn't keep himself from smiling if he tried. The fact that she was already thinking about a next time pleased him, and his mind started sprinting with ideas for all the different dates they could go on. *Not a date*, his practical side tried to remind him, but Archer ignored it. The time for logic had passed; it was time for his emotions to take over. He might have to spend time deciphering between real emotions and lust, but he could do that. Lust was definitely a part of whatever was happening between him and Jo, but somewhere between that first elevator ride and the message she just sent him, he had developed real feelings for her. He wasn't sure if those feelings were mutual, but these work sessions of theirs could be a good way to find out.

Another chime came in and brought Archer out of his head.

Farrow, J: **If you are this afraid to tell me, either I really am that scary, or your opinions on toppings really are that horrible. I'm waiting...**

Archer smiled and typed out his reply.

Hayes, A: **Okay, don't hurt me, but my favorite pizza of all time is spinach, roasted red pepper, pineapple, and pepperoncini.**

Archer started at the computer for a good two minutes waiting for a reply to come in, but instead he heard a knock. He looked up to see Jo standing there, leaning against the wall of the open door of his office, a grin on her face. "We are totally getting that pizza for dinner instead of Thai food," she declared before sitting down in the chair across from him. "I love a little sweet and spicy on my pizza and no one will ever split one with me, so I end up never getting it. I am dying for this pizza now."

A wide grin formed on his face, so wide the muscles in his cheeks protested. It was silly, but knowing that they enjoyed the same pizza toppings gave Archer an immeasurable amount of joy. No one ever wanted to split that pizza with him either, so he ended up having to eat it over the course of a few days on his own. It was nice to finally have someone to share that with. "Well, then. Where should we order from?"

Half an hour later, Jo and Archer had moved into the conference room with their laptops, tablets, and other work materials along with a piping hot pizza from Pie in the Sky. Archer had never had pizza from there before, but Jo recommended it. She had been right about the diner, and if the smells coming from the box on the table were any indication, she was right about this place too. Archer had snagged a couple of waters and napkins from the break room and now passed one over to Jo. She smiled in thanks and flipped open the lid of the pizza box. They both inhaled the smell of freshly baked dough and sweet pineapple before diving in and grabbing a slice for themselves.

"This looks amazing," Archer said to her before taking a bite of the pizza. The burst of sweetness from the hot pineapple and the bite from the spicy pepperoncini was just what he needed, and he moaned at how good it tasted. He looked up to see Jo enjoying her own slice, a look of absolute bliss on her face. Archer pictured that face underneath him on his bed and he nearly started to choke on his food.

"You okay?" Jo opened his water bottle for him and passed it over.

He nodded and took a swig of the icy liquid to help wash down the pizza and cool off his libido. It was barely working and he was still coughing when Jo scooted her chair closer and rubbed her hand up and down his back. Archer tried not to lean into her touch, but her hand on him felt so nice that he couldn't help himself, and he shifted in his chair to give her better access, arching into her hand like a cat. He heard a soft chuckle next to him and looked over to see Jo smirking at him.

"You angling for a back rub, Hayes?"

Archer shrugged, enjoying her teasing along with the touches. "Hey, since you're already there I figured I would give it a shot," he said with a smile. The image of her rubbing his back and other places came to mind and he nearly started choking again.

Jo stopped rubbing and gave him a firm pat on the back. "Let's land the university as a client, and then we can talk about back rubs."

Archer grinned at her and grabbed his slice again. "Then let's get to work. The sooner we get this done, the sooner you can get back to my massage," he quipped.

Jo rolled her eyes at him, but she was still smiling as she grabbed her laptop and opened it up to the university's athletics page. It displayed some of the same marketing they had seen time and time again, and while the old adage "If it ain't broke, don't fix it" came to mind, there was just something so tired about seeing football players fiercely staring down the camera with a look of intimidation. Did that really sell tickets nowadays? Archer highly doubted it.

"I took a peek at their social media pages and I think that would be another area we could punch up a bit." Jo clicked over to some of the college's sites and scrolled through as he munched on his slice. "It looks like it's mostly game-day reminders and posting pictures of the star athletes, but other than that it's pretty banal."

Archer hummed in agreement. "They've probably been relying on their reputation for so long that they haven't really bothered to step up their marketing game." Tale as old as time. Rather than evolving along with the rest of society or trying to appeal to new demographics, people relied a lot on reputation and name recognition to keep them going. Archer had a feeling that was true for the firm he was currently employed at as well.

Jo nodded. "I bet that's exactly it, and now that their enrollment numbers have plateaued, they're finally ready to join the rest of us in the twenty-first century," she said with a bright smile.

"Okay, so what's the plan?" Archer asked as he finished off his first slice, wiping his greasy fingers on a napkin.

"I'm so glad you asked." Jo clicked over to another page that had videos of the colleges dance and cheer teams. "I'm thinking we highlight the cheer teams and post some of their videos to the main athletics socials. They're the ones that get people fired up for the game, right? So why not show them doing their thing?" She clicked over to an outline on her computer. "Seeing your spreadsheet this morning gave me so many ideas. It's a little rough right now, but I think we can get something together pretty quickly if we work hard."

Archer gave her a dubious expression. "I don't know, Jo. You're always coming in late and leaving early, on your phone all day and chatting with the other consultants. I'm not sure you have the focus." Jo had more focus than all of them put together, and he was happy that he was able to snag even a tiny bit for himself.

"Ha ha," she snarked before playfully slugging him in the arm.

Archer grabbed at the area she hit and feigned hurt when really he wished she would touch him in any capacity again. "I'm surprised with an arm like that you don't have more boxers as clients."

Jo scrunched up her nose at him. "Ew, no. Finch likes to handle the boxing world and I wouldn't go near anything he does with a ten-foot pole."

"Yeah, he's quite the character," Archer replied diplomatically. He had other words to describe the misogynist clown, but he would save those for when they weren't still in the office.

Jo raised her brow. "That's definitely one way of putting it." Her smile was sad, but it brightened the longer she looked at him. "At least I still have you and Blake. I'm not sure what I would do if you guys weren't here anymore."

That she counted Archer along with her other friend at work was touching. They'd certainly come a long way from the icy glare she shot his way on his first day months back. "Well, I don't plan on going anywhere anytime soon." As much as he could tell this place was a dead end, he wanted to put in at least a year and Jo was giving him more reasons to stay with each passing day.

"Good," Jo said quietly before turning back to her laptop, her cheeks turning a beautiful shade of pink.

They spent another two hours going over the areas

where Liberty U was flailing in their marketing campaign and strategizing the different ways they could improve them. When they finally reached a breaking point, Jo slammed her laptop shut and leaned back in her chair. "I think that's plenty for today," she sighed before covering her yawn with a hand.

Archer stretched in his chair and felt his back pop. He definitely needed a good stretch before bed tonight if he didn't want to hobble in the next morning, giving Jo more reasons to dog him about his age. "Agreed." As much as he wished he could prolong their time together, they both needed a break, so he gathered up his things.

Jo put all of her stuff in her messenger bag before collecting their trash and walking it over to the can at the front of the conference room. Archer met her there with her bag and she smiled as she took it from him. "Thanks." Her smile was tired as they walked to the elevator in silence. Once again he wondered who took care of this woman. If the position was available, he was more than happy to apply.

The trip down to their cars was a quiet one, but Archer didn't mind it. They were both overworked and leaning up against the back of the elevator, but the silence felt relaxed, comfortable. It wouldn't even have felt out of place for Jo's head to lean against his shoulder, or for him to hold onto her hand as they rode down the elevator. In fact, it felt a little out of place for those things to not be happening. The chime sounded and the doors parted, signaling an end to what was the most relaxing few minutes he'd had all day. Archer pressed his palm to the small of her back and led her out of the elevator and through the doors to the parking lot. Jo peeked over her shoulder at him and smiled sweetly.

Archer walked the two of them over to their cars, his SUV right next to her convertible. It hadn't been a conscious thing, at least that's what he told himself, but it had been happening more and more and he wondered if maybe he hadn't been parking there on purpose in hopes of running into her even more than he already did. Jo opened the door and put her things inside before turning back to him. She had pulled her hair up into a high ponytail as the night went on, and Archer couldn't help himself from reaching up and tugging on one of the curls that had shaken itself loose, letting his finger linger on her neck.

Jo's sky blue eyes narrowed slightly as she looked at him. "I'm really bad at this," she stated strongly, looking unsure of herself for the first time since Archer had met her.

"Bad at what, Freckles?" His brow furrowed in confusion. Jo was so take-charge in just about every situation he had seen her in so far that her seemingly feeling off-kilter was perplexing.

Jo's smile was shaky as she replied, her honeyed voice low. "I'm really bad at knowing when something is more than what it seems to be. I don't really date, and I know this was just a work thing, but it felt like a date." She stepped closer to him and her floral scent hit him like a comforting wave he wouldn't mind floating in for as long as she'd let him. "How did it feel to you?"

Archer took a deep breath and stared into her eyes. "It felt like date to me too," he confessed boldly. No need for him to be less than honest, and since they weren't holding back feelings, he decided to not hold back his touch anymore either. Archer ran his fingers down her neck and shoulder, feeling a jolt of pride when it caused her to shiver. The pride faded when he realized how out of his depth he was with romance, though. It had been a very long time. "I don't really date much either, so I'm not sure I'm much better at it than you are," he admitted wryly.

Jo tiled her head in thought. "Do you like that it felt like a date?"

Like it? Archer had loved that it felt like a date. He wanted more nights like this. Nights, days, weekends. Whatever he could get, he wanted. "Very much. You?"

Jo reached over and placed her hands on his chest. "I liked it," she said huskily. "I really, really liked it." She licked her lips, her gaze laser focused on his, but just as he was leaning in, she leaned back and blushed. "I really want to kiss you right now," she said firmly despite her actions saying otherwise.

Archer placed his hands on her hips, rubbing his thumbs against the soft fabric of her pants. "Well, I'm certainly not going to stop you," he said with a smile.

She chuckled and smiled at him, but she had a pained expression on her face. "I'm supposed to be doing better than this though," she whined before her forehead hit his chest.

Archer huffed. "I might need you to explain that last comment or I might start taking things personally," he remarked, suddenly wondering if she thought he wasn't good enough. He thought they were a great match, so to hear her doubting it already was a little disconcerting.

"Sorry." Jo warm breath fanned across the open collar of his shirt before her gaze lifted to his once more. "My friends said I need to actually go out on some dates and not mess around with fuckboys," she confessed and held up her hands in supplication immediately. "Not that you are a fuckboy. Quite the opposite, in fact, which is why I don't want to screw things up by falling back into old habits."

Archer nodded, though he was still a little confused after her admission. "So, let me see if I have this straight." He moved his hands up to her arms and rubbed them up and down, hoping to comfort her and soothe his frayed ego at the same time. The more he touched her, the more he found that it centered him, and he needed that at the moment. "Your old habits were to rush into things with guys who weren't necessarily serious boyfriend material, but you don't want to do that with me, so we can't kiss?"

Jo smiled. "Yes, exactly," she said, agreeing with his assessment. "Well, I mean, eventually we can kiss."

Archer smirked and leaned in closer to her, his cheek brushing hers in a barely there touch that still managed to sear his skin. "And when is eventually?" He hoped it was soon because she was far too tempting and he wasn't sure how much longer he could hold out before getting his lips on hers.

Jo exhaled shakily. "I-I'm not sure. I might have to consult some people," she said swaying closer to him.

"You do that." Archer moved closer to her ear and rubbed his nose along the shell of it before whispering to her. "Because for me, eventually can't come soon enough." He brushed his lips against her cheek in a feather light kiss before pulling back completely. It was difficult to not kiss her fully, but if she saw a future with him, waiting would be worth it. "Goodnight, Freckles."

"G'night," she whispered, a mix of shock and happiness on her face.

Archer walked over to his car and hopped in, but he didn't bother to start it until she was safely in her car and pulling out of the lot. During the drive home, he replayed their evening together, going over every soft word or even the smallest of touches, again and again as he got home and relaxed on the couch, and once more as he lay in bed. Yes, they would kiss eventually, and he already knew it would be spectacular. When he finally managed to fall asleep, there was a smile on his face and dreams of Jo dancing through his mind.

## Chapter Thirteen

*Jo*

The days following Jo's work dinner with Archer that felt a lot like a date, but actually wasn't technically a date, were a strange mix of horrible and wonderful. The horribleness came from the fact that there had been more meetings than usual and she had been forced to interact with some of her more annoying colleagues at work at least once every day, but it had been worth it when Archer would sit down next to her at the meeting and send smiles her way or nudge her foot with his. They were small touches, but they sent a shiver of excitement through Jo's body and she was actually finding that she enjoyed the anticipation that was building up in every fiber of her being.

When she admitted to being bad at dating, she was sure he was going to run the other way, but instead he divulged his own insecurities and agreed to take things at her pace. Going slow wasn't something she was used to. Normally, Jo would see a guy, flirt for ten minutes or so before heading back to his place for some good sex, then she'd be home before the guy's sheets cooled. Taking her time felt nice, and she wondered if their being together would be even better because of the delayed gratification.

A smiled played across Jo's face as she thought about all that gratification, and she was so lost in her thoughts that she didn't notice someone had entered her office until Blake was waving a hand in front of her face to get her attention. "Earth to Jo," he said, smirking at her when she finally pulled herself together and looked up at him. "Girl, I want some of what you're on because you looked like you were in heaven just now."

Jo chuckled and her cheeks warmed with a blush. "Well, when it comes to this, I am definitely not willing to share." There was no way she was sharing Archer with anyone. He was all hers.

Blake leaned back, giving her a searching look. "Do I need to go grab a bowl of popcorn for this?" He sat down in the chair across from her and waved away his question with a flick of his wrist. "Never mind. Your expression tells me I'll probably need a cigarette afterward instead."

Jo laughed and chucked her pencil at him.

Like the former baseball player he was, Blake caught it deftly and put it back in her pencil cup. "Spill it, lady. Who's the new man?"

Jo shook her head. "I don't have a new man." It felt like she did, but she and Archer were still feeling things out, so he wasn't really hers yet. They hadn't had time for another working dinner or even lunch this week, but they did have their moments in the meetings and sometimes in the mornings they would come into each other's offices to talk and flirt. It wasn't a lot, but Jo had cherished each interaction because it brought the two of them that much closer together.

"I was giving you a chance to come clean, but since you feel like playing coy, I'll just go ahead and tell you that I know you and Archer have something going on, and I am here for it," Blake cheered, clapping his large hands together. "Details, please."

Jo sighed and leaned back in her chair. "Not many details yet. We're taking things slow," she admitted. "Keep this under wraps, though. I don't need any more hassle from The Idiot Brigade."

Blake looked offended and placed a hand over his

heart. "Girl, you know I would never throw you to the wolves like that and I'm offended you'd even mention it."

Jo leaned across her desk and squeezed his other hand. "Sorry, Blake. I know you wouldn't say anything. I just..."

Blake held up a hand to stop her from speaking. "You want to protect this because you actually like him." When Jo nodded, he had a wide smile on his face once again and patted her hand. "Okay, then. My lips are sealed, but hopefully yours won't be for very long." He winked as he stood up and turned to the door, waving at her over his shoulder and chuckling at his own joke as he left the room.

Archer stepped into her office seconds later, shooting her a curious look. "What were you guys getting up to in here?"

He sat down in the same chair Blake had and made himself comfortable, unbuttoning his cuffs and rolling up his sleeves to the elbow, giving her giving her a peek at his sturdy, muscled forearms. Jo watched and closed her mouth tightly to contain the moisture that was pooling inside. She knew he had a great body, but it was always so covered up in his suits. Even when they were at the gym downstairs at the same time, he wore track pants or shorts and never took his shirt off. She was dying to see what was under those layers of clothes.

When she moved her gaze from his arms to his eyes, she saw the chocolate-brown orbs lit up with amusement. "See something you like?"

The answer to that question was a definite yes, but Jo flicked her eyes to the ceiling and scoffed, trying to play off the fact that she was totally ogling him. "Please," she said before looking back to her laptop and pretending to check her email.

Archer placed his hands on her desk and stood, leaning over into her space. Jo had to tilt her head back to look at him, spying pupils that were dark and a look so intensely wanton she felt weak in the knees. "Please, what, Freckles? You want to see a little more? All you have to do is say the word and I will be there in a heartbeat."

Jo swallowed thickly and blinked up at him, her own heartbeat kicking into overdrive. She did want to see more. So much more, but she also wanted to keep her promise to herself that she would actually try this time, and that meant not giving into her baser urges, the ones currently screaming at her to climb that man like a tree. Jo exhaled slowly and opened her mouth, but before she could say anything, her cell phone pinged with a call. She glanced at it and saw it was her dad. He knew how busy she always was at work and wouldn't call if it wasn't important.

"I have to get this," Jo said to Archer before picking up the phone. "Pops? Is everything okay?"

"Hey, Jo. It's Cooper," the deep voice of the head mechanic at her dad's auto shop came through the line and Jo instantly panicked. Cooper wouldn't be calling from her dad's phone if something bad hadn't happened.

"What's wrong with Pops?" Jo asked, already packing up her things in a rush. Her eyes flashed up to Archers' and she saw the hunger in his gaze replaced with concern.

Cooper sighed. "Everything is okay. He got a nosebleed and was having some trouble breathing, so we called an ambulance. The medics are here now and are recommending he go to the hospital to get checked out, but he won't budge. I stole his phone to call you because if anyone can convince him to go, it's you."

"Thanks, Coop. Will you put him on the phone?"

Jo pinched the bridge of her nose as she struggled to stay upright. She couldn't believe her dad was being so stubborn about this. Didn't he know how much she needed him? What would she do if something happened to her dad?

"Hey, Joley-bear." His voice was raspy and weak. Her mind immediately went down a rabbit hole of worst-case scenarios, shoving her anxiety into overdrive.

Tears welled up in Jo's eyes and she tried to rapidly blink them away, but the minute she felt Archer's hand covering hers and giving it a squeeze, one fell away and rolled down her cheek. Jo flipped her hand and interlaced their fingers, deriving as much strength from his grip as she could. "Pops, will you please go with the paramedics? I'll meet you at the hospital and I can drive you home if you don't have to stay overnight." Jo really, really didn't want this to be happening right now, but it was, so she took a deep breath and exhaled slowly to calm herself. Someone needed to be in control of the situation, and that was her. She needed to keep it together for her dad.

"They're making a fuss over nothing, Jo," Pops whined. "It was just a little nosebleed, and after a nice hit from their O2 machine, I'm as good as new. No hospital visit required."

Jo sighed, happy it didn't sound like something more serious but worried it was also the calm before the storm. "Daddy, please?" Only on rare occasions did she ever call her father "daddy," but it always slipped out when she was afraid, and right now she was scared to death that something was going to happen to him and she would be all alone. Jo glanced down at her and Archer's intertwined hands and looked at him with a sad smile. Maybe not totally alone, but still. Jo needed her dad.

Her father gave a tired wheeze on the phone.

"Okay, Joley-bear. I'll go with them," he acquiesced. "But I better be out of that hospital before dinner because I'm not eating lousy cafeteria food."

Jo's laugh was watery, but it was nice to smile when something like this was happening. "Thanks, Pops. I'll be there as soon as I can. Will you give the phone back to Coop for a second?"

There was some mumbled shuffling on the line before Cooper's voice came back through. "What's up, Jo?"

"Hey, thanks again for calling," she told the man before gathering up the courage she needed to ask for a favor. Jo hated asking for help, but right now, she needed it. "Look, I know Saturdays are always really busy, but do you think you guys can handle tomorrow on your own? I really want Pops to rest up. I can come in and help out too if need be."

Cooper chuckled on the other end. "I appreciate the offer, Jo, but the boys and I can handle it. We'll be happy to take care of the shop while Bob gets a well-deserved weekend off."

Jo exhaled in relief and nodded at no one in particular. "That's great, Coop. I'll keep you posted on what's going on with Pops," she promised.

"Thanks, Jo. Take care." The line went dead but Jo still heard her dad's tired wheezing ringing in her ears.

Sometime during that whole conversation, Archer had moved next to her and draped his arm over her shoulder, the other still holding onto her hand. The feel of his body, warm and solid next to hers, was the only thing keeping her standing. "Everything okay with your dad?"

Jo felt her chin wobble, but she tightened her lips together and shrugged a shoulder. "I don't know. He has high blood pressure and was having trouble breathing, so I'm going to meet him at the hospital." She went to close her planner and saw the big, bold lettering outlining a meeting scheduled for an hour with her, Archer, and some businesses they hoped to help tie into their marketing campaign with the university. "Shit," Jo said to herself. "I forgot about the meeting."

"I've got it covered, Jo." Archer rubbed his hand up and down her arm as he reassured her that he could handle everything. Jo knew he could, but not pushing herself to do it all wasn't something she was used to. "You go take care of your dad."

Jo turned to face him. "Are you sure? That's a lot of people to coordinate with." It would have been a lot of work for the two of them. With her gone it would be nearly unmanageable, but if anyone could do it, it was Archer.

Archer smiled and ran his hands down her arms before grasping both of her hands. "Are you saying you're not confident in my abilities?"

Jo smiled and he smirked.

"There it is." He leaned down to kiss her forehead, his lips soft and another welcome distraction from the bad turn her day had taken. "I've missed that smile the last few minutes."

The butterflies that seemed to be a permanent fixture in her stomach when Archer was around took flight once more, and Jo was in danger of getting teary-eyed again. He was saying and doing everything she needed to feel better about the current situation, and she wished she could take him with her to the hospital where he could continue to be a stable force for her. "I don't doubt you," she professed, meaning it in more ways than one. He had proved himself more than capable at work and right now, he was proving that he was able to handle her at her most vulnerable too. She leaned up and kissed his cheek, the slight stubble that was always there tickling her lips. "Thank you, Archer."

When Jo leaned back, his eyes were wide and a smile tugged at the corner of his mouth. "While I don't love the circumstances that brought it on, I sure do like the sound of my name on your lips," Archer said, placing his hand on her back and steering her out of her office and to the elevator. "Let me know if you need anything else." He nodded to her as the bell chimed and the elevator doors parted.

"I will," Jo promised. "Thanks again." The amount of gratitude she felt toward this man could not be measured, but she would try to pay him back somehow, even if it was only in some small way.

"Anytime, Freckles." Archer winked as the doors closed and the car started its descent.

Jo leaned against the back wall to hold herself upright. Now that she was alone, the worries that Archer helped keep at bay flooded back in, and she grabbed her phone from her bag to make a few calls. She never liked asking for help, but if there was ever a time to get used to doing that, it was now.

****

Four hours, two rounds of hospital tests, and one stop by Greens on the Go later, Jo was escorting her dad into her childhood home and steering him straight over to the couch. "I'm going to go get your medication and then we're going to have dinner and a nice long talk," she declared.

His annoyed grumbles trailed after her as she went to the medicine cabinet of the master bedroom to grab his blood pressure pills. It turned out that even missing one small dose could cause enough of a problem that led to his nosebleed and breathing problems from earlier. Jo had been grateful that it was nothing more than that, but the doctor did say that her dad needed to reduce the amount of stress in his life, so Jo was on a mission to get him to do just that.

Jo walked back into the family room with his pills, a glass of water, and some silverware for their dinner. Eating out on the couch was practically a tradition. They had done it quite a lot while she was growing up, always with a game on in the background as they ate dinner consisting of whatever the two of them had managed to throw together from the items in their pantry. It wasn't the typical sit-down dinner some kids were used to, but it had been fine with her. Talking and watching sports had become another one of their special things, and while she was tempted to flip the television on and disappear into another game with him, they really needed to talk.

Jo sat next to him on the lumpy fabric couch that probably dated back to when they first moved in and handed him his pills and the water. "Here you go," she said, placing a fork on his salad and watching to make sure he took the pill before eating anything.

Her dad washed down his medicine with a large gulp of water and picked up his salad, looking around the room and inspecting it with a furrowed brow. "Why does this room look different?" Jo shrugged a shoulder, feigning ignorance, but she had always been a crap liar and her dad saw right through her. "Joley-bear, what did you do?"

With little energy or desire to hide much of what she had done, Jo blew a raspberry out through her lips. "I might have made a few calls to take care of some things." She had been avoiding his gaze, but when she finally made eye contact with her dad, he did not look amused and just stared at her until she gave up holding back any more information. She tossed her hands up in the air. "Fine. I may have called Gigi and she might have volunteered to clean your house up."

Pops narrowed his eyes at her. "And?"

"And Millie might have put some of her casseroles and other food in the fridge so you don't have to cook anything." When he simply raised one eyebrow at her, she divulged the rest. "I also told Coop that you weren't coming in tomorrow and I called Barb's Diner and said if they served you anything other than boiled broccoli I would contact a lawyer."

"Jo," her dad exclaimed, highly annoyed. "You cannot threaten to sue my favorite restaurant." Her dad shoved his salad across the coffee table in a huff. "I'm not a child, sweetheart."

His actions spoke to the contrary, but she knew she was the reason for his petulance, not a lack of maturity on his part. "I know you aren't," she protested. Why was he so annoyed? She should be the one mad at him for putting his health at risk. Didn't he realize just how upset she had gotten at the thought of losing him? "I'm just trying to help, Pops."

"Well, you're suffocating me with all your help," he spat out.

Jo reared back, upset and holding back tears again.

Her dad took one look at her stricken expression and wiped his hand down his face with a sigh. "I didn't mean that." Pops suddenly looked a lot more tired than he already had, and she couldn't help but feel responsible. Maybe her brand of "help" wasn't doing as much good as she had hoped it would.

She leaned against her dad, resting her head on his shoulder. "Yeah, you did," she told him sadly. Jo knew she was a control freak when it came to just about everything, but even more so when it came to her dad. She choked down the tears that threatened to spill and decided to just tell him how she really felt. "I can't lose you too, Daddy." She sniffled, and when his big arm came around to grip her shoulder, she gave into the urge to cry and let a sob loose.

Her father rubbed her arm and made the same shushing noises he did when she was little. Jo had always tried to act tough, but when it came right down to it, she was just like everyone else. Big, scary things like the possibility of losing the only parent she had left got to her, and she didn't try to hold it back anymore.

When her crying stopped, her dad tilted her face up to meet hers. "I know you don't want to lose me too, Joley-bear, but it's going to happen eventually. You're strong and tough, but even you can't control everything."

She nodded sadly. "I know, but I can still try," she implored. Trying to control everything had been her modus operandi for the last twenty odd years. She didn't know how to act any differently.

Her dad chuckled at that and smiled at her. "You do try, and while I appreciate everything you do to keep me around, I need to be able to live my life how I want to, sweetheart. I can't have every part of my day managed by my well-meaning, but very restrictive daughter. It's pretty miserable."

Jo took a deep breath to calm the hurt she felt at having caused so much trouble for her dad. "So you want me to back off and let you eat as many burgers as you want?" She wasn't sure she could do that. Jo had never liked giving up control, but she had in a small way with Archer earlier when she let herself be vulnerable in front of him, let him handle the meeting all on his own. It had been difficult for her to do that, but it hadn't been all that bad. Maybe she just needed to wade into the no-control pool one tiny step at a time.

"Kind of, yeah." Her dad laughed and she lightly

slapped at his arm. "I don't want you to stop caring about me, Jo. I just want to be able to do a few things that bring me joy without feeling like I'm letting you down."

Her heart sunk at hearing how her restrictions had made him feel guilty. The stress she was causing him was probably doing more damage to his health than any greasy burger could. "You aren't letting me down." Her dad was the greatest and she hated that her actions had caused him to feel that she could possibly be disappointed with him. He knew his health better than she did, and it was long past time she remembered that. "I want you to have joy in your life. I'm sorry if I've been the fun police for too long."

Her dad smiled and shook his head. "Not the fun police," he reassured her, tilting his head slightly. "Maybe something less extreme, like the fun mall cop."

Jo chuckled and gave her dad a big bear hug. "I promise to not be so down on fun," she vowed, but she leaned back and gave him a stern look. "But you're still taking the weekend off to rest and I want you to seriously think about giving Coop more responsibility at the shop. He's smart and can take some stuff off your plate."

"I will. He said as much himself the other day anyway." Pops reached for his salad container and peeked inside, looking over at her with a frown. "Do you think maybe I can dig into one of Millie's casseroles instead of munching on this? That girl can cook and I'm not really in the mood for rabbit food."

Jo smiled. "Sure." She hopped up to serve them both a nice helping of Millie's vegetable lasagna. "She also made some of her homemade garlic bread. Do you want a slice?"

An undignified snort reached her ears and she turned toward the family room. "Like you even have to ask," her dad called out to her, turning on the television to the sports network.

Jo chuckled and took their plates out to join him. It felt like old times, and while the urge to remind him to drink more water and go easy on the bread the entire time they ate was very palpable, she managed to hold herself back. It was a small step forward, but she was confident she could keep going. Thinking of confidence brought her favorite coworker to mind, and she pulled up their text thread from a couple of hours earlier.

Archer had messaged her a selfie with a big thumbs up after the meeting with the promise to email her and catch her up on Monday. He'd also asked how her dad was, and after she updated him with the all clear, he wished her a good weekend and they hadn't texted much more than that. She clicked on the selfie and admired his wide smile. Jo never really thought of herself as a relationship person, but the more time she spent with Archer, the more she realized that she just hadn't let herself consider the possibility before. Relationships were volatile and unpredictable, so she never bothered, but she wanted to try with him. Now, she just had to figure out how she could give up her desire to manage everything without losing herself in the process.

## Chapter Fourteen

*Archer*

Saturday night at The Tap House Bar and Grille was pretty busy—people were packed in like sardines, but Archer didn't notice a single one of them. His mind was still firmly with Jo. He wondered how she was doing after the scare with her dad. She had never looked frightened before, and to see such a formidable woman brought low had tugged at his heartstrings. He had been so tempted to just wrap her up in his arms and offer her some comfort, but they were taking things slow and hadn't defined exactly what that meant. Were they a couple? Were they just feeling things out? Jo mentioned kissing eventually, but people kissed all the time without it meaning they were official.

God, he sounded like a confused teenager. Archer was so out of the dating game that he had no idea what was going on. He felt totally inept, and he hated that feeling. When he saw a problem, he wanted to fix it. Not that Jo was a problem, but his mixed-up head certainly was and he wasn't sure how to see things more clearly. Hence his current state of moderate inebriation and his sitting position, his arms draped over the top of the mahogany bar and his eyes trying to fix themselves on one point in the distance, but failing to do so.

"You okay over there, Arch?" Caro asked, her voice filled with amused concern.

Archer had been so busy at work that he hadn't had time to hang out with his sister, so when she texted that Todd was going camping with the boys and she was available to go out, he of course said yes and the two found themselves at the local watering hole.

Archer lifted his head from where it had been resting on his arm and stared at his sister. Caro looked really happy, and Archer felt the sting of envy pierce him once again. He hadn't wanted to admit to that though, so he tried his best to put on a smile and fake it for his sibling and closest friend. No need to bring Caro down with his weird mood. "Yeah, I'm okay." He scrubbed a hand up and down his face to try and erase some of the conflicted emotions he was feeling, raising his beer glass to his mouth but setting it back down before taking a drink. "No, I'm not okay," he confessed. Why was he trying to hide his feeling when he clearly needed help?

Caro frowned at him, her expression filled with warm regard. "What's wrong? Is it the job?"

"No. The job is great. Well, not great, but it's a job, you know," Archer told her as he shook his head, his hair falling into his eyes.

The strands were disheveled from running his fingers through it so many times that day and almost every minute since he had witnessed Jo falling apart in front of him. At first he had been worried for both her dad and for her, but that morphed into a frustration at not knowing exactly where they stood. His need to comfort her had been so great that not being able to do more than handle a simple meeting for her ate away at him. The feelings Archer had for Jo had developed rapidly and were getting deeper by the minute. Every small glimpse she gave him of the real person behind her tough exterior just made him want her more. Hell, he was pretty sure he was already in love with her and they hadn't even kissed yet. Archer pulled up the sleeves of his faded college hoodie to cool off, the swirl of emotions causing his body to feel too hot and his skin too tight.

"What's the problem, then?" Caro asked,

completely oblivious to the turmoil going on in his head.

Archer sighed heavily. "There's this woman at work," he started, trying to keep it vague as to not get Caro's hopes up. She had been bugging him to give her a sister-in-law for almost a decade now. "She's headstrong, single-minded, stubborn, and impatient." He ran his hands through his already tussled hair and yanked at the ends. "And she argues with me over every little thing, from how I drink my coffee to how I use the wrong color pen for my contracts. She's driving me insane."

Caro's brow furrowed. "So report her to human resources or something if she makes you uncomfortable."

"I can't," Archer grumbled before taking a pull from his beer, hoping the dark stout would wash the bad taste out of his mouth from complaining about Jo. She had been all of those things, but she was so much more to him now and he didn't know what to do about it. "It's more of a playful teasing now, and I can admit that maybe I haven't always been as cordial to her as I could have been." Archer scratched at his jaw before peering over at Caro sheepishly. "There's another reason why I can't report her behavior."

"What's that?" she asked, and Archer blushed at the thought of what he was about to admit out loud.

He took a deep breath to fortify himself and summoned the courage to speak. "I'm pretty sure I'm in love with her," he blurted, his head collapsing back onto his arms. From the corner of his eye, he caught Caro covering her mouth to stifle a laugh. He appreciated his sister keeping her amusement to herself, as he wasn't sure he could handle the ridicule.

Instead of teasing Archer, Caro rubbed his back gently and smiled. "Welcome to the club, brother. It's not all hearts and cherubs, but it's not all storm clouds either."

"Easy for you to say," Archer complained at the wisdom she was attempting to impart to him. "You and your husband are solid. I have no idea how to pursue this woman. We're in this weird holding pattern, and after all the pranking and stuff we've done to one another, I'm not entirely sure how to proceed."

Caro chuckled at him. "You're pretty smart. I'm sure you'll figure it out."

He rolled his eyes and drank some more of his beer. Another hour went buy, and he switched to water so that he wouldn't be too hungover in the morning. For the remainder of the evening, he and his sister talked about how he was adjusting to life in Willow Creek, and how Caro was thinking of asking Todd for another baby. He encouraged Caro since the idea of another nephew or niece to play with sounded like a good idea to him.

Caro's mouth opened to let out a big yawn. "You okay if we call it a night? I'm wiped."

Archer looked at her and nodded. "I'm fine with that." He could tell how tired his sister was, and while he had been grateful for her company, he could use some alone time to get his head straight. Or attempt to, at least. He stood up and pulled his sister into a hug. "Go enjoy your quiet house and get some rest."

"You know it," Caro said. "Keep me appraised of the situation with my future sister-in-law."

Archer shook his head and retook his seat at the bar, turning to signal the bartender for his tab. He didn't want to be the sad guy drinking alone at the bar and there was only one other person's company he wanted at the moment.

Archer slid his phone out of his pocket and navigated over to his text messages. He clicked on his thread with Jo and looked over their last interactions. His thumbs hovered over the keyboard to type out a new message, but he hesitated. She was probably taking care of her dad all weekend. Would he be bothering her, or would she welcome the message? He shook his head and closed the thread, opening up the app to order a driver instead. They really needed to have that talk about where they stood because he was all twisted up about it, but at least if he knew Jo felt the same way, it would make his being a jumbled mess of emotions a little more bearable.

\*\*\*\*

Monday morning finally rolled around and Archer felt a lot better than he had Saturday night, partly because he spent most of Sunday morning lying around and doing nothing, which was always a nice treat, but also because he had decided to just go for it where Jo was concerned. He was going to ask her out on a date, not a working dinner or a little hang out like they had at the diner, but a real, actual date. He had been so enthusiastic about his plan that he immediately came up with the perfect day for the two of them to share.

He was going to drive them down to Atlanta for a day of hiking and roaming around all the local markets before ending with a baseball game where they could dine on hot dogs and enjoy the ballpark atmosphere. Archer knew that baseball was her favorite sport, and she had mentioned not being able to go to a game in a while, so he thought it would be a great way to make her happy.

As he strolled into the office with a smile on his face, he greeted everyone he passed with a friendly "hello." Even the colleagues who he would be happy to never interact with another day in his life got at least a friendly nod—he was in that good a mood. When he made it to the break room, Jo was pouring coffee into her preferred mug. It read "nobody asked you" in bold black letters against a stark white background. It was very on-brand for Jo, and he chuckled every time he saw it.

Archer stopped in the doorway to take a moment and admire her beauty. She was wearing a silky, dark blue top with thin straps and tight capri pants that formed nicely against her tight ass. He couldn't help moving toward her; she was like a planet and he was caught in her gravity pull.

Jo she turned at the sound of his footsteps on the tile flooring and shot him a bright smile. "Good morning." She passed him his own plain black mug filled with coffee, and his heart twinged at the domesticity of it all. "I made it just how you like it."

If this had been two months ago, Archer would have thought she was trying to poison him, but now he knew better. He took a gulp of the hot, sweetened liquid and sighed. "Thank you," he said, licking a few stray drops off of his lips. "How did the rest of your weekend go?"

"Huh," she said, and he smiled when he saw she was staring at his lips. "Oh, my weekend? It was good." Jo nodded, walking off toward her office, and he followed like the lovesick fool he was. "My dad promised to take things easier, and I promised to not treat him like a baby by trying to manage every little part of his day," she explained as she entered her office and sat in her chair. Archer leaned against the door and slowly sipped his coffee. Jo looked at him with a smirk. "Would you believe he called me controlling?"

Archer gasped. "You? Controlling? I can't imagine anyone saying that to you," he quipped.

"Right?" Jo laughed lightly, the sound filling his heart with joy. "I mean, I'm like the most reasonable, flexible person in the world," she replied as she clicked her mouse a few times. Her eyes moved over the screen rapidly, her smile widening. "Oh. My. God. This is amazing!" she exclaimed before looking up at him, her blue eyes sparkling with delight.

"I've finally been declared Sexiest Man Alive? It's about time," he joked and watched her roll her eyes, but the smile was still on her face.

Jo shook her head at him. "I'm not sure there's room enough in this office for you and your ego," she joked before waving him over to look at her computer screen.

Archer walked over to her side of the desk and leaned down, taking a hit of her flowery scent, an aroma he had finally discovered was gardenias. The temptation to fill his apartment with the flower so it always smelled like her was strong, but he resisted, hoping that Jo would be there enough on her own to make that happen. While he basked in her sweet smell, he admired the smooth column of her neck that was exposed to him. Jo's hair was in a high ponytail, and if he lowered himself just the tiniest bit more, he would be able to kiss up and down her neck all the way to her bare shoulder, where he would nip and suck at her skin until he left his mark. The possessive instinct was a new one, but it was there nonetheless. He definitely wanted to lay claim to this woman, and soon.

"Isn't this fantastic?" Her voice interrupted his meanderings and Archer finally moved his gaze from her body to the email she was pointing at.

"Shit," he muttered. He read over the message from the athletic director of Liberty U inviting them and some of the other marketing consultants he assumed were also going to pitch for them to a college baseball game that afternoon. Well, there went his big plan for their date. A major league game and a college game were two vastly different experiences, but it still felt like the wind had been knocked from his sails when he read about how they would get a guided tour of the stadium as well as a meet and greet with the coaching staff afterwards.

"I know, it's awesome. I haven't been to a live game in ages and this will be so much fun." Her enthusiasm was wonderful, but not contagious, and his heart sank a little more at not having been the one to make her so happy.

Archer schooled his expression to hide his disappointment. "It will be great." His voice went higher than normal, so he cleared his throat before grabbing his mug and walking over to the door of her office. "Shall I drive?"

"That would be great, thanks." Jo shuffled some papers along her desk. "We can go over the meeting I missed in more detail and can talk strategy before we arrive at the ballpark."

"Sounds like a plan," he agreed before walking back to his office. Great. Not only were his plans for their possible date in need of an overhaul, but they would spend all of their time together today working, or talking about work. He had been so eager for today so that the two of them could take a step forward, but with one email, it felt like he was taking about two steps back.

Later that afternoon, once they had strategized in the car, gone through the stadium tour with about a dozen other marketing consultants, and watched most of the baseball game from better seats than he would have been able to score for a major league game, Archer and Jo sat and enjoyed a cold soda as the bottom of the twelfth inning stretched on. The Liberty Tigers and Plymouth Bears were tied with a score of five each and neither team could seem to get a hit to end the game.

It was hot, and the late afternoon sun caused his skin to feel like he was being roasted alive. He had long ago ditched his tie and rolled up the sleeves of his shirt, but it did little to help the situation. Archer was certain he looked like a sweaty mess, but when he glanced over at

Jo, she looked as fresh as when they had arrived, not a hair out of place nor a drop of perspiration to be seen. He was ready to leave and dive into an ice cold pool, but Jo looked as if she could stay and watch another twelve innings.

"How are you not dripping in sweat?" He fanned himself with some papers from his messenger bag. "I feel like boiled chicken."

Jo smiled at him and shrugged a shoulder. "I guess I run cold," she said before narrowing her eyes at him. "How are you not used to summers in the South? You're from Alabama."

Archer raised his chin defiantly. "It's a drier heat in Alabama," he insisted as he continued to wave papers in front of his face to cool off.

Jo snorted. "Whatever you need to tell yourself, Sugar."

She turned to look back at the game, but he didn't. He was too busy staring at her to care what happened out on the field. It hadn't helped that she had given him a little nickname of her own, and his inner thirteen-year-old squealed in delight. This woman had him wrapped around her pinky finger and she didn't even know it. Or she did and delighted in dragging things out just to torture him. Either way, he was actually good with it because it meant being around her more.

The crack of a bat finally broke his concentration on Jo and his eyes shot to the field. The player from Liberty U had managed to knock one that looked like it was going to sail damn near out of the park. The two of them stood up and watched as the ball flew past the outfielders and landed in the last row of seats over in left field. Jo cupped her hands around her mouth and hollered before clapping loudly. Archer smiled at her enthusiasm and joined in with the celebration.

With the game finally over, they gathered their things and made their way past other spectators and down to the field, where they were told they'd get a few moments to speak with the coaching staff and ask them any questions they might have. Archer and Jo mostly stuck to themselves, not mingling with the other marketing consultants, who were essentially their competition, as they all spoke with the staff about what kind of marketing they like to see for their teams, how much time players and coaches really had available to work with a marketing firm, and answered any questions the staff had for them.

The entire time they were speaking with them, there was one athletic trainer who would not stop staring at Jo and it was really pissing Archer off. Damn possessive tendencies. When they were finally done with their question and answer session, Archer started to lead them back toward his car when the guy that had been staring at Jo jogged over to them.

"Jojo?" the tall, muscular guy called in their direction, and Jo spun around to look at him.

After a few moments, recognition lit up her face and she smiled at the man. "Holy shit. Thomas?" She took a step toward the guy and Archer immediately went on high alert.

The man nodded and walked up to Jo before scooping her up in his arms and spinning her around. Archer felt jealous and envious at the same time. This guy was built like a brick house and looked good despite having spent all day in the heat. He, on the other hand, could feel his damp undershirt sticking to his body and was pretty sure his face was as red as a beet from being out in the sun all day.

"It's so good to see you, Jojo," Thomas gushed before putting her down and leaning back to look at her.

"Still beautiful as always."

Jo blushed and giggled like a schoolgirl, kicking the jealousy Archer had been feeling up at notch. He had never made her giggle like that. "Thank you." She playfully slugged the guy on the arm. "Look at you. Wow, you really filled out." Jo gave the man a blatant once over, not that Thomas seemed to mind, if the toothy grin he was flashing her was any indication.

"I finally hit my growth spurt the year after you graduated," he explained before his eyes flicked over to Archer. "Sorry, man, I didn't notice you there."

Archer nodded, not believing the man for a second. "No worries," he said, holding out his hand for a shake. "Archer Hayes."

"Thomas Bigsby. Jojo and I were at college together for a time," he explained before turning back to Jo, his expression fond. "It wasn't the same after you left." A mock pout appeared on his lips and Archer had a difficult time containing a groan at the man's antics.

"Doubtful," Jo replied with a smile. "I'm sure you handled yourself just fine, especially if you were packing all the muscles you are now." She squeezed the man's admittedly large biceps, and Archer peered down at his own, wondering if she was into beefier guys. He was no slouch and spent plenty of time hitting the weights, but he was leaner than this Thomas by a decent measure.

"They helped for sure, but it was probably more to do with my linebacker boyfriend than anything else." Archer raised his brows at this wonderful new development. Boyfriend? Thomas saw his expression and smiled. "I, uh, had some trouble with people not liking a gay equipment manager for the baseball and softball teams, but Jo always managed to keep people in line or put them in their place. After she left, my boyfriend took over as my protector. Or, I guess I should refer to him as my husband now," he said, flashing a gold band on his hand.

"That's amazing, Thomas." Jo pulled the large man into a hug. Now that Archer knew he wasn't interested in Jo, the jealousy he'd been feeling faded away. He didn't love feeling envious, so they really did need to talk about what they were to each other before he spiraled any further.

"Thanks, Jojo." Thomas peered to the side and noticed someone waving him toward the locker rooms. "Look, I need to head out, but I want to see you again. It's been too long." He handed Jo a card and kissed her cheek. "Call me."

"I will definitely do that," Jo promised before pocketing the card and waving goodbye. She turned to Archer and smiled. "Ready to go?"

Archer's fingers made their way through his damp hair and he nodded. "Definitely ready to get out of this heat." The air conditioner on his car would be getting a workout today for sure.

"We should go get dinner," Jo suggested as he opened the door for her. His heart soared and he smiled at her. "We can talk over everything we learned today and update our strategy."

"Right. Good idea." He took a deep breath as he closed her door and rounded the hood of his car. *Wonderful. Another non-date,* he thought to himself as he started the car. He looked over at Jo to see her already messing with the radio dials to pick a station she liked. Despite his slight disappointment, Archer smiled at her and steered out of the parking lot. It might not be a real date, but it was still time with her, and while he wanted much more than that, he could be patient. After all, Jo was the type of woman worth waiting for.

## Chapter Fifteen

*Jo*

The ride from Liberty University to the Thai food restaurant across the street from their office was a long one, but it flew by fairly quickly. The conversation had mostly been centered on work, which normally would have put Jo in a bad mood, but it had been pleasant enough. Talking with Archer came as naturally as breathing, and she liked it. Everything was easier with him. Whether that was because of his laid-back nature or her trying harder to actually get to know him, she wasn't sure, but it didn't matter because she wanted to just sit back and enjoy every minute of it.

During the ride, they tweaked their marketing strategy based on what they learned at the ball game. After finding out that players and coaches often had downtime between warm-up and the start of the game, they decided to include having members of staff and the team do small video profiles or thoughts on the upcoming game for social media posts. Social media was a huge part of marketing nowadays, but Liberty U hadn't quite gotten that message. Jo was confident that their strategy would be the winning one, and she said as much to Archer as he pulled into the parking lot of their office.

"Well, I think that we've got a solid approach for our presentation," Jo posited as she unbuckled her seatbelt and opened her car door, Archer nodding at her in agreement.

After hopping out of the car, she walked over to her own to drop everything but her purse in the convertible, peeking over her shoulder to get a look at her coworker. Was he still just a coworker, though? He felt like a lot more than that. At the very least, Archer was a friend, but he was also a friend who she had developed romantic feelings for over the last few weeks. The more time Jo spent with him, the deeper those feelings got. It was like he had sneaked past all of her defenses when it came to keeping guys at arm's length, but she wasn't even mad about it.

Her friends had challenged her to get serious about someone, and she had. No one was more surprised than her, but what she hadn't foreseen was how happy she would be about it. When she had promised to shake things up at their birthday dinner, Jo figured she would give it a shot, but ultimately go back to meaningless hookups, but that hadn't happened. It was nice to have another person to rely on, to care about you and show that care in so many different ways, and Jo was over the moon that that person turned out to be Archer.

As if to illustrate her point about how thoughtful he was, Archer rounded the hood of his car and grabbed her hand. She smiled as he intertwined their fingers and looked up to see his brown eyes lighten. "Is this okay?" he asked, nodding to where they were joined. "I was taught to always hold hands when you cross the street. You know, for safety."

Jo nodded and smiled knowingly. "Of course. Safety first and all that," she remarked as they crossed the street to the restaurant.

Except once they were across the street, he didn't stop holding her hand as he opened the door for her, as they approached the hostess stand, or as they walked to their table, only finally dropping it to pull out her chair for her before taking the seat across. They perused the menu for a few minutes before deciding to split a few dishes family style, or rather, her deciding that's what they would do and Archer willing to go along with it. Once their server had gone to place their order and they were alone again, he reached across the table and grabbed her hand once again.

She flipped her hand so that they were palm to palm, and gave him a questioning look. "Still for safety purposes?" she asked with a smirk.

A smile pulled at the corners of Archer's mouth, but the expression on his face wasn't amused—it was meaningful. "No," he replied, shaking his head slowly. "This is because I want to." He tilted his head and searched her eyes. "If that's okay."

"It's more than okay." She meant every word as she squeezed his hand.

The fluttery winged creatures that had taken residence in her stomach weeks ago were having a field day tonight, batting around her insides and causing her to feel the anticipatory nerves that were equal parts thrilling and terrifying. Jo took a breath to try and calm herself, even though she enjoyed the feeling more than she'd thought she would.

All of these cheerful, contented emotions were becoming more familiar and she enjoyed having them. The only downside was that small amount of fear that followed after. There was the wondering if or when these emotions would go away, and thinking how horrible it would feel to lose something you hadn't even known that you wanted, but now that you were so close to having it, you couldn't imagine going back to the life you led before.

Jo wanted what she and Archer were building toward, but she was also afraid of how to go about getting it. In the past, she had never been one to shy away from a challenge, but this one was so different from anything she had ever done before that is was a bit daunting. The last time Jo felt her heart truly break was when her mom died, and she didn't want to feel that pain again. But as she looked at the man sitting across from her, she decided it might be worth the risk of trying.

Archer peered at her skeptically as he stroked his thumb along the back of her hand. "Where did you go just now?" He asked, his face filled with curiosity.

What emotions must have been playing across her face for him to ask that? She wasn't sure how to answer his question without giving too many of her feelings away, and she didn't know if she was ready to take that big of a step just yet. "I was just thinking about life and how it can take some interesting turns," she told him. It wasn't a lie, but it wasn't the whole truth either.

A smile came across his face and he chuckled. "Tell me about it," Archer said, taking a sip from his water glass. Jo tried not to watch his throat bob as he swallowed, but she couldn't help it. The man was handsome and made something even as mundane as drinking water seem sexy. "I never imagined that I would leave Montgomery for a small city in Georgia, but here I am."

Jo jumped at the subject change, both to take her focus off her own emotions and to get the chance to learn a little more about her colleague. "You moved here to be closer to your sister, right?"

Archer nodded. "That was most of it," he said with a wistful smile. "Being closer to Caro, my sister Caroline, and her family was a big draw, but I also felt like my career had stalled a bit back home. I was at a large firm, but I was just another cog in the machine there. I thought that being a bigger fish in a smaller pond would be better, but..." he trailed off, but Jo had a feeling she knew what he was talking about.

"But you didn't realize that the pond was more

like a dumping ground for a chemical plant and most of the other fish were three eyed mutants?" She offered with a smile.

Archer barked a laugh and sat back in his chair. "I don't know if I'd go quite that far, and I would never think of you as a mutant fish," he replied.

Jo nodded. "Of course you wouldn't because I'm not a mutant. I said most of the other fish. I'm clearly the beautiful mermaid taking pity on all the poor creatures by gifting them with my presence." She brushed her hair off her shoulder dramatically.

Archer chuckled and played with her fingers. "Okay, mermaid. Than what does that make me?" His expression was playful and she loved seeing it. More and more, she was figuring out she loved a lot of things about him.

Jo tapped her chin in thought before grinning at him. "You can be my pet seahorse," she explained like it should have been obvious. Archer was closer to a sexy sea god or strapping sailor than anything else, but she wasn't going to feed his ego like that, at least not until she had teased him a little first.

Archer held his free hand to his chest, looking playfully offended. "Pet seahorse? I don't even get to be a shark or something cool like that?" He acted put out, but the light in his eyes let Jo know he was enjoying her good natured ribbing.

"There are no sharks in ponds," she challenged, enjoying the amused look on his face.

"But there are mermaids and seahorses?" He raised one eyebrow and smirked. Yup, definitely more like a sexy sea god.

"Obviously," Jo stated before taking a drink from her water glass to cool her down. Lusting after Archer was turning the temperature in the room up by a zillion degrees. Another subject change was in order. "And Blake is clearly a swan." The man liked to preen around the office in his fashionable suits and other attire. Deservedly so because he always looked absolutely flawless.

Archer shook his head, but the smile stayed on his face. "Alright then. Pet seahorse it is," he conceded just as their server arrived with their food.

Everything smelled wonderful, the spices wafting through the air causing her stomach to growl. They passed the different dishes back and forth to one another until their plates were piled high with veggie spring rolls, chicken satay, and green curry with rice. Archer took a bite of the curry and groaned as he chewed it. Jo's eyes shot up to see the blissful expression on his face, and she had to take another drink of water to cool off again.

Hearing the sounds of pleasure coming from his mouth did things to her, like make her clit pulse as her panties flooded, and all she could think about was taking him back to her place for some quality time in her bed. *Keep it in your pants, Jo*, she thought to herself. They hadn't even kissed yet, but that didn't stop the images from flooding into her brain, and she shifted in her seat to try and relieve the pressure building in her core.

Archer looked over at her. "You okay?"

Jo fanned herself with a folded napkin. "Yea, I'm okay. The curry's just a bit spicy is all." She wasn't sure he bought her cover story, and from the light in his eyes, he could definitely tell it was him making her sweat, not the food.

Archer glanced at her still full plate and smirked. "Sure," he said before taking a bite of a spring roll and groaning even louder than before.

Jo glanced around the restaurant to see a few people shooting looks their way, so she kicked him under the table. "You're making a scene with your moaning," she scolded, her cheeks turning red with equal parts embarrassment and arousal.

"You love it." He winked before taking another bite of food.

Thankfully, he kept quieter this time, but he was right about what he said. She did love all the sounds he made and was looking forward to a time when she could hear them without a live audience present. Archer could be as loud as he wanted in her tiny apartment, though. She didn't care one fig what her neighbors might think. Jo rolled her eyes at Archer anyway to prove how unaffected she was, but she doubted she was convincing anyone. She certainly wasn't convincing herself.

The two of them ate in weighted silence for a few minutes. Their gazes were locked on one another's, but they didn't say a word. The air was thick with tension between them, and it took all of Jo's concentration to not climb over the table and sit in his lap. "So how do your dad and Delaney know one another?" Jo needed to get her mind focused on anything other than how all of Archer's behavior affected her, making her think all kinds of naughty things. Thinking about her boss and Archer's dad was a sure fire way to do just that.

Archer blinked at her and wiped his mouth with the cloth napkin from the table. "Uh, they knew each other in college. I guess they pledged the same fraternity." He took a sip of water and shrugged a shoulder. "They weren't in the same year, and I don't think they really spoke all that often, but my dad says those kind of connections last a lifetime. That's probably why he pushed so hard for me to join the frat when I was in college."

"Did you?" Jo asked, looking at him and having a hard time seeing him as a fraternity brother. Archer seemed more the type to sip scotch or enjoy a craft beer, not the type that would do a keg stand at a frat party, but hey, college was a long time ago and not all fraternities were as stereotypical as the ones she'd seen.

Archer snorted. "Hell no," he said emphatically. "I had to endure way too many entitled jerks at my private high school. I wanted to do nothing but blend in when I went to college."

"I don't think you could ever just blend in anywhere," she confessed, her cheeks instantly warming at the admission.

Cockiness shined from his chocolate brown eyes and a smirk came across his face. "Oh yea," he remarked, looking way too pleased with himself. "You think I stand out in a crowd, Freckles?"

Jo pressed her lips together before biting the lower one. Archer did stand out, but not because he was insanely attractive or well-dressed, though he was both of those things. There was just something about Archer Hayes that set him apart from others. Maybe it was his innate charm or devil-may-care grin, but she had never met anyone like him, and the warm feeling in her chest that realization created was both scary and amazing.

"Yes. I do," she admitted boldly. She searched his eyes and confessed something she hadn't known she would until that moment. "You're the only one who ever has. For me anyway."

A mixture of shock and thrill filled his gaze and his smirk changed into a genuine smile. "Thank you," he said, leaning in closer toward her, but he backed up again when the server returned to the table.

"Can I get you two anything else?" The petite woman asked, her smile friendly.

Archer looked over at Jo and she smiled up at the server. "Can we get the check and a couple of boxes?"

179

The server nodded and came back with both quickly.

"You want all these leftovers?" Archer asked her as he slipped some cash into the billfold. He scrutinized her for a moment before a chuckle escaped his mouth. "I get the sense that you live off of take-out."

Jo snorted. "I would be offended by that if it weren't so completely true." She proceeded to pack up the food, making sure to distribute it evenly among two boxes. "I can't cook to save my life. My dad and I lived off grilled cheese and soup or dinners at the diner for most of my childhood. My friend, Millie, she is this total domestic goddess, and once she tried to teach me how to make a few different dishes, but I think she finally wrote me off as a lost cause when I burned the spaghetti."

Archer laughed, the deep, throaty sound making her feel warm all over again. "How do you even burn spaghetti?"

Jo chuckled and stood, grabbing her box of leftovers and passing Archer's over to him. "I have no idea how I did it, just that my place smelled like burnt noodles for two days," she explained as they left the restaurant.

Archer reached his hand out as they came to the curb of the street, and Jo took it without thinking. He smiled at her and they raced across the street back to their cars in the parking lot. It was almost 8:00, and while she was tired, she also didn't want the night to end. There was one thing she was worried about, though. Jo was a little nervous that she would slip into sex-mode if they went back to either of their places, so it was probably best to end the night now. Her stomach sank at the thought of leaving him, but there was no way she would risk screwing this up.

Jo glanced over at their work building, the one she

would be seeing again in less than twelve hours, to take her mind off it. "I'm almost tempted to sleep in my office to avoid the commute," she joked as she opened her car door and put her food on the passenger seat.

Archer placed his leftovers on the roof of her car and stepped closer to her, pressing his hands against both sides of the vehicle, trapping her between them. "You could always come home with me," he suggested, his deep voice causing goosebumps to break out across her skin.

"I don't know if that's a good idea," she confessed, but her hands slid up his chest and gripped the front of his shirt. Clearly her mind and body were on two separate wavelengths.

Archer leaned closer and brushed his nose against her hairline, inhaling her scent before he moved over to the side, where his lips skimmed over her cheek and made their way down her neck. "You always smell so good. I want this smell all over my car, my apartment, my bed," he professed, the tenor of his voice going impossibly lower as he nibbled at her earlobe.

Jo's knees melted like butter on a hot frying pan and she sent up a silent prayer in the hope that she didn't collapse. She was enjoying his words and his touch far too much. "I want that too," she breathed out, her hands tightening on his shirt even more. Jo did want that, and she wanted it for more than one night, but their working together was complicated, and they needed to be one hundred percent sure before they did anything they couldn't take back.

Archer moved his hands from the car to her hips and grabbed onto her before he pressed himself against her, moving his mouth down to her shoulder where he licked and sucked on the skin. Jo could feel the evidence of his arousal pressing up against her, and while she really,

really, *really* wanted to make use of it, she had to keep her wits about her. He bite her shoulder lightly, and a moan broke free from her mouth, but she released the grip on his shirt and pressed lightly against his chest and he stopped what he was doing immediately.

He leaned back and looked into her eyes, pupils blown wide with desire and hunger, but there was concern there as well. "I didn't mean to…"

Jo reached her hand up and placed the tips of her fingers over his lips. "You didn't do anything wrong," she vowed, her heart beating wildly as she moved her hand away from his mouth, her fingertips tingling along with the rest of her body. "Believe me. Everything felt very, very right."

"I'm a little confused then," he replied, his brow furrowed. She didn't blame him for being confused as she had been Little Miss Mixed Signals from the moment they met. Jo hated being that girl, but the signals in her own brain and body were at war at the moment, and she needed a little clarity before jumping into bed with him.

Jo nodded and moved her hands to rest on his shoulders. "I'm not trying to mess with your head, I swear. I really want to go home with you, Archer." She watched as the corners of his mouth twitched with a smile.

"But?" he asked.

"But we work together, and you make me feel things I haven't felt in a really long time, ever, really. I don't want to screw it up," she whispered. Jo wasn't usually this shy or willing to admit when she was less than sure of herself, but the whole being-vulnerable-in-front-of-a-guy thing wasn't exactly normal for her either. All kinds of new feelings and experiences were happening with Archer, and she was once again grateful that he was such a patient and understanding person.

"Ah," he said with a nod. "Well, I don't want to screw anything up either, so if we need to still take it slowly, I get that." He looked at her affectionately and smiled. "I do have one question, though."

"Go for it." She commanded, relieved that he wasn't pushing her. His hands squeezed her hips one last time before they were sliding up her arms. "Can we kiss yet?" he asked, looking like a hopeful puppy with his big brown eyes and lower lip sticking out just a little more than usual.

Jo smiled at him, imagining this was the same face he probably made as a little boy when he wanted ice cream for dinner. She played with the hair at the nape of his neck with her fingers, enjoying the way the silky strands felt against her skin. "I think we can make that happen," she said, tilting her head up to meet his.

His smile turned from that of a puppy to one of a hungry wolf seconds before his mouth was on hers. Archer's lips moved against hers with speed and skill, and Jo had a hard time believing he had been out of the dating game as long as he proclaimed to have been. The man kissed like he had been practicing his entire life, and she desperately tried to give back just as good as she received. Her grip in his hair tightened as she ran her tongue along the seam of his lips to get him to open up for her, and when he did, she drove her tongue in with enough force to extract a groan from the man she was trying to devour. His mouth was warm and he tasted like the spices from their dinner along with an underlying flavor that was all him. It was one she was eager to taste again and again, already addicted.

Jo continued to savor the flavor of him on her tongue, wanting more and more of it the longer they kissed. His hands moved from her arms to her neck, and he tilted her head to deepen the kiss as he backed her up against the car, her body sandwiched between it and his strong body. His erection was impossibly harder than before, and when he bucked it against her center, she gasped and whimpered before she dropped her hands from his hair to his ass so she could give it a rough squeeze, kneading the firm globes in her hands. Archer ground against her again, their tongues gliding against one another in sync with the movement of their bodies as they pressed deeper into one another.

A car honking as it drove by caused Jo to break the kiss, but her hands were still on his backside and his were still on her, one tangled in her hair and the other gripping her side like he was afraid she would try to run if he didn't have a hold of her. Jo wasn't going anywhere. That kiss had told her just about everything she needed to know. Their chemistry was off the charts to be sure, but the whole time they had been exploring one another, she hadn't once thought about leaving, she hadn't worried about a thing, hadn't really thought at all. Jo had simply felt, and what she had felt was safe, cared for, and loved. Jo licked her lower lip, enjoying the spicy taste of Archer that had lingered there.

"Go on a date with me. A real date," she said, winded from their kiss as the two of them stood there, faces close and breathe mingling together. They had been out together before, but it was always work adjacent. Jo wanted him all to herself, no work talk, no work clothes, just the two of them.

Archer smirked, his chest rising and falling rapidly after their little make-out session. Was it still technically just a kiss? Jo was too happy and turned-on to put much effort into figuring it out. "Is that a question or a command?"

Jo arched an eyebrow. "Does it make a difference?" She slid her hands up and down the round globes of his ass, memorizing the feel before clutching it one last time.

His head moved from side to side, a low growl rumbling in his chest. "Absolutely not," Archer admitted, that wolflike smile back on his face before he brushed his lips lightly against hers one last time and took a small step back. "You can ask me or you can tell me. Either way, I'm yours, Freckles."

"Good." She reluctantly dropped her hands from his body and slid into the seat of her car, letting him shut the door. He leaned down on the side and she ran her fingers through his hair one last time. "How about Saturday night?" They will have presented their work to their boss already and would have all of Sunday to enjoy one another. Jo wasn't even going to pretend like they wouldn't end up in bed together, because after that kiss, it was as inevitable as the sun coming up.

Archer leaned into the car and kissed her firmly one last time. "Saturday sounds great," he said before tapping his hands on the inside of her door and grabbing his leftovers. "I look forward to it, Freckles." He smiled and headed to his own car.

Once he had it started, she pulled out of the parking lot and pointed the convertible toward her house. She couldn't stop smiling and thinking about that kiss the entire ride home. Now all she had to do was make it through the rest of the week without pushing him into a broom closet at work for a repeat performance. Jo thought about Archer and sighed. It was going to be a very long five days.

## Chapter Sixteen

*Archer*

The last few days had been agony for Archer. Being so close to Jo without actually getting to *be* with her in any sort of physical way was getting to him. Every morning she walked by his office, popping in to say hello, and every morning it took the entirety of his self-control not to pull her inside, slam the door shut, and take her right there on his desk if she'd let him. If they were able to touch or kiss at all, keeping his raging hormones at bay might have been easier, but they talked on Tuesday morning about keeping things professional at work, and while his mind agreed that it was the smarter course of action, his body was screaming at him to just go for it already. They had a date, an actual date and not some working dinner, scheduled for Saturday night. It could not come soon enough. The ice cold showers he was taking were getting old, and while there was no guarantee that they would be having sex after their date, even the possibility of it was enough to keep him going.

It wasn't just the sex that he was looking forward to, though that was definitely part of it. What he was most excited about was the fact that their relationship was moving forward, that they were progressing toward being something more than colleagues or friends. Archer was certain he was in love with Jo. Most of his free time was spent thinking about her, and he spent a good chunk of his time at work doing it too. Just yesterday, he and Blake had been grabbing coffee in the breakroom, discussing a campaign for the local baseball team, and when Jo breezed in to refill her mug, he lost track of the conversation and only realized what had happened after she left and he looked over to see Blake smiling at him.

"What were we talking about?" he had asked his work friend, only for the man to flash his pearly whites in a wide grin.

"We were talking about marketing, but I think I just found another topic of conversation that you are far more interested in," Blake had replied, a smirk on his face.

Archer wanted to stick with their rule of keeping things professional, so he had simply straightened his tie and started to walk back to his office. "Not sure what you're talking about." He had nodded his head in goodbye and escaped before he could give anything more away.

Blake had laughed at his back. "Whatever you say, friend," he called out, chuckling all the way back to his office.

A reminder chiming on his phone brought Archer out of his continual thoughts of all things Jo and back to the present. The meeting he and Jo were having with Delaney to go over their strategy for Liberty U was in ten minutes, and while he was confident in the presentation they had put together, he was less confident in his ability to concentrate on the task at hand while Jo was in the room with him.

"Hey." Jo peered around the open door of his office with a smile on her face. "You ready to do this thing? I want to get this over with so that we can make any tweaks Delaney wants without having to stay all night to do it." Jo rolled her eyes and Archer smiled, standing up and pulling on his jacket.

"You don't want to pull an all-nighter with me, Freckles?" he asked, grabbing his notes and walking over to her. He leaned down to whisper in her ear. "I would make it worth your while."

Jo hummed happily and swayed toward him only to shake her head quickly, her blonde hair whipping his neck. He looked to her face and she scowled at him and slapped him lightly on the chest before taking a step back. "You cannot say things like that to me right now," she whisper-hissed, wiggling in her tight little skirt and sleeveless blouse. Archer was suddenly grateful for the heat wave they were experiencing because it meant Jo wore a lot fewer pantsuits. "I do not want to be turned-on during this presentation."

Archer smirked, pleased with both his effect on her and being able to witness her body move like it had just now. He reached over to her hand to give it a squeeze. "At least you won't have to present holding your notes in front of your pants. It's like I'm in eighth grade all over again," he mumbled, flicking his gaze down to the tenting in his slacks.

Jo's eyes followed his gaze and widened before meeting his again, her exhale coming out slowly. "One more day," she said to him, her eyes molten as she licked her red painted lips. "We just have to wait one more day."

She shifted on her feet and picked up her things from where she had dropped them on the chair, and Archer smiled as they walked out of his office toward their boss's. "Are you saying you expect me to put out after the first date?" He splayed one hand over his chest. "I will have you know that I am no hussy." For her, Archer was a total hussy, but part of the fun of being with Jo was their banter. As happy as he was that their relationship was progressing, he didn't want to lose the playfulness they had going either.

Jo smiled over her shoulder at him as they approached Delaney's office. "Suit yourself, mister prim and proper, but at the end of the date, I'm having an orgasm. You can decide whether or not you want to be a part of it," she said with a wink.

A full-color cinematic of the two of them making that orgasm together immediately started playing in his mind and Archer groaned. "Dammit, Jo," he chided with no real heat in his voice. He was merely momentarily frustrated with his body's instant response to her, and needed to slide his notes in front of his trousers again.

Jo cackled lightly as they approached Delaney's assistant. "Hey, Janine. We have a two o'clock with Gavin."

Janine nodded, her red hair and purple glasses bobbing as she did. "He's ready and waiting for you both." The middle-aged woman nodded her head to the door. "Good luck, you two."

"Thanks," he and Jo said in unison before smiling at one another and heading through the double doors of Delaney's office. It was great to finally be in sync with her on more than one level.

Gavin Delaney rose from his chair, his smile almost blinding as the fluorescent lights of his office bounced off his veneers. He gestured toward the two chairs in front of him and Jo and Archer took a seat. Jo crossed her legs, causing her skirt to ride up even more, and while Archer loved the view of her long, smooth legs, he didn't like that his boss was currently leering as well.

Archer scowled at the older man and cleared his throat. "Shall we begin?" he asked, drawing his boss's attention away from Jo. He did not like the way he had been looking at his girlfriend. Or maybe girlfriend? Colleague you were in love with and were probably sleeping with the next night but hadn't had the whole define your relationship discussion with yet? That was a mouthful, and Archer suddenly added another item to his to do list: make things official with Jo.

Gavin nodded. "Certainly. You don't need to do a dry run of your entire presentation or anything, but I would like you to go over the major points."

Thank goodness for that. Archer wanted this meeting behind him, even more now that he noticed the way his boss was eyeing Jo like a piece of meat.

"Of course." Jo seemed oblivious to their boss' lewd gazing as she grabbed her tablet and swiped along until she got to her notes. Archer tried to forget about their boss's leering and focus. He glanced over at Jo, smiling at how organized she was. It was impressive, but then again, everything this woman did impressed him. When she found what she was looking for, Jo looked over to him and then to their boss before starting. "We're suggesting an entire update to the athletic department's marketing. Their social media platforms are currently underutilized to an almost alarming degree, and they just aren't tapping into markets that are available to them. For instance, the female and LGBT+ athletes aren't given half as much promotion as the male athletes, and that could really help broaden the fan base and get kids from those communities interested in coming to Liberty." She looked over to Archer with a small smile and he nodded. It was his turn.

"We've also spoken with some businesses that would love to partner with Liberty. Advertisements at games, providing gear and food for the athletes, and product placement in sponsored social media posts would help bolster the athletic department's revenue and visibility," he explained to Gavin before passing over some of the figures and numbers they ran.

Archer and Jo spent the next twenty minutes going into even more detail on their presentation, and at the end of it, Archer fully expected his boss to be excited about the direction they had chosen, so the look of confusion on the man's face when they were finally finished was startling.

"I'm not sure that your focus on social media is the right way to go," the older man said with a frown. "What about newspaper ads and radio spots?"

"Radio spots?" Jo asked, a polite smile on her face, but when she looked over at Archer, he didn't have to be a mind reader to know what she was thinking because it was the same thing he was. Hardly anyone listened to the radio anymore, especially not those in the age range they were targeting. Podcast commercials could maybe have an effect, but radio? Not so much.

"That's certainly an option." Archer was trying to respond diplomatically, but it was difficult in the face of such an outdated suggestion. "Though, we may want to focus on steering the university toward using technology that is more current. Our demographic probably doesn't listen to much radio." Archer was having a hard time coming to grips with his boss's request for radio spots. If he had suggested using radio ads for college-aged kids at his other firm, he would have been laughed right out of the building.

Delaney grunted while tapping his fingers on the desk. "While your approach is certainly... inclusive," he said, treating the word like it was spelled with four letters instead of nine, "I'm not so sure this is the best way to win the contract. Switch the focus to more ads and less of the social stuff and I think you're golden."

Jo smiled, but Archer knew all of her smiles so well by now that he could tell this was her *get fucked* smile. "I really think that we should keep our focus where it is." Somehow, she managed to keep her tone of voice mild despite her visible irritation. "If you look at our numbers again…" she started, but Gavin cut her off with a raised hand.

"Make the changes, Jolene," he directed, voice firm. He glanced at Archer and nodded curtly. "You're dismissed."

Jo opened her mouth, but snapped it shut, stood up, gathered her things, and walked toward the door. Her body was stiff, and he didn't have to be a body language expert to read the tension and anger in the square set of her shoulders. Archer nodded at his boss before following her out of the office and over to the stairwell entrance. She opened the door so forcefully it banged against the wall, the loud sound hurting his ears as he stepped in behind her.

Archer watched as she paced back and forth on the cement landing, breathing harshly. Jo was frustrated, and he was too, but more than that he was confused as to why their boss would want them to take such an out-of-touch approach to marketing.

"I can't believe this." Jo's voice was high. She was clearly past the point of frustration and tipping into anger. "This is so typical. We come in there with great ideas, but we leave with the direction to present a marketing strategy from forty years ago." She continued to pace back and forth, shaking her head. Her blue eyes blazed with annoyance as they met his. "How are you not as pissed as I am?"

Archer shrugged a shoulder. "I think I'm still adjusting from that trip back in time we took a few moments ago." He smiled, hoping the small joke would lighten things up.

Jo stopped pacing and huffed a laugh before coming up to him and collapsing her head on his chest. "This isn't fair. We worked so hard and now we have to go in with a presentation that would be laughable if it wasn't so irritating."

Archer reached over and rubbed his hand up and down her back. "Don't worry, Freckles." He lowered his voice, making it as soothing as possible. Her shoulder relaxed and she wrapped her arms around his waist, pulling him closer in a hug, his mouth ticking up at the feel of her body against his. "We're not going to present something laughable."

Her face tilted up to see his and she smiled sadly. "Is it because we're going to call in sick and make someone else do it? I vote for Finch and North."

Archer chuckled but shook his head. "No. It's because we're going to do the presentation we worked our asses off on and win that contract," he said, firmly committed to their work. They had put together a fantastic presentation, and he wouldn't feel right with himself if he tossed all that aside to phone it in with Gavin's suggestions.

Jo smiled, but her brow furrowed. "What about Delaney?"

"Delaney can suck it." Archer reached a hand up to her head, idly playing with her curls while she chuckled lightly in his arms. "Besides, I've always been the type to beg forgiveness rather than ask permission."

Jo's smile turned sly. "You're the type to beg, huh?" Her gaze flicked to his mouth and she licked her lips.

"Only under the right circumstances." Archer tipped his head down to hers.

The kiss started out slowly, with the both of them merely getting a small taste of one another, but once Jo whimpered, his control snapped and he licked her lips before going all in, his tongue snaking its way into her mouth. Their tongues and lips moved together in synchronicity, their coffee and mint flavors mixing together over and over until they were both out of breathe. If it wasn't for a door a few floors below them slamming, Archer was sure they might have just stayed like that in the stairwell for the rest of the day, and he wouldn't have had a single complaint about it.

"Come over tonight. I don't want to wait anymore," he admitted, brushing his lips lightly over Jo's on more time. Jo stared at him, her pupils wide and only reflecting the slightest hesitation. Archer leaned over to her ear. "I'll beg if you want me to."

Jo's shiver was visible just before she leaned into him and groaned. "I don't want you to beg." Her voice was low and husky, causing him to shiver as well. "At least, not here."

"Does that mean you'll come over?" Archer wanted nothing more in the world than for her to say yes and for the work day to be over right that minute.

Jo nodded, her blonde ringlets bounding up and down. "Yes," she replied happily, leaning up the slightest bit to kiss his cheek. "I don't want to wait either."

Air whooshed from his lungs. "Thank God for that."

Archer's reply elicited a chuckle from her rosy lips and he couldn't help but smile at the sound. He opened the stairwell door for her and ushered her outside first. They walked back to their offices next to one another, their hands brushing every now and then, each pass sending shivers of anticipation up and down Archer's spine.

"See you tonight, Freckles." He kept his voice low so no one would overhear. It was more about keeping her all to himself than it was about remaining professional.

Jo simply smiled in return. It was a new smile, one with such affection shining back at him that if he didn't know better, he would call it her love smile. Archer was already over the moon for her, so maybe it wasn't totally out of the question for her to be in love with him too. He sighed and stepped back into his office. Tonight couldn't come soon enough because he was done waiting, in more ways than one.

## Chapter Seventeen

*Jo*

It wasn't normally a great idea to push a classic car beyond its capabilities, but this was not a normal situation. Jo was practically redlining her vehicle in an attempt to get home, shower, and change before heading over to Archer's place. After reenacting the old seven minutes in heaven game in the stairwell, she was more than ready to take their relationship to the next level. It had been a long six months of no physical release with another person, and while she had been going out of her mind previously, her need quadrupled as soon as she and Archer became a thing.

Jo had always embraced her sexuality, exploring her body by herself and with a guy who struck her fancy for the night in order to figure out exactly what she wanted, but this was different. She wasn't just excited about the possibility of sex and orgasms, though the thought of both had her squirming in the seat of her car as she sped toward her apartment. It was the wholly new experience of being with a man she cared about, a man she was pretty sure she loved, which had the anticipation building to a crescendo.

Love. The word brought a grin to her face, one that widened the moment her small apartment was in sight. After parking her car crookedly, something she never normally did, she sprinted up the stairs and through the door. Once she was inside, she made her way over to the bathroom, stripping off her work clothes and tossing them around the room as she went. Jo waited impatiently for the water to warm up, and as she did, she caught sight of herself in the mirror. Her eyes were wild and her hair had that end-of-the-day frizz all curly girls had to deal with, but the thing that struck her most was how absolutely, blissfully happy she looked. There was a glow about her she wasn't sure had ever been there before, and if this was the result of falling in love with someone, she should find a way to bottle and sell it because she'd make millions.

Jo rolled her eyes at herself and jumped in the shower, washing her body thoroughly and shaving just about everywhere. After drying off and smoothing some cream over her curls, she decided to just moisturize and slap on some lip balm in lieu of her normal makeup routine. Archer would have to get used to seeing her au natural soon enough if they were going to be more than what they were now. Jo really, really hoped that would be the case because she couldn't get enough of this happy feeling in her chest, the one that made her want to burst at the seams with how giddy she was inside.

Jo thought about what to wear and paused. The closet was bursting at the seams with her pantsuits and other professional attire, and her dresser was mostly filled with jeans and t-shirts. There was no real in-between with her, and for the first time in her life, Jo would have killed for one of Gigi's floral dresses or even one of Millie's thrift store finds. While she mulled over her lack of choices, she stepped over to her lingerie drawer and dug around, smiling when she found something she had bought a long time ago and never really had reason to wear, until now. She slipped on the bubblegum pink lace bralette and matching lace thong, giving herself a once-over in the floor-length mirror that rested along the wall and smiled approvingly. With her blonde hair down and the pink of her undergarments, Jo looked and felt like lingerie Barbie, something she hadn't thought would feel as empowering as it did.

Jo had never lacked for body confidence, embracing the scars from playing sports that were sprinkled across her body, the sometimes-awkward limbs that came with being a little on the taller side, and the just-barely-a-handful pair of breasts that she had been rocking since high school, but this was different. Before, Jo would dress for herself, not truly caring if the guy liked what he saw or not. If he was taking her home, she assumed he did, and then when they got there, she would take what she needed, make sure he got his, and leave.

This felt different. She was still dressing for herself, loving the look she was sporting, but she also wanted Archer to like what he saw. In addition to that, making sure he got everything he needed from their coupling mattered more than it had with other men. Jo wouldn't call herself a selfish lover, but her concern for the other person always came second. Tonight, she wasn't thinking that way, already wondering what ways she could put Archer first and smiling when a wicked plan started forming in her mind.

After throwing some clothes and toiletries into an overnight bag, Jo made her way toward the door. The wool peacoat she wore during the two or three months it was actually cold enough in Willow Creek to warrant it hung on the hook, and she smiled as she slipped it on. It didn't cover much, but just enough for her not to feel embarrassed about making the walk to and from her car for the evening. A pair of white heels completed her outfit, and Jo made her way down the steps to her car.

As she slipped inside, the soft leather brushing against the bare skin of her legs, her phone pinged and she nabbed it from her purse, smiling when she saw who it was from.

Archer: **Dinner has just been delivered and will be hot**

**and ready for you when you arrive.**

Jo smirked while her thumbs flew across the screen to rely.

Jo: **Fantastic. I'm starving. See you in five.**

Ignoring the fact that Archer's apartment was at least ten minutes away, Jo once again pushed her car to the limit, peeling out of her spot and pointing the vehicle toward his place. She really was starving, but not for dinner, and she hoped that the food he had delivered wasn't the only thing hot and ready for her when she got there.

In record time, Jo pulled up to his apartment complex, which was really more of a collection of cottages covered in varying shades of blue siding. Archer's place was dark blue, and Jo smiled when she parked in front of it. She was nervous, but the excitement she also felt was overriding it at the moment, and she needed that to keep her confidence high. Jo was about 99% certain that he would like her surprise, but there was always that small chance that things could go sideways. She did her best to ignore that niggling one percent as she grabbed her bags and walked up to the white wood door.

One deep breath and small pep talk later, she knocked on the door and waited about two seconds before it swung open, revealing a freshly showered Archer in dark wash jeans and a collared shirt. His hair was damp, but other than that, he looked totally put together for an actual date night and she seriously considered bolting, but that was before she caught the look in his eyes as he gazed at her. His expression was dreamy, like she was the best possible thing to ever show up on his doorstep. With the addition of his affectionate gaze, the courage to stick to her plan solidified.

Archer gestured for her to enter, which she did, dropping her bags on the floor before she walked further inside. The apartment was very masculine, very him. Beige walls adorned with various sports memorabilia and black and white photos of some now-defunct baseball stadiums, dark wood flooring covered in patterned rugs underneath the brown leather couches, and a kitchen filled with stainless steel appliances and what looked like a professional-grade coffee maker filled the space. It was perfectly decorated and completely spotless, but it was also cozy with a throw blanket lining the back of one of the couches and a couple of throw pillows at the corner. The whole place was a perfect reflection of the man that lived there: perfectly put together, but real and approachable.

Jo spun to look at him and smiled. "I like your place." She took one last look around to catch anything she'd missed.

"Thanks," he replied, taking a step toward her. His smile was wry and one of his eyebrows was raised. "Aren't you hot?" He nodded at her coat.

Jo took another breath. *It's now or never*, she thought as she undid the tie at her waist. "Scorching," she replied, peeling the coat from her body and letting it fall to the ground.

As he took in her lingerie, Archer's eyes widened, roaming up and down her body until he finally brought his brown eyes back up to hers. They blazed with heat and hunger, and Jo couldn't keep the slow smile from spreading across her face.

"Fuck," he breathed out, taking another step toward her. His hand reached out and he ran the backs of his fingers across the lace strap of her bralette, the slow motion and feel of his hand causing her whole body to tremble and her nipples to pebble. "What about dinner?" He nodded to the pizza box that rested on his counter, but his eyes never left hers.

Jo grinned. "I love cold pizza." Her hands slid up his chest and into his hair. She pulled his mouth down to hers, but stopped just before they touched. "And I'm hungry for something else."

Archer groaned and slammed his mouth down on hers, his hands finding their way to her hips and pulling her body closer to his until she felt like they might blend into one person. Tongues darted out and slipped into mouths that didn't belong to them, hands grabbed at exposed flesh and tugged at hair until they were both worked up into a frenzy. Jo managed to get one of her hands between them and palmed his erection, but Archer grabbed her wrist and pulled it behind her back. Jo's brow furrowed in confusion, but he was still too busy ravaging her mouth to explain. She had wanted to put him first tonight, so she finally broke the kiss to ask him about it.

As she caught her breath, she found the words she wanted to ask. "Did you not want...?"

Archer cut her off with a chaste kiss to her lips, bringing both her hands around his neck and sliding his down her body to cup her ass. He pulled her into him again, and there was no mistaking the erection he was sporting, so clearly he was aroused. "I want to do everything with you, Jo." He gazed into her eyes, his pupils dilated and his chest heaving. "You're always trying to rule over every outcome and you work so hard all the time. Let me have the wheel so I can take care of you for once."

Jo was still a little confused. "I can take care of myself." The reply was automatic, a knee jerk reaction anytime she felt like her abilities were being challenged.

"I know you can, Freckles." Archer smiled, brushing his lips lightly over the skin of her cheek. "But you shouldn't always have to, and I want to show you another way," he purred in her ear before sucking the lobe into his mouth.

The sensation caused her head to tilt toward him, and she wanted so badly to give him all the control, let him be in charge of her pleasure, but it was hard for her. "I don't know how," she moaned out, half in complaint at her inability to relinquish control and half because he continued to lick and suck on her ear, her neck, and her shoulder.

"Let me help you. I want to help you." His voice was husky, but the words were steady. "Do you trust me?"

There wasn't a question in her mind as to whether or not she did. Jo trusted Archer with everything.

She leaned back, cupping both his cheeks and staring into his eyes so he would see the conviction in her face as well as hear it in her voice. "I trust you, Archer. I…" she started to tell him that she loved him, but was too nervous to finish. "I trust you."

Archer beamed at her, and while she was fairly certain he knew exactly what she was going to say, he didn't let on. "Thank you, Freckles." He kissed her forehead, the tip of her nose, then finally her lips. After a second the fire that had been burning between the two of them reignited and they explored each other again, only this time with more fervor. A moment later, Archer was finally grabbing her ass and lifting her up to him. Jo's legs wrapped around him instantly and she kicked off her heels as he walked the two of them down his short hallway, but Jo paid no attention to her surroundings as he did. She was more than happy to put all her focus into what was happening between the two of them.

Archer's body shifted next to her, and their bodies parted as he laid her down on his bed. He stood up and winked at her before spinning around and going over to a tall wardrobe. When he turned back, his smile was nervous as he walked back over toward the bed carrying handcuffs and a blindfold. Jo tried to keep her face calm, but clearly her surprise showed because he held his hands up in surrender as he approached. "This is just an idea I had and by no means necessary," he explained calmly before sitting down next to her.

Jo leaned up on her elbows and eyed the accessories he had brought with curiosity. She was definitely not opposed to trying something new. Her past experiences had varied widely and she was never one to judge a kink—well, most kinks anyway—but oddly enough she had never tried any kind of bondage. She never trusted anyone enough to put herself in such a vulnerable position, but Archer was different.

Jo ran a finger along the smooth, hard metal of the handcuffs that rested in the palm of Archer's strong hand. They felt cool to the touch, and the idea of her hands being bound in them turned her on more than she thought possible. Maybe she wasn't as much of a control freak in bed as she'd thought. Jo looked up at Archer and smiled wryly. "Is this something you do with everyone?" She didn't want to talk about past lovers, but she was curious to see if this was his thing or if maybe it would just be their thing, something they only did together.

Archer head shook slowly from side to side. "No, I've never done this before, but I thought it could be fun." His eyes bore into hers, and she could see he was nervous. "With the right person."

"And you think I'm the right person?" Jo sat up fully, taking the blindfold from his other hand and running her fingers over the silky black fabric, already picturing it over her eyes. Maybe over his in the future.

"In more ways than one," he confessed.

Jo's eyes shot up to his, and he didn't have to put

words to the feelings that were shining through. Archer loved her, and he trusted her enough to ask for something he had wanted, just as she trusted him enough to try it with him.

Jo leaned into his space and kissed his lips. It wasn't simply a kiss of want or need, but it was also one of devotion and tenderness. Archer was the guy she'd never thought she would have. A guy who understood her, saw her for who she really was, and wanted her both in spite of and because of it. Any remaining fear she had at declaring her love for him melted away, and when she pulled her lips from his, she stayed close enough so that he could hear her whisper. "I love you."

Archer leaned back to look into her eyes, and when he saw her smiling up at him, his own grin widened and he looked about as happy as she had ever seen him. "I love you too, Freckles," he proclaimed, cupping her cheek with one hand as he leaned his forehead against hers. "I love how strong and confident you are, I love how much you care about other people, and I even love how much you tease me even though I should probably hate it. I love you so much it feels like my chest is going to burst. I have so much love for you, I'm not sure what to do with it sometimes."

Jo touched her hand to his and licked her lips, leaning back onto the soft mattress beneath her. "Maybe you can show me how much you love me." Her voice shook the slightest bit as she took the blindfold and covered her eyes, making sure to tie it tightly enough that she could see nothing and that it wouldn't slip.

"God, you're perfect," Archer breathed out, and Jo felt the bed shift as he stood again. His warm hands grabbed her wrists and he cuffed one after the other, winding the chain through the metal rods of his bed frame. He leaned down to her ear, and she felt his hot breath as it rushed past her skin. "If you ever want me to stop, just tell me."

"Shouldn't I have a safe word?" Her lips curled up into a smirk at the question.

"'No' is a word that will always work with me, but if you want something more specific, you can have it," he told her, humor laced in his voice.

Jo hummed as she thought. "How about … foul ball." The smile on her face widened when Archer barked a laugh from above her.

"Whatever you want." Then he was on her again, kissing her deeply, his mouth and tongue exploring hers, but other than that, he didn't touch her at all. When he pulled back and seemed to disappear completely, a small whine left her mouth. "Don't you worry, Freckles, I'm going to take very good care of you." Footsteps walked away from her and then the room was quiet except for the low hum of the air conditioner and her own breathing, but that silence was broken by the sound of a belt clinking and a zipper being undone. Jo was a little sad to not be able to see the show, but the lack of sight made her other senses heighten. She could hear him removing his pants and shirt, and she could sense him coming closer once again, like she could feel the air swirling around just before he was next to her. "Are you ready?"

Jo swallowed the lump of anticipation and nerves that clogged her throat. "Yes." Her voice was far breathier than it ever had been, but the conviction in her tone was unwavering. Jo trusted him. She didn't know what to expect, so she jumped slightly at his initial touch, but soon relaxed back into the bed. Archer's warm hands ran the length of her arms from her wrist to her shoulder. Up and down his fingers brushed against her skin, causing goosebumps to break out all over her body and her nipples to form tight buds. His hands found the base of her neck and he leaned down to kiss her, moving his tongue against hers the moment she opened for him.

This lasted minutes, maybe even an hour. Time ceased to exist when she was with him like this, and she couldn't believe how wound up she was just from touching and kissing, but Jo felt like she was already getting close to coming already. When he broke the kiss, she whimpered again, but that quickly turned into a moan when she felt his mouth close over one of her nipples through the lace of her bralette.

"I love this on you," he admitted before diving back down to her other breast and repeating his actions there. The slight scratch of the fabric was instantly soothed by the warmth and wetness of his mouth and tongue, and the strange combination of the two had her legs squirming as she looked for release. Archer popped of her chest. "Ah, ah, ah. Not just yet, Freckles." He moved her legs apart so she couldn't create the friction she so badly needed. "I'm in charge, remember?"

"Please," Jo whined, not caring that she was begging him for release. She wanted to come so badly, but she already knew the answer before he gave it.

"I love when you ask me nicely, but remember, patience is a virtue."

Archer pushed her bralette up to her neck and took her breasts into his mouth again. He continued to nip and suck at her while his strong hands ran up and down her sides, tickling her ribs in a way that made her shiver instead of laugh. Soon enough she was a panting, mewling mess, and everything he did drove her higher, but anytime she thought she was close, he would back off, kissing her side or her belly before starting up again. As he kissed his way south, he took the sides of her thong and pulled them down her legs. Jo breathed a sigh of relief. Finally, he was where she needed him most, and while she loved the buildup, she wanted more than that right now.

Archer kissed his way up her legs, and when Jo let out a small grumble of discontent, he merely chuckled and kissed the top of her thigh. "Soon, Freckles. Very soon."

"Not soon enough," she retorted, earning herself a gentle swat on the leg. She laughed lightly, but it soon died on her tongue when Archer threw her legs over his shoulders and dove into her center, driving his tongue inside her before licking all the way up to the bundle of nerves that had been screaming for attention.

Jo moaned and writhed against him, her hands reaching for him despite the restraints. She wanted to touch him, to run her fingers through his hair while he ate her, but not being able to also felt freeing in a way. The metal bit into skin until she finally let go of her need to control, to manage, and just let him do whatever he wanted, enjoying each sensation he created with his hands, his tongue, and his whole being immensely. She was so worked up that she was almost ready to come, but just as she almost got there, he backed away again.

"Not so funny now, is it?" His breathe fanned across her slippery center, but it wasn't the friction she desired in that moment.

Jo started to grumble, but before her reply got out, his tongue was back, licking and sucking at her as he drove two long, blunt fingers inside her.

Jo's back bowed off the bed and she continued to try and move her hips against him, but he used his free arm to hold her body in place. After a few minutes, she was nothing more than a pile of whimpers and moans, babbling nonsensically as he drove her closer and closer to the edge of bliss. She needed to come so very badly.

"Please, Archer. Please make me come." She was

craving the release more than she had ever craved it in her entire life. A low grunt was the only reply he gave before he curled his fingers up and sucked hard on her clit. "Oh, fuck," she shouted as she came, the orgasm more powerful than any she had ever experienced.

Her whole body felt like it was wired, electricity running through her veins and in her blood as small flecks of light appeared behind her eyelids, looking like the sparklers she used to ignite on the Fourth of July. It was bliss, her legs practically vibrating as the pleasure rolled through her in waves. If she thought he was going to quit at that, she was sorely mistaken because Archer doubled his efforts, holding her pussy hostage until she came twice more in rapid succession, animalistic sounds she'd never made or heard before ripping from her throat as she did.

Jo wasn't sure how much time had passed before Archer slipped the blindfold up over her eyes because she was fairly certain she had been transported to another plane of existence entirely. As her eyes adjusted to the dim light of his bedroom, she looked up at Archer to see him peering down at her with a concerned expression. "Was that too much?"

Jo was still catching her breath, but she still managed to utter two words to let him know just how well he had done. "Home run," she breathed out, and his smile was all the reply she needed. Jo looked down to see that Archer was fully disrobed and looking very much like she had dreamed he would. Planes of lean muscle covered his body with just a smattering of dark brown chest hair covering his pecs. Her eyes moved south and widened at the very obvious and very large erection he was sporting. When Jo brought her eyes back up to his face, he was smirking, and she just rolled her eyes at his well-earned cockiness. She wriggled her hands, the chain of the handcuffs rattling against the bed frame. "If it wasn't obvious, I really, really enjoyed that, and we are one hundred percent doing it again, but right now I want to touch you."

"Are you sure?" he asked, licking her release from his glistening lips. "Because I could keep going. Tasting you is something that I could do all damn day."

Jo smiled at that, and while it would be fun, she really did need to get her hands on him and make him feel just as good as he made her. "It's a good thing neither of us has to work tomorrow then," she teased, wiggling her hands once again. "Now get these off me so I can get you off."

Archer chuckled before using the key to release the cuffs, and after tossing them on the nightstand, he rubbed her wrists and hands to get the feeling back even though they felt perfectly fine. Still, it was nice having someone take care of her, and she tried not to blush at the gesture. Jo must not have done a very good job, because he looked at her lovingly before brushing his finger across her pinked cheek. "Love seeing you blush, Freckles."

Jo smiled, bringing his fingers to her mouth for a kiss before she raised up on her knees and stripped off her bralette. "Thanks." In one swift movement, she was straddling his lap. "Now let's see all the ways I can make you blush." She lowered her mouth to his in a kiss that wasn't just the promise of more sex—it was the promise of more everything, and she couldn't wait to get started.

## Chapter Eighteen

*Archer*

Holy shit. Tonight was already the best night of Archer's life and it was barely getting started. Having Jo walk into his house and drop her coat to reveal herself decked out in sexy lingerie was amazing, but the highlights came after that. First when she placed her trust in him to let go, to give him the reigns when it came to her pleasure, and then when she confessed that she loved him.

Archer knew he loved Jo. It all started from the moment she walked into the elevator on his first day, her blonde curls bouncing and her smile lighting up his whole world. They may have hit a few bumps along the way, but he wouldn't trade that for anything since it's what led them to where they were now, and that was madly in love with one another and finally getting to express that both verbally and physically.

The physical part of the night had been all about her so far, and that was fine by him. Watching Jo finally letting go and relaxing into the pleasure he could give her made him feel so many emotions. He felt touched and honored to have earned her trust, and he was pleased that he could be the one to give her the release she so sorely needed. He wasn't so cocky as to think that he was the only man to ever give her an orgasm, but he was the only one she had ever had enough faith in to hand over the reins.

That was something that made his chest swell with affection and pride, pride in himself for being that kind of man, and pride in her for being able to do something that was usually so difficult for her. Jo didn't let just anyone have control, so someone she did relax like that need in front of must be pretty damn special. That's exactly how she made him feel. Archer felt like the most special man on the planet at the moment, and if the smirk that appeared on Jo's face as she broke their kiss was any indication, he was about to feel a whole lot more than that.

Jo ground her hips against him, running her sex along the shaft of his rock-hard erection, the warm wetness sliding over his skin causing him to groan with anticipation and also from the need to stave things off before he came right then. Eating her out had driven his body into a frenzy, the sweet taste of her and the noises she made driving him closer and closer to his own release until he was worried he was going to blow against his bedsheets. He was almost there again as she gyrated on top of him, her body moving in ways he had dreamed about for months. Archer's entire body felt hot, like his blood was pure gasoline and she was a lit match that would cause him to burst into flames at any given second. He was also so tightly wound that he was pretty sure another minute of this was going to cause him to snap.

Jo leaned down to kiss his lips briefly. "Looks like I finally got you to blush, didn't I, Sugar?"

Archer smiled at the repeated endearment, and leaned back, raising a brow at her. "Sugar?" He didn't mind the nickname, liking it actually, but most of his blood was not in his brain, so that might change when it was back to functioning properly.

Jo nodded her head, her curls bouncing along as she did. "Uh huh," she muttered, doubling her efforts to drive him mad with her rubbing all over him. "We both know that out of the two of us, you're definitely the one that's sweet." She leaned down again and kissed him, this time more fiercely and with purpose. She drove her tongue inside his mouth and reached her hands up to his face, tilting his head to the side to give her more access and deepen the kiss. When she popped off his mouth, she licked a stripe up his neck and over to his ear where she nipped at his lobe for a moment. "I love the way you taste." She purred the words into his ear and he got closer still. Jo leaned back and pushed against his chest to get him to lie back on the bed. "I want more."

As much as Archer loved Jo giving her control over to him, her taking it was equally as sexy. "Be my guest, Freckles. It's all for you, anyway," he said, a smile on his face as she explored his body.

Jo's hands drifted over the bulges on his arms and the ridges of his torso. He wasn't a vain man, but he knew he looked pretty good without his clothes on, and it seemed that Jo was in agreement with that. She dipped down and ran her tongue over his nipple, the warm sensation feeling better than he remembered, and she ran her other hand down his side to hold onto his hip, still grinding herself against him the entire time. He would call her a tease, but he did the same thing to her, so it was only fair.

Jo continued to kiss and suck her way down his torso until her teeth nipped at the ridge just below his hip bone. Archer's dick was so hard he was sure he could use it to hammer nails, and it was leaking steadily, more than ready for her. Her blue eyes that were alight with desire met his, and she winked at him just before she licked him from root to tip, bobbing her head down to take him into her mouth. A moan slipped out from between his lips, and she took that as encouragement to continue, but if she didn't stop, things were going to escalate quickly. Too quickly.

"While that feels fucking fantastic," he panted

out. "I want to be inside you when I come." Her head popped up and there was a small pout on her face, so he echoed her words from earlier back to her. "We have all day tomorrow. Right, Freckles?"

Jo smiled as she crawled back up to his face. "I'm going to hold you to that." She reached between them to give his dick a few good pumps with her fist. "I want to see if you taste as sweet as you act."

"Fuck," he groaned, grabbing her fist from his erection and bringing it up to rest on his chest. "That smart mouth of yours is going to make me come all on its own."

Jo's smile was both amused and pleased. "We're definitely trying phone sex sometime." She lined her center up to him, but paused before going further. "We can use a condom if you want, but I'm on the pill and clean, so I'm good with this if you are."

Archer's eyes widened at the thought of taking her bare and he nodded, taking her narrow hips in his hands. "I'm clean too. We're good to go."

She chuckled at his eagerness, but he didn't care if she knew just how badly he wanted her. Jo didn't say another word, simply humming contentedly and smiling as she slid down, sheathing him inside her. "You feel so good," she told him, her voice breathy.

"God, you too." It wasn't the most eloquent reply Archer had ever come up with, but he was having a hard time forming words at the moment. Jo felt so warm, so wet and snug. Her walls gripped him tightly and when she rolled her hips, he was pretty sure his eyes disappeared into the back of his head. "Fuck."

"That's sometimes what they call it, yes," Jo remarked, a light chuckle in her voice.

Archer would have swatted her for her sass, but he was too busy enjoying the sensation that her laugh caused as her walls contracted around him. After another delicious roll of her hips, Jo leaned back and placed her hands atop his thighs. They were warm, soft, and lightly brushed against the hair on his legs as she braced herself, searching for a new angle that would please herself and him until a low moan from her rosy lips told him she'd found what she was looking for. With her body on display for him, Archer ran his hands from her hips up to her chest and gently massaged her breasts, pinching the pink buds at the tips until he could feel Jo clenching around him.

"I'm so close," she breathed out, and Archer was too. He was dangerously close to coming, but he needed her to get there again one last time. She wanted to please him, but he wasn't done pleasing her. He would never be done pleasing her.

Sliding one of his hands down her taut stomach until he was at the junction where their bodies were joined, Archer explored until he found her swollen nub once again. He caressed and pressed on the bundle of nerves until he heard the telltale signs of her orgasm. Her eyes were closed tightly, her breath was coming in short bursts, and all her muscles were tensed. He sped up his thumb and reached his other hand up to cup her face.

"Look at me, Freckles," he commanded. Her blue eyes with the pupils blown wide flew open and met his. He looked up at her with every ounce of love that he felt and smiled. "I love you."

The movement of her body never faltered, but her expression went completely serene as he spoke the words to her. "I love you, too." The confession came just before she did, her eyes never leaving his and he stared in awe at the look of pure bliss on her face.

"Thank fuck," Archer gritted out as her walls squeezed him like a vice as he spilled inside her. He bucked his hips up to meet hers, their eyes never leaving each other's the entire time they found their release, and while having sex with someone was already intimate, their connection felt like it went even deeper after what they'd shared. It was as if they had peered into one another's souls and recognized something that they had been missing for a long time and finally found it in the other person.

Jo slowed her movements and leaned down to him for another kiss. It was slow and sensual, a bow on the wonderful present that they had just shared. Archer rubbed the bare skin of her arms and back as she kissed him, finally reaching his hands up to cup her face. When she leaned back to stare at him, he saw so much love in her expression that he could feel tears prickle at the corner of his eyes. Most of his life had been spent in privilege, but he had never felt as rich and accomplished as he did when she looked at him like that. He was going to marry her someday, and while that thought might scare some men, it only made him feel lighter and happier than he ever had.

A smile pulled at his mouth, and while he felt nothing but joy, earning Jo's love and her trust wasn't something he was going to take lightly, and he wanted her to know that. "Thank you, Jo."

Jo leaned her forehead against his and smiled. "Thank you," she replied and brushed her lips against his briefly. "That was the best sex I've ever had."

Archer shook his head. "I'm not thanking you for the sex." At her raised brow he smirked. "Well, not just the sex." He rolled their bodies so they were on their sides facing one another on his bed, legs intertwined as he cupped her cheek and ran his thumb over the freckles he couldn't get enough of. "Thank you for thinking enough of me to give me your love and your trust. I won't squander it."

A shy smile overcame Jo's face. It was a smile that was rare because she was shy so infrequently, but it was one that he loved just as much as her others. "I know you won't," she told him, reaching her hand up to cover his. "You're an amazing person. You're smart, funny, loyal, and I know that you can handle me at my best and my worst." She chuckled lightly. "I think I've known that for a while, which is probably why I found you so irritating at first."

A smirk broke out across his face. "Come on, Freckles. Be honest. You were irritated with me because of how much you wanted me."

His teasing earned him a wry smile, but it was filled with love. "I will neither confirm nor deny that." Jo moved onto her back and stretched like a cat. The view was nice, and he was already feeling the stirrings of another round in him when both of their stomachs growled. Jo barked a laugh and lightly slapped her stomach. "Clearly some replenishment is in order before we go for round two." She sat up and looked around the room for her clothes. After a minute, she peered at him sheepishly from behind her curls. "Think I could borrow a shirt?"

Archer pulled himself up to sitting and kissed her cheek. "Freckles, you can borrow whatever you want. What's mine is yours." He slipped off his bed, pulled his white trunks on, and padded over to his dresser to grab one of his t-shirts for her. Jo slipped it on, and while it was a little big on her, that old college t-shirt had never looked better. She sashayed over to the doorway, totally bypassing her undergarments. "Do you want to borrow some boxers, or…"

Jo stopped with her hand on the doorframe and peeked at him over her shoulder. "Thanks, Sugar, but I'm good." A knowing smile pulled across her face "I don't plan on being dressed for very long." With that, she walked out the door and back out into his kitchen.

Archer dropped the shirt he had grabbed for himself to the ground and jogged after her, knowing that following Jo was what he would be doing for the rest of his life.

****

The rest of Friday night and all of Saturday passed by in a haze of cold pizza, sex, sleeping until noon, more sex, and finally reheated pizza for dinner. Jo spending the entire weekend in his apartment felt right, and Archer had already decided he was going to ask her to move in with him as soon as he could. Lying there last night with Jo in his arms and the thought of waking up next to her every day playing in his head had helped him drift off into the most restful sleep he'd had in ages, though he was currently being stirred from that sleep in the most curious manner. His body felt heated all over, and he was incredibly aroused.

Archer blinked his eyes open, letting them adjust to the light coming in through the plantation blinds, just as the sensation of extreme pleasure rippled through his body. It took a second for his mind to play catch up, but when it did, he peered down at the mass of blonde curls currently waking him up in the best way possible. He reached down and ran his hand across Jo's cheek as her warm mouth engulfed his hard cock, her hand holding the shaft like someone might try to snatch away her new favorite toy.

"Freckles," he breathed out, and she popped off him long enough to wink before going back to what she was doing.

Archer laid his head back and enjoyed the feel of her tongue as she licked and sucked her way up and down, working her hand in time with her mouth in what would end up being the best blowjob of his life. They definitely needed to move in together because this was better than any alarm clock. Her hand sped up and he felt a tingling in the base of his spine. He was close, and she was so good at what she was doing. If they gave out gold medals for fellatio, she would be the Michael Phelps of the sport. Jo hollowed her cheeks and seemed to be trying to suck his soul from his body.

"You're making me come." It was the only warning he could manage as he panted just before he shot into her mouth, fireworks exploding behind his eyelids. Jo worked him through his orgasm, swallowing every drop before slowing her movements and stopping all together.

Jo crawled up his body and leaned down to kiss him. Archer could taste the saltiness of his release on her tongue, and thinking about what she had just done to him got him hard again already. He groaned and deepened the kiss before she leaned back and ran her fingers through his messy hair. "Good morning." She laid her head down on his chest and sighed happily, and he wondered if she could hear how fast his heart had been beating. It beat for her now. Only for her.

"A very good morning indeed," he smirked. Jo's body shook as she chuckled and she looked up at him, her sky blue eyes shining with mirth. She continued to stare at him for a few minutes until he couldn't stand not knowing what she was thinking for another minute. "What?"

Her smile widened and she leaned up to kiss him briefly. "Nothing. I just like waking up next to you." A slight blush came over her cheeks and she ducked her head bashfully.

"I like it to." If there was ever a time to broach the

subject of living together, it was now. "In fact, I was thinking just how nice it would be if we did it every day."

Jo looked up at him and smiled brightly. "Really?"

Archer nodded and rubbed his hand along the planes of her bare back. "Really. I like having you in my space," he confessed. There was no way he would be able to go to work with her every day and not drag her back home with him at night anyway, and Jo brightened up his apartment considerably.

Jo arched a brow at him. "What if I want you in my space?"

Archer laughed and held her body tighter to his. "Then we'll be in your space," he relented. "I don't care where we live, Freckles, as long as we are there together."

"Me too," Jo admitted, reaching up to cup his face. Her brow furrowed slightly. "I like being with you."

Archer smiled. "Well, that's good, but I'm not sure I love the confused look on your face as you said that," he proclaimed.

Her blue eyes rolled at him playfully, her favorite pastime it seemed. "I'm not confused about you," she admitted, and some of the tension in his body disappeared. "I'm just surprised at how easy everything is between us. I thought this would be harder, but it's not." Her face turned to him and he could see his love for her reflecting back to him. "I feel more at peace now than I have in a very long time."

"I think that's all the orgasms talking." He was joking, but he knew exactly what she was talking about. Once they'd let go of their inhibitions and just leaned into the relationship, it was incredibly easy.

Jo slapped his shoulder and chuckled. "It's not the orgasms. Well, not just those, but it's a lot of things. I can be myself around you and that's not something I'm going to take for granted."

Archer smiled and stroked her hair. "Does that mean you'll move in with me?"

"Yes," she replied immediately, not a sliver of doubt present in her voice. "I would love to move in with you." She laid her head back on his chest, a contented sigh coming out as she did. Her phone pinged and she reached over to the nightstand where it had been charging. "I can't believe I almost forgot."

Archer sat up and held onto her. "What is it?"

"Pancake Sunday," she said with a trace of sadness. "I almost forgot pancake Sunday." She peered over her shoulder at him and smiled sadly. "I guess I was too busy being happy."

Archer leaned over and kissed her shoulder. "It's okay to be happy, Jo. I think your mom would want that for you."

She nodded. "She would." Her voice was firm as she stood up. Her hand reached down to his and she squeezed it. "Do you want to come?"

The breath whooshed from his body and he smiled shakily. He knew how much those breakfasts with her dad meant to her, so for her to include him was a huge deal. "I would love to," he confessed. The smile that she beamed back at him was everything, and Archer knew in his heart that this would be the first of many pancake Sundays to come.

## Chapter Nineteen

*Jo*

Pancake Sundays with Pops had always been sacred, so Jo had been nervous about taking Archer with her. As it turned out, her anxiety was all for naught. Her dad had been so excited to meet Archer and the two of them got along instantly, talking about sports and fishing, something she hadn't even known Archer was a fan of until her dad invited him to join him down by the river sometime. Jo basically spent most of their brunch at the diner with her mouth agape at how easily two parts of her life had slotted together like a couple of puzzle pieces. The two men spent their time together teasing her about her various quirks and eccentricities. It hadn't bothered her in the least. Jo was fine being the butt of a few jokes in exchange for seeing the happy, carefree smile on her dad's face. She hadn't once thought to remind him to drink his orange juice or make plans for a walk after their meal. Letting go of the things she couldn't control and focusing on being happy was her new priority, and right now, she was overjoyed.

It was finally Wednesday, the day of her and Archer's big presentation. They had discussed sleeping in their own apartments to make sure they got a good night's sleep beforehand, but when their goodnight kiss in the parking lot rounded the fifteenth minute, the two of them decided to call it, and he slept over at her place. The small apartment seemed even smaller with his large body in it, but she liked seeing him on her couch, in her bed, and wearing one of her small pink towels in the morning when he stepped out of the bathroom after his shower.

Just thinking about it again made her chuckle as she gathered up the materials for their presentation that were scattered around her office. Their presentation was digital, but she had also printed hard copies for the members of the athletic department to look over later should they want to. She also slid her and Archer's business cards into the back of the hard copies so that they could call with any questions they might have. If everything went well today, the only question would be: "when can we sign a contract with you?"

Getting the Liberty U account would be huge, and she could finally get that promotion up from junior agent. The money that came along with the promotion was less important now that she promised her dad she would stop micromanaging his life, but she would still like to pay off her student loans and save up in case he ever needed her help. Trying to control every little thing her father did wasn't something she was going to do anymore, but she still cared for her dad and would be there for him in a heartbeat.

It was nice to not feel the constant tug of worry about her father, and her body felt lighter and more relaxed because of it. That could also be attributed to the amazing sex she was having, but Jo wasn't going to think about that right now or she would get ideas in her head about doing it in Archer's car. She did consider it for about half a second before shaking her head. Nah, they would never make it to their presentation on time.

A knock on her door drew her attention away from sexy times with Archer and over to the man standing there. "Good luck on your presentation, Jolene," her boss called over to her, his smile looking more smarmy than usual. He took in her outfit, his eyes lingering on certain parts of her body a little too long, and Jo suddenly wished she had worn about five more layers of clothes. "It's nice to see you in a skirt."

"Thanks," Jo said flatly, not loving her boss commenting on her choice of clothing. She was used to him telling her to smile more or giving her weird looks every now and then, but this was the first time he made a more forward remark. Jo looked down at her outfit. When she got dressed this morning, the purple polka dot sleeveless blouse and black pencil skirt seemed like a smart choice. Now she wished she had thrown a parka over the whole outfit.

She was saved from any more of her boss's creepy observations when Archer appeared in the doorway. "Hey." His head swiveled between her and their boss with a strange look on his face. "We should head out so we're not late."

"Good idea." Delaney slapped Archer on the shoulder and grinned. "Good luck to you both." With that, their boss left her office and headed back toward his own.

Archer followed Delaney with his eyes before turning back to her with a furrowed brow. "What did he want?"

Jo shrugged a shoulder and finished putting all her materials in her bag. "Just to wish us good luck and to make an unnecessary comment about my attire." She would definitely be putting that in her journal later today.

"He what?" Archer demanded, sounding angrier than she thought he would.

"It's nothing." Jo brushed it aside like she normally did anything that made her uncomfortable and breezed past him and over to the elevator. It was nothing that hadn't happened before, and while she was sick of all of it, right now they had a presentation to concentrate on.

Archer was hot on her heels, and when the doors opened and they stepped inside, he punched the button for the bottom floor, then stood directly in front of her. "It's not nothing, Jo. He shouldn't be talking about your clothes."

"I know that, and you know that, but clearly he doesn't know that." She sighed, tired of dealing with the outdated ideas and attitudes of older men. Jo reached up and pinched the bridge of her nose. "Can we not talk about it right now? We need to focus on the presentation and not our skeevy boss." Her head tilted back and hit the wall of the elevator. "It's not like there's another agency around here to jump ship to anyway."

The elevator dinged and deposited them on the ground floor. Archer led her out with the palm of his hand on her lower back. "I know there isn't, and I know you don't want to leave your dad." He escorted her over to his car and let her in the passenger door, always caring for her even when she was in one of her moods. Once he was inside as well, he started the engine, but turned to her before driving anywhere. "We could start our own agency."

Jo snorted. "Good one." She pointed out the windshield. "Let's go. I don't want to be late." The last thing she needed was to feel rushed during their presentation when her boss had already thrown her off her game with his weirdness.

A hand reached over and turned her cheek. Jo was facing Archer, and his expression was dead serious. "I'm not joking, Freckles. We could do it. We could even try to poach Blake and some of the admins who are tired of the outdated business model too."

Jo considered his words for a moment and opened her mouth to protest that it wasn't possible, but maybe it was. They had the knowledge and the contacts, but money would definitely be an issue. "It's too expensive, and I don't know about you, but I don't have the kind of capital it takes to start a business. I'm still paying off college debt."

Archer's brown eyes lit up. "We could get a business loan, or borrow from my dad," he explained, seeming to get more and more excited at the possibility. "I don't want to play the nepo baby card, but my dad has more than enough to invest and has a ton of contacts from his media business we could use. We'd be hitting the ground running."

Jo bit her lower lip as she thought more about it. Being her own boss would be amazing, and she wouldn't have to deal with the Idiot Brigade or Delaney any longer.

Archer reached over and pulled her lip free. "Just think about it, okay?"

The car started moving and Jo tried to relax into her seat, but her body was wired at the prospect of the two of them starting their own sports marketing firm. She already enjoyed working with Archer and they were moving in together. Was it such a big leap to start a business with him too? It was putting all her eggs in one basket, but when Jo peered over at the man next to her, she smiled. If she was going to take that kind of leap with anyone, it would be him. Archer made her feel safe enough to take that kind of chance. Jo had already risked her heart and it paid off big time, so maybe one more risk wasn't such a bad idea.

****

The Liberty U presentation went off without a hitch, and any qualms she had about starting a new agency with Archer flew right out the window the moment they started explaining their marketing plan to the athletic department. Jo and Archer worked so seamlessly together that it was like they had been doing this for years instead of mere months. Their banter was witty and light, their transitions seamless, and even the question and answer portion went well with neither of them speaking over the other or fumbling their answers. Most members of the committee making the decision seemed to love their ideas about spotlighting athletes individually and in groups as well as pushing for more inclusion of female and LGBT+ students, smiling and asking lots of thoughtful and interesting questions. Overall, it went as smoothly as it could have, and Jo was certain the two of them had secured the contract for Elite Marketing.

"We rocked that presentation so hard." Jo's voice was filled with the glee she felt, and she couldn't help but bounce in the seat next to Archer as he parked back in the office lot.

"Hell yeah we did." Archer put the car in park and leaned over to kiss her on the lips. "We make an amazing team." His eyes were bright and his smile was wide.

Jo was so in love with him and couldn't wait to start the rest of their lives together, beginning with starting a new agency. "Let's do it," she said, excitedly. "Let's start our own agency."

Archer beamed at her before slamming his mouth down onto hers again. When they finally came up for air, he ran his hand into her hair and pulled her forehead to rest against his. "This will be so great. We're going to do great things together, Freckles," he promised.

"I know." She was still nervous at the thought of making such a big change, but she felt safe with the knowledge that Archer wouldn't let her down. Jo brushed her lips against his lightly. "You have that thing with your family tonight, right?"

He nodded and groaned as he pulled away. "I still wish you would come with me." There was a pout in his voice and on his lips. "Just because it's my brother-in-law's birthday doesn't mean you're not welcome."

Jo smiled and ran her fingers through his silky brown locks. "I know, and I'm excited to meet your family. I would like to wait until it's just dinner and not a whole party with a bunch of people I don't know." She opened the car door and stepped a leg out. "I'm better one-on-one anyway."

Archer waggled his eyebrows comically. "Don't I know it." He laughed.

Jo shook her head at him and shut the door. "You're lucky I love you," she told him through the open window.

His expression turned serious. "Don't I know it." He blew her a kiss. "Love you too, Freckles."

"Have a good time, Sugar." Reluctantly, she stepped away from the car and waved as he left the lot.

With a heart full of happiness and many other feelings for Archer, Jo walked over to her car with her bag and dug around for her keys. When she couldn't find them, she grumbled and looked up at the office building. She must have left them there. It was nearly 6:00, so there should still be someone left in the building. Jo sped inside and into the elevator, and a short ride later, she was out the doors and into the offices of Elite Marketing. There were a few people left in the space, but they were packing up and leaving for the day. Jo made her way to her office and for once was actually grateful that it didn't have a working lock on the door.

When she spotted her keys on her desk, she did a little victory dance and grabbed them before hightailing it toward the double doors so she could go home and grab a nice, long shower before scarfing some leftover takeout and hitting the sack. Jo and Archer had decided to sleep in their respective apartments for the evening so they could catch up on sleep. Jo smiled at the memory of the repeat conversation, wondering if their appetite for each other would ever be satisfied enough for them to make sleep a priority. They would have to figure it out if they were going to live together and work together, something Jo also couldn't wait to make happen.

"Is that you, Jolene?" A voice called from her side.

Jo tried to smooth out the annoyance that was probably evident on her face at hearing her boss's voice. It was there basically every time she heard Gavin Delaney say her full name.

"Yes, it's me." Jo turned to face him. He was standing in the doorway of his office, his graying hair looking a little matted after the long day. "Did you need something?"

"I do." He nodded his head for her to come into his office.

Jo walked over, noticing that his assistant Janine was gone for the day. After she got inside, he shut the door behind her and sat in one of the chairs in front of his desk, patting the seat of the one next to him. That alone was unusual, and her Spidey-senses were tingling, but she ignored them, wanting to just get the interaction over with so she could go home.

"I had a very interesting phone call from my friend at Liberty U."

"You did?" Jo asked happily. She hadn't anticipated that the university would make a decision that quickly, but she and Archer had knocked it out of the park earlier, so it wasn't a huge surprise.

Gavin nodded, but he wasn't smiling. "He found it interesting that you would focus your attention on marginalized athletes instead of their superstars, a strategy I had thought we had agreed would be the smarter way to go," he reminded her.

*Shit.* Her stomach dropped, and Jo wished Archer was there with her to help smooth things out, but she was on her own. "Well, Archer and I thought that going with something more modern would be a good idea, and the committee seemed to love it." They had been nothing but smiles after the presentation, but clearly there was another person stuck in the past that they hadn't accounted for whose smile had been less than genuine.

Delaney scoffed. "I can't speak to that, only to what my friend told me." He looked over at her and raised a brow. "Disobeying the boss isn't senior consultant behavior, Jolene. It isn't even junior consultant behavior, if I'm being honest, and we need people here who we know we can count on."

Jo swallowed thickly. She and Archer had the beginnings of a plan to start their own business, but it was just the barest of ideas at that point. While she would love to flip Delaney the finger and march out of there with her head held high, she and Archer both still needed jobs. Suddenly, it sounded like she was in danger of losing hers. "I apologize for the misstep, but I really do think the university liked our pitch," she explained, searching for a way to keep her job. "What can I do to prove myself?"

Jo steeled herself for what was to come. Probably having to go back to minor-league stuff like proofreading other people's press releases or being the gopher for the senior consultants, running back and forth between departments for other people. *Kill me now*, she thought to herself just as Gavin reached over and ran his fingers along her kneecap before moving them further up her leg, inching up the hem of her skirt. Jo froze momentarily before pulling her leg away from her boss just as he got to her thigh. When her eyes met his, she did not like the predatory look she saw there.

He raised a brow at her. "Come on, Jolene. This is

how things are done. I thought you wanted to prove yourself," he stated, his voice eerily calm for what was currently happening.

"I do," she said, standing and grabbing her things. "But not like that." She backed away toward the door, not wanting to spend another minute in the man's presence.

Delaney stood, buttoning the coat of his jacket. "You know," he said as he rounded his desk, "I thought you were more of a team player, Jolene."

The audacity of the man was staggering, but she was too eager to get away from him to tell him off properly. "I am, but only if the team is worth playing on. I quit." Jo swung the door open. "And the name is Jo, asshole." With those as her parting words, she walked out of the office and over to the stairwell. She didn't want to wait for the elevator, so she booked it down the stairs as quickly as possible, not stopping until she was out of the building and safely inside her vehicle.

It wasn't until she looked in the rearview mirror that she saw she had started crying. As she looked at her tear-soaked face, her lower lip wobbled and a sob broke loose. Never before had she ever been made to feel so small, so dirty, and her stomach turned at the thought of what had just happened. It could have been so much worse too, and thinking that had her opening her car door and throwing up the pretzels she had eaten on the way back to the office in Archer's car.

*Archer.*

Jo wanted nothing more than to drive over to his apartment and curl up in his lap, but he wasn't there. He was with his family.

*Family.*

*Archer's dad is friends with Delaney.* Jo wiped her mouth with the back of her hand and leaned back in to start the car, her thoughts disjointed, and bouncing around until she was in a state of near panic. There went any chance of his dad helping them with their business, and now she was out of a job too. She swiped at the tears streaming down her face, tears of anger and sadness. Jo didn't remember the drive home or even the walk up to her apartment, but she did remember getting into the shower, hoping to scrub away any remnants of the last hour from her body. If only she could scrub it from her mind, but it was there, playing on a loop, and she wasn't sure what to do about it.

The one person she wanted to talk to was unavailable, and with his dad and Delaney connected, it was complicated. Archer said he loved how strong and confident she was, but at the moment, she felt anything but. It wasn't rational, but the idea that he might not love her anymore because of it had her leaving the shower and collapsing onto her bed, still soaking wet and only in a towel. Her body curled in on itself protectively as she cried, hoping that sleep would come quickly to take her away from her troubled thoughts.

## Chapter Twenty

*Archer*

The birthday party for his brother-in-law, Todd, lasted longer than Archer would have thought, especially for a weeknight. It turns out that when you get a bunch of teachers together and they have a school holiday the next day, they want to party all night long. Archer called it a night at 10:00, saying goodbye to Caro, Todd, and his group of teacher friends before heading out. He didn't want to be completely dead on his feet the next day, and he guessed Jo must have felt similarly because she didn't respond to his goodnight text. He seriously considered driving over to her place and crawling into bed with her, but if she wasn't responding to texts, she was probably asleep. Archer didn't want to risk waking her. They had been keeping each other up a lot the last week or so with their marathon lovemaking, but he was happy to keep that going. Caffeine and sugar existed for a reason after all, but if she needed rest, he could give her one night at least.

A smile played across his face as he walked through the doors of Elite Marketing, the thought of more nighttime activities with his girlfriend putting an extra spring in his step. The small plastic box containing a gardenia in his bag added to his giddiness. He hadn't thought he would be able to find the flower to gift to Jo, but luckily the grocery store near his apartment had some in the form of a corsage. It wasn't a bouquet, but Archer hoped it was at least better than a vase filled with berries.

He was just reaching into his bag to grab it when Blake rushed up to him. "Delaney's called an emergency meeting." The man spoke in hurried whispers and snagged Archer's arm, steering him over to the conference room.

Archer followed along and grabbed a seat next to the man. He looked around and saw every other marketing consultant in attendance with one exception. Suddenly very concerned, he turned to Blake. "Where's Jo?"

Blake frowned. "I was just going to ask you," he said, his voice filled with worry.

Before either of them had more time to ponder the location of the missing woman, Delaney entered the room, a fixed expression on his face. "Let's get this started, shall we?" He stood at the head of the table and passed papers around to each of the men. "These accounts are now under your purview. You will need to make time in your schedule to get up to date with each one until we are able to hire another consultant to take them back over."

"Another consultant?" Lowell North asked as he shuffled through his papers.

Archer was only half listening as he was too busy taking in the names of his new clients. They were all athletes or companies that had been working with Jo. A pit formed in his stomach and he looked over at Blake to see that the man had just made the same connection he had. "Where's Jo?" Archer asked, his tone less than friendly as he directed the question at their boss.

Delaney's expression shuddered for a moment before becoming a mask once again. "Jolene has decided to part ways with the company." His voice was flat and he looked completely unfazed by the occurrence. "Not surprising given she was turned down for a promotion after she decided to go rogue with your presentation yesterday."

Archer balked at the insinuation that it was all her

fault or that doing what was actually in the best interest of all involved was going rogue. "We both decided it was the better strategy. If she got reprimanded, then I should too," he insisted. There was no way he was going to sit there and let her take all the blame.

Delaney waved away Archer's statement. "Jolene has a history of thinking outside the company's values, and it doesn't matter because she left of her own volition and you all have new clients to focus on. Now, get to it." He exited the room quickly with no time for further questions. The pit in Archer's stomach turned into a heavy brick. Something wasn't right, and he needed to get to the bottom of it.

"Ding dong the witch is dead," Chadwick muttered, eliciting a few chuckles from the other agents. "Fuck off, Chadwick." Archer was tired of coddling these assholes. He stood and stormed out toward his office, hands balling into fists and teeth nearly cracking as he ground them together. Why hadn't Jo called him and told him what happened? He took out his phone and opened their messages, balking when he didn't see anything new since the day before. *I thought she trusted me?* His thumbs flew across the screen as he messaged Jo.

Archer: **Are you okay? Delaney said you quit. Call me please.**

Archer stared at his phone, hoping a response would come through right away, but there was nothing. He took out the keys to his office, but paused just as they were near the lock. Sidestepping his door, he moved over to Jo's office and opened it, flicking on the light and taking in the scene before him. Her desk still had the neat piles of file folders that were always present and her laptop was open. When he stepped behind her desk and saw her personal effects still there, he knew something was wrong. Jo didn't decorate her office. It was clean and efficient, much like her, but she did have three items that gave the smallest glimpse into her life outside of work.

There were two picture frames, one of a young Jo with her parents and another of her with her two friends, Gigi and Millie. He had yet to meet the women, but Jo spoke of them fondly, and if they were granted a place on her desk, they must be incredibly dear to her. The last item was a baseball stress toy. With as tightly wound as his woman was, Archer was surprised she hadn't crushed it into tiny pieces by now. His mouth twitched at the corner with the desire to smile as he pictured it, but that wasn't happening until he found out what the hell was going on.

Archer glanced at his phone one more time, but there was still no response. He looked up from the device to see Blake enter the office.

"What the fuck happened?" the man asked him.

His head shook sadly and he shrugged a shoulder. "I have no idea, but I am definitely going to find out," Archer vowed.

As he passed by Blake on his way out the door, the man stopped him with a hand on his forearm. "If you get a hold of her, will you tell her to call me? I know just about everyone here is afraid of her, but we know different," he said, a sad smile on his face.

"Yes, we do." Arched patted Blake on the shoulder before going into his own office, shutting the door behind him.

Firing up his laptop, Archer proceeded to go through his calendar to clear his schedule for the day, pushing everything back to the next week or even later than that. Next, he navigated over to his bank account and checked the balance. With a little fine tuning, he would have more than enough to pay his rent and food bills for the next year if he depleted his savings. If he were to quit his job right then, something he was seriously considering doing, he would at least be able to survive for a while until he figured things out. It would be so much easier to pull the trigger on that if he just knew what happened with Jo.

There were still no notifications from her on his phone, and he was tired of waiting. He dialed her number and listened as it rang and rang before going to voicemail. *You've reached Jo…* it started, but he hung up and hit redial. He repeated this four times until finally a voice answered the phone, but it wasn't the one he wanted to hear. "Hello?" The sweet voice asked, and from way Jo had described her friends to him, Archer would bet a good amount of money he was speaking to Millie.

"Hi. Can I speak with Jo, please? It's urgent." He spoke as politely as he could for someone who was currently in the dark as to their girlfriend's whereabouts and slowly going insane with worry.

"Let me just check." There was some shuffling and mumbling on the other end before the voice came back on. "Jo isn't up for talking at the moment." There was some more shuffling and the sound of a door shutting before the voice spoke again. "Look," the woman said, her voice soft. "I'm not going to tell you what happened because it's not my story to tell, but I think that if you could come over to her place right now, that would be very helpful."

Archer huffed a breath. "Are you sure? She won't even talk to me or return my texts." Even as he spoke the words he was grabbing his messenger bag and keys from off his desk.

"She's just afraid," the woman explained.

"Of what?" Jo wasn't afraid of anything. "What the hell happened to her?"

The woman sighed. "She's afraid of losing you,

and even though we both know better, this is still pretty new to Jo, so she might be needing extra reassurance at the moment," she said, the love for her friend clear in her tone. "Will you come over?"

Archer nodded even though he was on the phone. "I was never planning on not coming." He took a deep breath to calm his racing heart. "Thank you, Millie."

"Oh," she squeaked in surprise. "How did you ... you know what, never mind. You're very welcome. We'll see you soon."

Then her voice was gone and Archer was out the door, walking as quickly as his long legs would take him. A few administrative assistants and other consultants gave him inquisitive looks as he passed by, but he ignored them. He had somewhere far more important to be.

****

It took twenty-five long minutes to get to Jo's apartment, and Archer's gut had been churning the whole time. She wouldn't have quit because of a reprimand or lack of promotion—she had worked there six years without one and held on. Jo had endured so much for so long, it would have taken a lot more than that to tip her over the edge. Archer wondered briefly if their plan of starting their own firm let her feel okay with quitting, but then why was she afraid he wouldn't love her anymore? He would always love her, and the lack of sense this whole situation made was giving him a migraine. His fingers rubbed at his temples as he made his way up the stairs to her place.

After one last deep breath to try and calm the swirl of emotions inside his body, Archer raised his fist to knock. A moment later, a petite but curvy brunette with thick-framed glasses opened the door. Her checkered skirt and flowy white blouse gave off a studious vibe, and

237

although he already knew she was there, he could tell right away that he was looking at Millie. Jo had described her librarian friend to a T. "Hi Millie," he said politely, sticking his hand out to shake. "It's nice to finally meet you."

"Likewise, Archer." Her voice was as sweet as honey with a smile to match. Archer could instantly see why Jo liked her. "I wish it were under better circumstances." Millie opened the door and gestured for him to enter.

Archer had been in Jo's apartment before, so the small space and cottage style furnishings were familiar to him. What wasn't familiar was the sight of Jo on her bed. Her normally bright eyes were bloodshot, her hair was up in a messy bun, and her baggy t-shirt covered her legs, which were pulled up to her chest. It wasn't her appearance that caused his steps to falter though. It was the downcast expression on Jo's face that had him worried. Millie walked over to Jo and kissed her cheek and whispered in Jo's ear. After getting a nod, she walked toward the door.

"I'll be back later with some food and a few other things," Millie promised before tossing a smile and nod of encouragement in his direction then disappearing out the door.

Archer turned to Jo. Her face was filled with trepidation, but as he got closer, he saw the love that she had for him was still in her eyes, and he sighed with relief. Whatever had happened, they would get through it because they loved one another. He reached his palm out to her and waited with baited breath to see if she took it. When she did, his shoulders relaxed and he ran his thumb over the back of her hand. "What happened, Freckles?"

Jo lifted a shoulder a few times and her eyes darted around the room before meeting his again.

Whatever had occurred, it was a lot more than her not getting a promotion. "After you left for the party, I realized I left my keys upstairs." Her voice sounded raspy from crying and it gutted him that he hadn't been there to comfort her. He squeezed her hand to encourage her to continue, and after letting out a shaky breath, she did. "I went inside and grabbed them off my desk, but on my way out, Delaney called me into his office and shut the door."

Jo paused, and the rock that had been present in his stomach from the moment the work meeting started felt like a boulder. Archer did not like the direction this story was taking. "What happened in his office?" He sat on the edge of the bed while silently hoping that what he thought had happened hadn't.

Moisture shone at him from Jo's blue eyes, and he ran the back of his finger under the right one to catch a stray tear. "He said that his friend called and told him about our presentation, and he was disappointed in the way I acted without approval. He said he needed people at the firm that could be counted on." She took another deep breath and continued, her voice shaky. "I thought I was going to get fired, and we hadn't made any solid plans for our firm yet, so I apologized. I said I was sorry for not getting his go-ahead first, but that I believed the university really liked our presentation." She looked over at him pleadingly. "They did, didn't they?"

"Yeah, Freckles, they did. We were awesome."

Jo nodded at his reassurance, though her eyes were still troubled and filled with unshed tears. "I didn't want to lose my job, so then I asked what I could do to prove myself." Another tear came loose and she swiped at it angrily, like she hated the fact that she was crying. Jo was strong and showing any vulnerability was hard for her, but she could always do that with him, and he wanted to remind her of that.

"Hey." He spoke softly, cupping her face and bringing their heads together. "You're safe with me, Jo. I love you, and nothing you tell me right now will change that." Archer would love this woman until the end of time no matter what, and he would spend the rest of his life proving it to her so she never questioned it again.

Jo sniffed and nodded her head. "I know. I just got scared." Her lip wobbled. "I love you too," she whispered.

"You tell me whenever you're ready. Okay?" Taking care of Jo was the only item on his to-do list that day. He wasn't going anywhere.

With another nod and one more shuddering breath, she revealed the rest of the story. "He reached over and touched my knee, and used his fingers to push up my skirt," she explained.

Archer's free hand curled into a fist, but he tried to swallow his anger so that he could be there for her.

"When I pulled away, he said he thought I wanted to prove myself, and I told him I did, but not like that. Then I quit, called him an asshole, and left." Her eyes went wide and met his. "I left my pictures," she started, but he shook his head at her.

"I grabbed them for you." Archer reached into his pocket and pulled out her stress ball. "I nabbed this too. I don't want you going around breaking things because you don't have your squeeze toy." He scrunched it a few times to demonstrate.

Jo's watery laugh filled the air and his chest lightened with the sound of it. "I do love a good squeeze toy." She sniffled again and wiped at her eyes on last time. Archer pulled her into his lap and cradled her, wrapping his arms around her in hopes of reassuring her that she was safe and sound right there. When she looked up at him, her expression was pained. "I'm sorry I didn't call you or answer your texts."

Archer rubbed his hand up and down her back, his desire to know why she kept her distance outweighing his need to keep things light for her sake. "Why didn't you?" he asked as he continued to sway her from side to side. "Did you think I wouldn't understand?"

Jo shook her head, the curls from her bun tickling his chin. "No, I knew you would understand, but the whole thing caught me off guard. I didn't know what to do. I was worried about not having a job, and then I remembered your dad and Delaney are friends, and I don't know." She jerkily shrugged her shoulder. "I thought it would be weird and messy and I just didn't know how to deal with it. I'm not great at dealing with emotions and big things like this."

The connection between his father and Delaney wasn't something Archer had even thought about until that moment, but he wasn't worried about it. "You're stronger than you give yourself credit for, and don't worry about my dad and Delaney. They know one another, but I wouldn't call them friends. Frankly, my dad will be appalled when I tell him what happened." He tucked her head further into his chest and stroked her cheek. "It will all work out," he promised. He wasn't sure exactly how, but he knew it would.

Jo sighed and her breathing got steadier. After a long moment of silence, he looked down to see that she had fallen asleep. Archer wanted to talk to her more about what had happened and help her figure out what her next steps were, but she was clearly exhausted from the whole ordeal and having to relive it with both Millie and him, so he let her rest.

After laying her down on her bed and tucking her covers up to her chin, he grabbed his bag and took out his laptop, opened a document, and typed out his letter of resignation. There were a few other moves he wanted to make too, but he would wait and talk to Jo about them. As much as he wanted to go on a rampage and destroy Delaney for what he did, it was her decision to make, so after he was done with his letter, he slipped off his shoes and climbed into bed with her. Archer wrapped her in his arms and snuggled her close, knowing that no matter what happened next, he had the love of his life with him, and that made everything infinitely better.

# Chapter Twenty-One

*Jo*

The feel of a warm body against hers had a smile pulling across Jo's face for the first time in twenty-four hours, and when she finally managed to open her eyes from a sound sleep, she looked up to see Archer smiling back at her. Even in his rumpled work clothes he looked good.

"Hey, Freckles." He leaned down to kiss her.

She leaned into him, relishing the feel of his soft lips against hers, not wanting to come back to reality just yet. Reality was where bad things had happened and she no longer had a job, but here in her little bliss bubble with Archer, everything was okay and she was happy.

Jo still felt guilty about not calling him immediately, but she had panicked. Archer seemed like he was fine with it because she was okay, but she would endeavor to do better in the future, not wanting to worry him or let her own concerns get in the way of their relationship.

When their lips finally parted, Archer was gazing at her with a veiled expression. He inhaled deeply and sighed as he shifted in the bed, moving them up to sitting. "What do you want to do about Delaney?" Both of his hands gripped hers, and she was grateful. Touching him helped her feel more settled, and she felt better prepared for what lie ahead.

Jo groaned and leaned her head against him. "I don't know," she whined, cringing at the sound of her own uncertainty. "I mean, Blake and I have been documenting how toxic that environment has been for a while now, but I don't know if that would be enough to file a complaint or start a lawsuit. I would love to do something about it, but I'm not sure what that is yet." She took a breath and exhaled slowly. "I definitely don't want it to happen to someone else, though."

Archer nodded and squeezed her hands again. "What can I do to help?" With those six words, he secured a permanent place in her heart. He wasn't telling her what to do or how she should handle it, he was simply there for her and it was everything she needed.

Jo interlaced their fingers together as they sat on the bed. "You just being here is enough for now." She gazed at him and smiled, beaming all her love over to the man who had quickly become her safe space, her rock.

"Let me know if that changes." He leaned over and kissed the tip of her nose. "I do have contacts in media and I'm sure if I dig around my business card file I can find the number for a lawyer."

"Oh, she already has a lawyer." Gigi's determined voice called from the doorway to the apartment before she strode in, dragging her brother Ford along behind her.

Jo really should reconsider her friends having an all-access pass to her apartment now that she had a boyfriend, but luckily, she and Archer were fully dressed and nowhere near having sex. Still, her friend should have at least knocked, but after the way Gigi had been there for Jo last night, she couldn't stay mad at the woman for long. After what she was now referring to as "the incident," Jo had called both of her friends, and they came rushing over, supported her all night long, even sleeping in bed with her so she wouldn't be alone. Gigi had to leave earlier that morning to open her tea shop, but Millie called in sick so she could stay with her, only leaving once Archer showed up.

Jo glanced at the clock and saw that it was only noon. She turned to her friend with a raised brow.

"Who's minding the tea shop?" Gigi was a trusting person, but she wouldn't let just anyone take charge of her business.

Gigi waved off her question and shut the door behind her. When she was closer to Jo's bed, she plopped down on the other side of her as Ford followed awkwardly behind. Gigi's brother had never been in her apartment before, and he looked slightly uncomfortable at being there now. Jo could hardly blame him. There was barely enough room between the bed and the couch for him to stand. "Mags is looking after things," Gigi explained with a smile.

Jo's eyes widened with the news that Gigi left her fiancé's eighty-something-year-old grandmother in charge of her tea room, but she assumed her friend knew what she was doing. "Good thing Thursdays are slow," she muttered, looking over at her boyfriend and realizing she needed to make introductions. "Oh, sorry. Archer, this is Gigi and her brother Ford—guys this is Archer, my boyfriend." It felt nice to call him that, though the title felt woefully inadequate for signifying just how important he had quickly become.

Archer shook both of their hands and nodded. "Nice to meet you both." He smiled at the pair of newcomers before turning to her. "Do you want me to give you guys some privacy?"

Jo's head shook adamantly, her mind made up before her mouth could form the words. "No. I want you here." She grabbed his hand again to link them together.

He looked down at their hands and smiled at her, the gesture telling her more than words ever could. Archer would be there for her no matter what, and that helped give her the courage to face whatever came next.

Jo looked over at Ford, who was looking around her apartment, his hands stuffed into his pockets. "I assume Gigi dragged you here to try and get me to file a lawsuit." Jo glared at Gigi, who had the decency to look sorry that she had spilled the beans to her brother.

Ford's green eyes met hers and he nodded.

She looked over at a puzzled Archer. "Ford is a lawyer," she explained and understanding dawned on his face.

"If that's something you want to do, I will definitely help you with that," Ford said, his expression friendly but serious. "Gigi filled me in on what happened, and without knowing all the details, I think you have a claim."

There was a hesitancy in his voice that Jo didn't love. "But?" She knew it wouldn't be easy, but she had hoped that the road forward wouldn't be as difficult as she was currently imagining.

Ford exhaled slowly. "Well, you would have to tell your story over and over again, and we would have to go through any evidence you have." His long fingers ran through his hair for a moment before he made sure to smooth it back out. "It would be helpful if we could establish a pattern."

A thought occurred to Jo, and she wished she had thought of it sooner. She had been so distraught about what happened and worried about her relationship with Archer to think of it, but now that she felt better, she wanted to harness her anger and do something. Not just for herself, but for others too. "There's a pattern." She hopped off her bed and grabbed her journals from her closet, dropping the heavy stack of composition books onto the mattress. "This is documentation of all the sexist behavior that has occurred." She lifted the blue-colored notebook from the bed and flipped through it. "And these are all the names of women I know who have complained to human resources about inappropriate situations and ended up leaving when nothing changed."

Ford took the notebook from her hands and looked through it, his eyes widening at the number of names listed. "This many women?"

Jo thought of Blake and nodded. "My friend Blake has been keeping track of stuff too." She really needed to call him and fill him in on everything. "He hasn't been a direct victim of harassment, but he's seen and heard plenty."

"Jesus," Ford muttered as he gathered the other notebooks. "If we can convince the others to come forward, we'll definitely have a stronger case."

Jo nodded, already trying to think of ways to convince the other victims to join her. Then her eyes took in Ford's expensive suit and his shiny watch and she deflated. There was no way she was ever going to be able to afford him as her lawyer. "I don't think I could afford to pay your hourly rate, though."

"I'll pay it," Archer volunteered automatically, and while she loved his knight in shining armor routine, she didn't want him using all his savings for this. They needed it if they were going to start up their own firm.

"No need." Ford's easy-breezy tone caused Jo to whip her head back in his direction. "I'll do it pro bono."

"What?" She and Archer said at the same time while Gigi just beamed with pride at her brother.

Ford shrugged like it was no big deal. "Trust me, this is the type of law I actually enjoy practicing. Helping people instead of protecting corporations," he muttered sadly.

"Thank you." Jo felt overwhelmed at the response from her boyfriend, her friends, and their family. They had never given her a reason to doubt them before, and they were once again proving just how fantastic a good support system could be.

"Knock knock," a sweet voice said from the doorway, and Jo looked over to see Millie peering in from behind the doorway. Her eyes widened behind her glasses. "Whoa. Full house."

Jo smiled at her friend and waved her inside. "Might as well come in and join us." The space was shrinking by the minute, but she didn't mind when it was filled with so many people she loved.

Millie pushed the door open to reveal two huge brown bags in her arms, which she was struggling to carry. Before Jo or Gigi could go help her, Ford quickly stepped over and lifted both bags easily. "Let me get those for you." He smiled at Millie before carrying them over to the counter in Jo's small kitchen and setting them down.

"Thanks." Millie's reply was shier than normal, no doubt from the fact that her crush was right in front of her. She was watching Ford with hearts in her eyes, and Jo really wished he would pull his head out of his ass and see what was in front of him. Watching Millie get constantly overlooked by the man she was in love with was getting old.

"Something smells amazing," Gigi said, walking over to help her brother unload the bags.

"Oh, it's nothing special," Millie mumbled as she came in and shut the door. She adjusted her glasses and smiled at Jo. "I thought you might get hungry later and I wanted you to have a home-cooked meal."

"More like a few home-cooked meals." Gigi smiled as she unloaded multiple food containers onto the counter. "These look great, Mills."

"I like taking care of people." Millie shrugged a shoulder as her cheeks turned pink from blushing. "Besides, I figured you had at least one other person here, so I made enough food for both of you."

Jo smiled at Millie before walking over and pulling her into a firm hug. "Thanks, Mills. You're the best." She leaned back and grabbed one of the containers, smiling when she opened the lid to see her favorite cowboy cookies. Jo had no idea how the woman made so much food in the few hours she was gone, but she was happy to benefit from it. "You have to try one of these." She turned to Archer, handing him a cookie before walking the rest back over to the counter. Archer groaned approvingly and gave Millie a thumbs-up. Gigi grabbed one before offering one to Ford, who managed to eat it in two large bites. Jo looked over at Millie mooning over their friend's brother as he ate her baked goods and decided to help her out. She grabbed a cookie for herself and took a nibble. "I'm jealous of your future husband, Mills," Jo said with a smile. "With food like this always coming out of your kitchen, he'll be one lucky guy."

"You really think so?" Millie asked her, sneaking a peek at Ford. The man was so oblivious to how in love with him she was it bordered on farcical.

"Oh yeah," Ford chimed in, nodding as he grabbed another cookie. "I don't know any guy who wouldn't love to be married to a girl like you. I'm surprised someone hasn't snapped you up already." He popped the cookie into his mouth and chewed it, missing the love pouring off the woman in front of him in waves.

Millie smiled, but it didn't quite reach her eyes. "Thanks," she muttered, sadly. It was obvious to everyone but Ford that his words had impacted her deeply. With the string of bad dating luck she'd been having, it was no wonder.

Jo stared at Ford with a scowl, as did his sister. Even Archer could be heard audibly cringing at his comment. "I guess some guys are just dumb," Jo said firmly, staring daggers at Ford as he reached for his third cookie.

"Yeah, well." With a humorless laugh, Millie gathered her purse and hiked it up on her shoulder. "I should get going."

"Mills," Jo started, but her friend just shook her head, her eyes looking a little watery.

"You all have a good evening." Millie walked out of Jo's apartment quickly, shutting the door behind her and taking a little bit of sunshine with her.

As soon as the door shut, Gigi pinched the bridge of her nose in frustration and glared at her brother. For a smart, big shot lawyer, the man knew even less than Jo had when it came to love.

Jo sighed and got back to the task at hand. "Okay, so what are the next steps with all this?" She swept her hands over her notebooks, eager to get things moving now that she had decided on a course of action.

Ford walked over and picked up the notebooks. "If it's all right with you, I'll take these and make copies, look through them and get a timeline set up for you." He opened his leather briefcase and stuffed them inside before pulling out his business card for her. "Here's my number. I'll call you with an update early next week."

"Thanks, Ford." As much as she wanted to scream at him for the way he continued to not see how amazing Millie was, she was also grateful for his help.

"You're welcome." Ford stepped toward the door and glanced at his sister. "I need to get back to the office."

Gigi nodded and grabbed her purse. "Drop me on the way," she told him, and like the dutiful older brother he was, he nodded and started down the stairs. Gigi stopped in the open doorway and peered at Jo over her shoulder. "You might want to think about telling your dad." With a nod, she left and shut the door behind her.

"Ugh, I forgot about telling Pops." She groaned as she fell back on her bed, her head landing next to Archer.

He ran his hand over her hair and smiled down at her. "Want me to go with you?"

Jo sighed and placed her head in his lap. "Yes, please." She lay there for a moment, enjoying the comfort being near him provided. "But let's save it for later. I want to stay like this a little while longer."

"That's just fine with me, Freckles." Archer leaned down to kiss her forehead. "I'm always happy to just be near you."

Her smile grew and she reached up to grab his neck. "Love you," she breathed out.

"Love you too," he replied, stroking her face with the back of his hand. They stayed that way, content to not leave the familiarity and warmth of the other person, something she knew they'd be happy to do for the rest of their lives. Jo had nearly fallen asleep again when the sound of Archer's voice stirred her once more. "Oh, I can't believe I almost forgot."

His body shifted underneath her and there was a rustling noise before a small plastic box appeared in front of her face. The flower inside it brought tears to her eyes. "Is this...?" She stopped speaking, her throat thick with emotion as she stared at the soft white petals, able to smell the sweet scent despite the box being firmly closed.

Archer ran his fingers through her hair, smoothing both her locks and her emotions. "It is."

Jo rolled to sitting, taking the box and holding it reverently, as if the blossom inside would wither and die if she made one wrong move. She'd smelled gardenias plenty of times in her perfumes and lotions, even seen a glimpse of a real one at the local botanical garden on a school field trip when she was younger, but back then the pain of losing her mama had been too great and she couldn't bring herself to look at it for more than a split second before turning away to hide her tears. As she looked at the flower now, however, she let them flow freely.

"Was it wrong of me to get this for you?"

Jo turned to Archer, loving his concern, but hating the doubt that had come along with it. She shifted, clutching onto the gardenia box as she moved onto his lap. "No, this is perfect." Jo opened the box, the powerful, almost tropical scent washing over the two of them. She took a deep inhale, a memory of her mama playing in her mind. "Mama used to have this hand cream that smelled exactly like this. She even used it on me a few times when my hands got too dry from all of the washing I had to do after rolling around in the dirt."

Archer brushed a curl behind her ear. "That sounds like you."

The fondness in his voice along with his love sealed up the cracks in her heart to where the tears trickling down her face were now of the happy variety. Jo leaned over and brushed her lips against his. "Thank you, not just for giving me the flower but for giving me so much more than I ever thought to want for myself."

"You're welcome, Freckles." When he leaned in and kissed her again, any thoughts of the past were pushed to the side along with the flower as the two of them tumbled back onto the bed, losing themselves in one another and the future they would build together.

****

The conversation with her father was going a lot better than Jo had thought it would. Her dad had only sworn a handful of times so far, and merely hinted at the fact that he could make a man disappear without a trace, never coming right out and saying that he wanted to kill her former boss. Overall, Pops seemed much calmer than she had expected. His face was still red with anger, so Jo placed her hand over his as they sat at his kitchen table and patted it.

"Remember your blood pressure, Pops," she reminded him. Jo might not be nagging him all the time anymore, but she'd be damned if he had a heart attack on account of Gavin Delaney.

Pops grumbled and raked a hand over his face. After a deep breath, his coloring looked a little less like a tomato as he placed his other hand over hers, giving it a squeeze. "Thanks, Joley-bear, but you can't fault a man for getting angry when his little girl is treated poorly." Her dad's voice was getting all growly, so she tried to calm him a little more.

"I'm not faulting you, and I'm not a little girl, but I get what you're saying." Jo looked over at Archer to see him smiling at her in encouragement. "But things might get a lot worse if a lawsuit is filed. I'm sure all kinds of things could come out about me. Some true, some not."

Jo didn't love the idea of her name being dragged through the mud, but if it meant making sure no one else got taken advantage of by that slime ball Delaney, she would deal with the consequences. Her eyes met Archer's again, and while there was that little niggling voice telling her he might not like hearing stories about her past, stories that included quite a few hookups, she knew he was stronger than that and would stay by her side. He'd proven that on more than one occasion, and she had no reason to doubt that now.

"Well, I don't care what's true or what's made up," her dad stated firmly. "I'm going to support you through this even if it means having to pull double shifts at the garage to help pay for everything."

Jo smiled at her father's willingness to go the extra mile for her. "While I appreciate that, you're supposed to think about retiring," she prodded gently. "Besides, Gigi's brother is doing it pro bono."

Her dad's eyes widened at that. "Well isn't that something," he said with a smile before his brow furrowed once more. "What about rent and stuff like that? I suppose you could always move back in here." He tried to look excited, but Jo knew the thought of having her around to nag him all the time was the last thing he would want, not that she was all that eager to move back to her childhood home either.

Archer tried to stifle his laugh, but a little broke out anyway and she glared at him, causing him to cough and straighten up in his chair.

"As much as I would love to be here and be the fun police for you…" Jo reached over and took Archer's hand. "We were already talking about moving in together, and with one rent payment and our savings, we should be okay for a while."

Her dad looked at Archer with a raised brow. "You think you can handle living with her?" he asked, earning a light slap on the arm from Jo.

Archer smiled and squeezed her hand. "I would love nothing more than to spend the rest of my life finding out." He winked at her and warmth spread through her chest. The rest of their lives together did sound pretty good, and even though they'd only known each other for a few months, Jo wasn't the least bit worried about moving too fast or making a mistake. Giving him up would be the mistake, and she was never going to do that.

"Well, more power to you, son." Her dad smiled at them as he shoved away from the table. "Now, how about we go out to celebrate you two moving in together. I'm thinking Barb's Diner could be good."

Jo laughed. "Any excuse for a burger," she

muttered before standing and heading over to give her dad a hug. "Thanks, Pops."

Her dad hugged her back, squeezing her until she thought her lungs would burst. "Love you, Joley-bear."

"Love you too." She and Archer held hands as they followed her dad to the door.

Her father peered over his shoulder at them and smiled at their joined hands. "Now, Archer. You better not tell me that you're a vegetarian or something or we'll have to rethink this whole you-two-living-together thing."

Archer barked a laugh and shook his head. "Uh, no sir. I have had the pleasure of partaking in the double cheeseburger at Barb's, though I will confess to having vegetables on occasion," he said, smiling over at Jo.

"Good man." Her dad walked out the door and over to her car.

"That he is," Jo said, leaning up to kiss her man on the lips. "He's the best man."

Archer reached over and kissed her again, but it was a lot less chaste than her kiss and the rest of the world melted away until they heard her dad calling to them.

"Hey now, save it for later. I'm hungry," he ordered, finding his way into the backseat of her car.

Jo just shook her head at her dad. "Guess I'm driving." She went toward the car, but Archer tugged on her hand, pulling her back to him.

"Can I?" The prospect of driving her classic mustang lit up his cocoa-colored eyes as he shot that puppy dog look at her once more.

Jo handed over her keys. "You're lucky I love you."

"I am." He kissed her hand and escorted her over to the car.

They spent the rest of the night visiting with her dad before heading back to her place, where she showed him just how lucky he really was.

## Chapter Twenty-Two

*Archer*

After spending time with Jo, learning about everything that happened and staying as calm as he could in the face of what she had gone through, Archer fully intended on going into work to hand in his resignation, gather his things, and possibly punch Gavin Delaney in the jaw. When he mentioned that last part to Jo, she smiled but reminded him that an assault charge was probably the last thing they needed, especially if they were going to start their own business, but she thanked him for offering.

He and Jo stayed up half the night making plans, including ending her month-to-month lease on her tiny apartment. They were moving her in to his place—their place—this weekend, and he couldn't be more excited about it. What he was decidedly not excited about was having to head up to his office to drop off his resignation. Archer thought about doing it via email—he owed them nothing after all and Jo already talked to Blake to fill him in on what happened, so there was no need for him to go in—but he wanted to be able to look Gavin Delaney in the eye and tell him what he thought of him.

Archer's dad had wanted to do the same after he explained over the phone on his way into work everything that happened, but Archer asked him to hold off. No need to give Delaney a heads-up that the news was spreading beyond the office. They needed the element of surprise when it came to the potential lawsuit, and Archer wouldn't put it past Delaney to try and intimidate former employees into not joining up with Jo.

Archer did accept his father's offer to help with some seed money and contacts for their business, though. He would forever be grateful to his dad for the help he was providing, and told him as much when they ended their call.

The ride up to the fifth floor seemed to last forever, giving Archer time to harness all his outrage and anger at the man who would now be his former boss. As soon as the elevator door parted, Archer marched straight over to Delaney's office, ready to let loose. He couldn't believe the man thought he could get away with such egregious behavior. "Where's Delaney?" he barked at the man's assistant, and winced when he realized how unhinged he sounded. Janine was a sweet lady and didn't deserve his ire.

Janine looked up at him with wide eyes. "Oh, he's out meeting with some clients all morning. He won't be back until at least three in the afternoon." The woman smiled and grabbed a pen. "Would you like me to jot down a message for you?"

Archer sighed. On the one hand, he was happy to not have to see the man, but on the other, he was pissed off that he hadn't been able to give him a piece of his mind. Jo had already called him out on his behavior, so Archer getting to do it too was really just to satisfy his inner caveman. "You hurt my woman, now I break fingers" and all that. He spun the envelope containing the notice of his immediate resignation in his hands before handing it over to Janine. "No message. Could you just make sure he gets this?" When the woman nodded at him, he spun on his heel and walked to his office. "Well that was incredibly anticlimactic," he muttered to himself before opening his office door and gathering the small number of personal items he had there.

Blake popped in just as Archer had stuffed the

family picture he had on his desk into his messenger bag. "Oh my god," he said in a low voice before coming over to Archer and giving him a hug. Apparently they were closer than he thought, and he made a note to take Blake out for drinks sometime. "When Jo told me what happened, I was totally shocked." Blake looked at Archer and tilted his head, pursing his lips. "Well, not totally shocked because the man had always been icky, and it's not like this place wasn't already problematic as hell, but still."

"I know. I didn't think it was that bad, but I guess I was fooling myself," he admitted, packing up the rest of his things in his bag and clipping it shut. He looked up at Blake with a frown. "Sorry to leave you here, man."

Blake lifted a shoulder and smiled. "Please." He picked some imaginary lint from his deep violet suit jacket. Jo was right about him being a swan because only a man as graceful and confident as Blake could pull that look off. "I can handle this place for another month or two until you guys get our new agency set up. I'm just sad I can't come with you now, but, you know, student loans don't pay themselves."

Archer clasped the man's shoulder and gave it a squeeze. "We'll get the plans for a jailbreak together as quickly as possible." He smiled at Blake and walked out of his office.

"No nail files in cakes, please," he said, walking Archer to the elevator. "I'm trying to watch my figure."

Archer chuckled and nodded at the man. "I'll get you a rock hammer so you can tunnel your way out instead."

The elevator arrived and Archer stepped inside, giving a small wave to Blake before the doors closed. While the morning hadn't been as eventful as he'd thought it would be, Archer was glad it was over. Now he could head back to what really mattered: the woman he loved.

**\*\*\*\***

"Do you think they'll like me?" Jo played with the hem of her light blue tank, her toes tapping anxiously on the cement as they stood in front of the door to his sister's house.

Archer smiled at her nervousness, but only because he knew she had nothing to worry about. "They're going to love you because I do, and also because you are the most amazing woman I have ever met." He paused just long enough to tilt his head down to kiss her. "If anything, they'll wonder what you're doing with me."

Jo smirked at him. "Everyone will wonder that," she sassed, earning a pinch on the side. She giggled and so he tickled her some more, loving the sound of her laughter and needing to hear more of it after the week they'd had.

It had only been eight days since "the incident" as Jo called it and their subsequent departure from Elite Marketing, but it had been an eventful one. With the help of her friends, they moved her into his place, remarking on how easy it had been since she didn't have a ton of stuff. There were some new additions around the apartment, like her baby blue duvet cover and a few sentimental knickknacks she kept from her past, but Archer enjoyed seeing evidence of her living there strewn all over the place. The space felt more like a home with her, and the thought of one day maybe making a home with her and a gaggle of blonde, curly-haired babies in the future had him smiling like a fool all day and night.

After they had settled in, the spent their days looking into starting their firm and working on her lawsuit. Ford felt confident he could get more people to come forward and kept them in the loop about everything. Archer couldn't believe they were getting his help for free, but he tried not to look a gift horse in the mouth. It seemed that it really did pay to have friends in high places. Things were moving quickly on all fronts, but that didn't scare him. In fact, one day when Jo met her friends for lunch, Archer had gone down to a jewelry shop and bought a ring. He figured he would wait until things calmed down to ask her to marry him, but he wanted to be prepared in case the right moment presented itself.

The idea of marrying Jo had him grinning like a fool again, and she turned in his arms to look at him. "What has you smiling so big?"

"You." He spun her in his arms before kissing her soundly on the lips. Jo's hands found their way to his rear and she squeezed him, but she dropped her hands when they heard a throat clearing from the doorway.

They parted and Jo smiled sheepishly at his sister while he rubbed the back of his neck. "Hi Caro," he said awkwardly, gesturing over to Jo. "This is Jo. Jo, this is my sister, Caroline."

Caro looked stern for only a moment before she beamed at Jo. "Oh my god, it is so good to finally meet you." Archer could see the giddiness in his sister's eyes as she stepped forward, linking arms with his girlfriend and dragging her inside. "I have heard so much about you and I am so excited that you're here." Caro peeked over her shoulder at Archer and looked at him with wide eyes. *She's gorgeous,* she mouthed at him, and all he could do was nod in reply. His sister was right—Jo was gorgeous, and she was his.

"Thank you for having me." Jo shot his sister one of her authentic, friendly smiles. As he watched them walk back to the dining room, he could already tell the two of them were going to be the best of friends.

After dinner, they found themselves out in the backyard to enjoy the evening weather with cold beers and good conversation. Todd was pushing Trevor on their tire swing and Timothy was up in his treehouse with his game system. "At least he's outside in the fresh air," Caro had said with an eye roll when her son had pulled out his gamepad and started tapping at the screen. The meal they shared had gone well, with Caro and Jo bonding over their mutual desire to live in nothing but sweatpants and Todd asking her all kinds of questions about cars. His brother-in-law was not a car enthusiast in the least, but he was inquisitive and loved to learn more about new things. Even his two nephews had taken to her immediately, talking about how her Mustang looked like some of their toy cars and asking when she would take them for a ride.

Caro took a sip of her beer before pulling a face and placing the bottle back on the table. "Blergh," she announced as she stuck her tongue out. "I don't get the appeal of beer. Give me wine any day."

"I'm good with either, but there's something about beer that makes me feel more relaxed," Jo admitted with a shrug of her shoulder. "Maybe it's because I only drink it with friends, but wine always makes me feel like I should be gossiping or talking trash."

"Oh, I love gossip." Caro leaned in closer to Jo. "And anytime this guy gives you a hard time, you can come over and we can talk trash about him." Caro peered over at Archer with a smirk. "I have so many stories of him acting like an idiot."

Jo's head whipped over to him, her eyes bright with amusement. "I think I'm going to need to hear these stories sooner rather than later," she told his sister with a wide grin.

"Uh-ho, no." Archer stood and grabbed Jo's hand.

"I think that's our cue to leave." His sister had enough embarrassing stories about him to keep them there all night, and he had other plans with his girl.

"No. Not yet," Jo and Caro pouted simultaneously.

"Please let her stay longer," Caro pleaded, sounding very much like her five-year-old son when he begged to stay up later.

Archer looked between the two women and nodded. "Fine." He gave Jo a kiss on her forehead. "But if you think I'm sticking around to listen to you besmirch my good name, you are mistaken."

Caro smirked at him. "Besmirch? I see that word of the day calendar I got you for Christmas is coming in handy."

"Oh, here I thought he was smart all on his own," Jo sassed.

"Behave." He pointed his fingers at his eyes and then at them. "I'm watching you." He slowly backed away from the table, smiling at two of the women who mattered most to him.

"As long as you aren't listening," Jo quipped, and the two women giggled at his back as he walked away.

"That looks like trouble," his brother-in-law remarked as he approached him and his nephew. Archer peered over his shoulder and saw Jo and Caro huddled together and talking before bursting out in cackles again. He might say otherwise, but he was actually happy the two were getting along so well, even if it was at his own expense.

"Eh." He shrugged a shoulder. "At least now your wife will stop bugging me for a sister-in-law."

Todd's eyes widened as he pushed his youngest son on the swing. "You thinking about marriage already?"

Archer nodded, a grin overtaking his face. "Not thinking, thought. Past tense. I already bought the ring," he confessed happily. "I just need to find the right time to ask."

"Have you told your parents?"

"I have," he confessed. The phone call had been an interesting one. Both his mom and dad cautioned him about moving so quickly, but he explained how in love he was, and ultimately they were happy for him. "I'm trying to convince them to come out here for Labor Day so they can meet Jo and her dad."

Todd smiled and reached over to squeeze his shoulder. "Congrats, man." He turned to look at his wife. "It's a wild ride, especially once you add kids to the mix, but there's nothing better."

"I believe it." He looked over at Jo, and when her eyes met his and she smiled before turning back to her conversation with his sister, Archer knew it was one wild ride he was prepared for.

Later that night as he and Jo lay in bed, her wrapped up in his arms with her head resting on his chest, Archer wondered just how he got so lucky as to meet the woman of his dreams and be able to start not just a business together, but a whole life. "I love you, Freckles," he told her simply because he loved being able to say it and loved that he meant it too.

Jo tilted her head up to him. "I know." She smiled at him. "I love you too."

With her words of devotion in his ear, Archer let out a happy sigh and let sleep claim him, knowing that she would be there when he woke up, and the next day, and the day after that. His brother-in-law was right— there was definitely nothing better.

# Epilogue

*Jo*
*Six months later*

The humid air of the rock climbing gym had her curls frizzing like nobody's business, but Jo didn't care one bit because she was having way too much fun with this year's birthday adventure. It was her turn to pick, so it went without saying that they would be doing something physical or sports related. Archer had taken her rock climbing a few times over the last six months, and she really enjoyed it, so she figured she would subject her best friends to it when they couldn't say no. She was fairly certain Millie would retaliate with a flower arranging class or something else Jo would likely never use, but that was fine with her because she was having a blast and it would be worth it. Twenty-nine only came around once, after all, and she planned on making the most of this next year.

The last year had brought some challenges, but also a lot of gains. Now that she wasn't solely focused on his mortality, Jo and her dad had gotten closer than ever. He was basically retired now, and Cooper was slowing buying into the shop to take it over completely one day, but her dad managed to find his way into his old business every now and then to catch up with his former employees and work on the odd car or two. When he wasn't doing that, her father was busy trying to steal her boyfriend.

Jo had always been a bit of a tomboy, but it seemed like her dad had finally gotten the son he'd always longed for. He was constantly taking Archer fishing, having him over for ball games, and was even teaching him a few things about cars. Jo was always invited, but she often declined, leaving two most important men in her life to bond all on their own. Besides, it meant she got to spend more time with her friends or Archer's sister. Caro was a laugh riot, and she and Jo got along like chocolate and peanut butter, which is often what they would end up eating as they gossiped about Caro's job or Jo and Archer's new business.

The marketing firm they started was doing pretty well. Creative Solutions was still a small firm, but after hiring Blake and a few new marketing consultants as well as some former administrators from their old office, it was quickly becoming one of the most sought-after places for sports marketing in their area. Liberty University contacted the two of them about their pitch, but ultimately declined in favor of a more-established firm. Jo was a little upset at first, but came to see that it was for the best. She'd been doing better about reminding herself that some things were just out of her control.

Their new firm wasn't relying on that business anyway. It probably helped matters that their biggest competition, Elite Marketing, had shuttered its doors after the lawsuit. They tried to settle out of court, but Jo and the twenty-three other women who joined her wanted everything dragged out into the light of day, and Ford used his considerable influence in the community to fast-track the proceedings.

It had been hard, and Elite's lawyers definitely tried to paint her and the other women as overly promiscuous, but the jury ruled in their favor and they ended up basically bankrupting the old firm. Jo considered using her share of the money she received to pour into her and Archer's new business, but she didn't want where the money had come from to taint her new venture, so she donated it to the local women's shelter instead. Because Archer's dad had invested in their new business, she was lucky enough to be in a position to be able to make that decision, and she was grateful for that.

Archer's parents had come to visit over Labor Day weekend and again at Christmas time. Jo took an immediate liking to both of them, and they seemed to enjoy her as well. His parents were definitely from another class, but the only way to tell was by their fine clothes and fancy car, because much like their son, they were down-to-earth and extremely personable. Jo thanked Archer's father profusely for his investment in their firm, but he waved it off like it was no big deal. "Parents support their children and the people their children love," was all he had said, and when she told her father that, Pops immediately made it his mission in life to befriend the man. The five of them had all had lunch together one day, and now Archer's dad and hers had weekly phone chats. It was nice to see her dad expanding his social circle, and it made her worry less about the future because she knew it didn't all rest on her shoulders anymore.

"Come on, Freckles," Archer called to her from a quarter of the way up the rock wall. "Racing is no fun if you aren't even going to try."

Jo craned her neck to look at him before clapping the excess chalk from her hands and starting her ascent. "You're going to regret pulling me from my thoughts, Sugar, because now I'm going to kick your ass." She gave him one final look before using all the strength she possessed to try and catch up with him.

Archer chuckled and continued to climb. "We'll see about that." He moved his hands from grip to grip easily, climbing with the ease of someone who had done this many times before. The race wasn't exactly fair, but that didn't matter to her. Jo thrived on competition, even with her own boyfriend.

"You can do it, Jo," Millie called from near the bottom of the wall. She was smiling up at Jo, one of her hands laced with her partner's. It was good to see Millie so very happy. Jo glanced at her other friend to see Gigi and Cooper standing with their arms wrapped around one another, and she smiled at just how well each of their birthday challenges from the last year had worked out.

With Millie's motivation ringing in her ear, Jo scaled the wall as quickly as possible, but still fell short of beating her man to the top. When she pulled herself up next to him, he leaned over and kissed her on the lips. "I win," he announced, his eyes bright from the exertion of his climb and the victory.

"I guess you do." She smiled, not minding the loss one bit. "But I have to say that the view from below you was worth losing the race." With a wink at her boyfriend, she grabbed her safety line and repelled down, Archer following quickly after her.

They landed with a soft thud and removed their harnesses. Archer leaned over to whisper in her ear. "If you like that view so much, maybe I can give you a private birthday show later."

"Oh, yes please," she exclaimed with a shimmy, excited at the prospect of seeing his firm booty on display for her again. "Best birthday present ever."

Archer chuckled and smiled at her, but his eyes narrowed and he twisted his lips in thought. "Would you like your other birthday present now?"

"You already gave me my other present." Jo shot a puzzled look his way. Archer had bought her season tickets to the local minor league baseball team, telling her that he would cover any work that needed doing so that she could go and enjoy the games with her dad. It was generous, thoughtful, and so him that she'd cried happy tears when she opened it.

His head shook and he ran a hand through his hair, climbing chalk still covering his palm. Archer huffed a breath and shrugged at his now-white-streaked hair. "I have another present for you." His voice was nervous as he tapped his hand against his side. "I've actually had it for a while and I've been waiting for the right time to give it to you, but anytime I'm with you seems like the right time, and I don't want to wait anymore."

"Okay," she said with a shaky smile. Jo wasn't sure what he was getting at, but his anxiety was making hers flare up. "You can give it to me now then."

Archer smiled before reaching into his pocket and dropping to one knee. An audible gasp could be heard and Jo would bet her car that it came from Millie. "Freckles, I love you more than I love pineapple and jalapenos on pizza. You are the strongest, smartest, most beautiful person I have ever met, and I would be a damn fool to not want to spend the rest of my life with you. Will you marry me?"

Jo's eyes filled with moisture as she took him in. He was sweaty and his hair was matted and covered in chalk, but he was still the most handsome, most thoughtful, most amazing man she had ever met, and she would be a damn fool to not say yes. "Yeah, Sugar. I'll marry you." Jo dropped down to his level and tackled him with a kiss. Claps, cheers, and a few catcalls could be heard through the room, but Jo was only paying attention to the man in front of her.

Jo had spent most of her life playing games, always trying to control the outcome, but only now, with the promise of forever with the man she loved, did she truly feel like a winner.

## The End

**EVERNIGHT PUBLISHING ®**

www.evernightpublishing.com